Preface

No matter how enchanted our lives may be, at some point we'll all wish we could push a "reset" button and start over. We secretly desire to become someone else living somewhere else. Don't worry, everyone has that fantasy. Most people don't do anything about it. Others have a harder time resisting the urge.

Fifty years ago, a person could start a new life by moving to another town. Get a new job. Get a new family. Change their name if they wanted to. If they moved to another country they might as well have been on the moon.

Nowadays, everything is so connected. If a person wants to start a new life, they'll have to really work at it. They'll have to untangle themselves from everything they know. They'll have to have a good plan. And they will have to embrace the unknown.

Unknown people. Unknown languages. Unknown cultures. New everything. It is a more complicated transition than most of us are prepared to make, but some people take to it right away.

My friend Orlando Braxton wanted a new life, so he went out and got one. The stories in this book are his. Some are short. Some are long. All of them are based on true events.

I couldn't make this book a biography because Orlando thought it was bad luck to write someone's life story while they are still living it.

D1403312

I asked if he could tell these stories to me in a straight timeline so I could make it a novel. Orlando said, *"Time means nothing to people who believe in reincarnation"*.

I took that as a *"no"*.

So here, in no particular order, is my friend Orlando telling some of his best stories about life on the other side.

Enjoy.

Bart Walters

Story List

White Linen Pants

Maid for Trouble

The Legend of Bangkok Bill

Chicken Fried Freedom

Persona Non Grata

Nothing for Christmas

The Princess and the Pop Star

Sure Bet

Lights out in Bangkok

World Class People Watcher

One of them

Crimes of Opportunity

Professor Thailand

"Let go, or be dragged"

-- Zen proverb

White Linen Pants

Normally, I avoid doing things I'm not good at, but I had to give the dating thing one more shot. It felt like I'd circumvented the whole human mating protocol for a few years. I'd quit dating women considered "appropriate" and had been through a long stretch of strippers, barmaids, and nail technicians. All of them significantly younger than me.

It's not that I didn't know how to get involved in a "meaningful" relationship. It's not that I hadn't been in some before. I just hate when it's over. The hurt. The disappointment. And the inevitable feeling that you've lost time that you'll never get back.

Accepting failure and wasting time aren't my strong suits so, I'd chosen disposable relationships with little or no emotional attachment. That's the best thing about dating strippers. There's not much chance of it ever working out.

And to be honest, it wasn't just relationships I was tired of. I'd become disenchanted with "America-World" in general. At the ripe old age of 39, I had become successful enough to have all the stuff I wanted. Houses, cars, and expensive toys were piling up and none of them excited me. I had become "hard to thrill". I didn't have any friends that were interested in the same things I was. Most folks that were my age were married and up to their ears in little league and dance lessons. I'd become a social outcast. A "fifth wheel". Every couple's "bachelor friend".

The only thing that did thrill me was travel. I'd scaled down my business to a point where I could conduct it from a laptop just about anywhere with a good internet connection. So, I started taking a few trips close to home in the Caribbean and Central America. I went to Costa Rica a few times and loved it. My partner and I had some business associates in Panama where I made some new friends and felt right at home. When I visited the Dominican Republic, I discovered my Spanish was better than I thought. It seemed that when I was somewhere else, I felt relevant again. I felt a sense of adventure. Life had more flavor. So, travel became my new vice.

As it is with most vices, I kept going a little farther each trip. One day I jumped on a plane and flew to Thailand. I checked my globe. You can't go any further without starting to come back. My uncle had been stationed there with the Air Force during the Vietnam War. When I was a kid, I used to sit for hours going through his old 35mm slides. White sand beaches, steamy jungles, and pretty girls; it all looked so other-worldly.

Thirty years later, I was still dreaming about and searching for an that ideal exotic paradise. In July 1999 I stepped off the plane in Bangkok and immediately knew I was on the right path.

By 2001, I had been back to Southeast Asia four times, traveling to different countries each trip. Cambodia, Laos, Vietnam, The Philippines. Each experience flew by way too fast. Two weeks just wasn't enough. At the end of my last trip, I got off the plane in my hometown during a nasty winter storm. Somewhere in the back of my mind the idea of a longer stay abroad was proposed, discussed, and decided upon. Next trip I'd stay at least a month, maybe longer.

While I had toyed with the idea of actually living outside the US, I wasn't ready to give up on America just yet. I realized it was me that needed to change and not the whole damn country. The social isolation was my own doing. I knew I was the guy with shit on his shoe.

So, after some serious self-reflection, I concluded that I should get off the strippers and try once again to find a compatible mate. A "real" girlfriend. This whole travel thing would be more fun with someone to share it with, right? A beautiful and intelligent woman to spend time and travel with ... I thought that would be the cure for my forty-something blues for sure.

I made the mistake of voicing this notion aloud and in front of my business partner's wife. She took it as a call to action. "Lando, I know just the girl," she said excitedly. "She's perfect for you".

She insisted. I resisted. I had no idea how I was going to find Miss Right, but I hate being "fixed up". For weeks she pestered me until I finally gave in.

"All right Kim, who is she?" I asked.

She rattled off a long string of statistics like she was reading the back of a baseball card. "Thirty-seven ... tall and slim ... reddish-blonde hair ... looks like a runway model". How could I say no? Arrangements were made for me to meet this all-star woman at a neutral location for lunch.

Well, it wasn't really a neutral site, we met at Dexter's, a hipster-before-hipster-was-a-thing wine bar walking distance from my condo. It is a place where I was comfortable and well known.

She arrived first, and I spotted her at the end of the bar immediately. Perfectly faded jeans, a crisp white dress shirt casually untucked, strawberry-blonde hair loosely piled up, and just a sprinkling of makeup. She was stunning. I could tell she wanted to appear as though she just "came as she was" and no special preparation had gone on for our meeting. The French pedicure gave her away, but she was a perfectly composed image of casualness. And she did look like a runway model.

"Colleen?" I asked hopefully.

"Orlando" she replied, holding up her I-phone with my picture on it.

I smiled ... she smiled back ... and it was clear that neither of us was disappointed.

To say we hit it off would be a severe understatement. We sipped Pinot Noir and talked non-stop for two hours. She was funny, she was smart, we read the same books and liked the same kind of music. She seemed genuinely interested in what I had to say. I couldn't wait for this little meeting to be over so we could have a real date. We made plans to have dinner and a night on the town that weekend.

I congratulated myself a dozen times on the way home for being brave and taking this leap. It had all the hallmarks of a life-changing moment. One of those days you look back on and say, "that's when it all started".

I wanted everything to be perfect. Reservations were made at the coolest restaurant in town, which just happened to be on the ground floor of my building. Colleen showed up right on time looking like a magazine cover in her white linen pants and an indigo silk top. Her hair was down and shoulder-length framing her flawless face. We sat in the bar to chat while a private table was prepared. Travis the bartender walked behind Colleen, gave me the two-thumbs-up signal, and mouthed a big "wow!" as he walked by.

Our conversation seemed to pick up where we'd left off earlier in the week. We took turns asking each other questions like a one-on-one version of The Dating Game. I found out Colleen had been married for several years and divorced only about 18 months earlier. Her ex-husband is a psychiatrist with an office not far away. I also found out that Colleen is a licensed counselor of some kind and actually works at her ex-husband's office.

She could feel me tense up when this bit of information came out and said, *"Don't worry. Our divorce was totally amicable. We weren't the right people for each other and we're both evolved enough to know that. Now we're really good friends".*

I just let it go. My opinion on these types of arrangements seemed irrelevant at the time, and I'm a sucker for words like "evolved".

I have no idea what we ate or if it was any good. We were so smitten by each other that none of it mattered. When the check was paid and the waiters properly tipped, we took a walk around the park at Lake Jasmine. It was a steamy summer night with just enough breeze to keep us from overheating. I suggested we have a drink at a place I know downtown that has good live music. Colleen latched onto my arm and said, *"Lead on Captain"*.

We arrived at Tanqueray's Bar around 8:30, clutching the brass rail and negotiating the narrow stairs that take you down to the underground lounge. Tanqueray's is a grotto-like boozer that is dark, cool, and oozing with character. The sawed-off little Bartender Dan howled when He saw me enter, "Lando!". He ducked under the service portal of the bar and gave me a big brotherly hug. Introductions were made and it became apparent to Colleen that I was a VIP customer there.

"The usual?" Dan inquired.

"Naturally," I said.

"And the beautiful lady?"

Colleen was undecided. We'd drunk a bottle of wine for dinner so I suggested she might want to continue on the wine.

When my drink came, she grinned like a she-devil and said, "What is that?"

Dan announced, "That my dear is double Keitel One Vodka Martini with three olives, a little dirty".

"It looks spectacular," Colleen said. "Can I try"?

She took a slurp of my drink, rolled her eyes in ecstasy, and signaled Dan to make her one too. I remember thinking, *"If that's what she's drinking, we may just fly to Las Vegas and get married tonight"*.

Two martinis in, Colleen felt compelled to tell me about her failed marriage and what led to the divorce. Her ex-husband isn't so much of a psychiatrist as he is a pill-doctor. He specializes in patients that like to medicate themselves into a better state of mind rather than actually deal with any behavioral issues they might have. They keep coming with problems and he keeps giving them pills.

He'd had a run-in with the law a couple of years ago and had his business shut down for prescribing pills after nothing more than a quick phone conversation with patients. Colleen started naming off all the different drugs he prescribed but I'm not a pill guy, so I didn't know what any of them were. According to her, if patients were depressed, he made them happy. If they were tired, he gave them energy. If they were anxious, he chilled them out. All the drama from his legal trouble strained the marriage. Colleen moved out while his office was shut down. He said she was kicking him while he was down. She felt guilty but wanted to distance herself from his smarmy little practice.

I was curious why she went back to working there when he reopened, but I was tired of the conversation already. The evening was moving along nicely before we veered off into that lane, so I ordered some more drinks and redirected her attention to the band preparing to start their first set. Colleen switched off the negative energy in an instant and perked right up.

The band was a group I know well. They play a kooky combination of reggae, blues, and funk, and soon the twenty or so bar patrons had gathered in front of the stage and were bobbing their heads to the music. Two big black girls got up from their table and began dancing near the corner of the stage and to my surprise, Colleen joined them. They all gyrated through a couple of songs cackling and encouraging each other. Colleen didn't have much rhythm, but she looked so sexy nobody noticed.

The other girls went back to their table to cool down and Colleen headed towards ours. About three steps away one of her knees went all wobbly and she almost fell. I got up to help her to her chair and she plopped down on it with a thud. Her face was flushed, and she had sweat running down her forehead. "Sorry," she said. "I guess I'm out of practice". I ordered her a bottle of water and a glass of ice. She held the cold bottle up to her neck to cool down and in a few minutes, she seemed to regain her composure.

The bar was filling up and getting a bit stuffy, so I suggested we go upstairs and get some air. She shot me a tight smile, agreed and I got up. She pulled herself up by holding on to my arm and I could feel her full weight. With my arm around her waist, I walked her to the door and waved goodbye to Dan. "Good luck buddy," he said with his greasy Dan-the-bartender grin.

As soon as we got out the door to the landing at the bottom of the stairs Colleen's legs and arms turned to rubber, and she collapsed into my arms. She didn't pass out, but she seemed to have no control over her body. I wrapped my arms around her waist and ask her what was wrong, but she just kept insisting, "I'm okay, I'm okay". Clearly, she was not okay.

I looked up the narrow flight of treacherous brick stairs and it seemed a mile long. I wanted to get her up to the street where we could get some fresh air. I tried three or four times to get her up the first few steps and it was useless. It was then I realized Colleen's not such a small lady. I'd say she's about 5'9" and weighs 130 pounds. I'm linebacker-sized, so if she were passed out, I could have just hoisted her up and carried the dead weight no problem. But every time I tried to help her, she started thrashing and squirming so much I felt like I was wrestling an orangutan.

Finally, I commanded, "Colleen, hold your breath". She inhaled deeply and when she held it, she stopped moving. I threw her over my shoulder and ran up the stairs with her like a heroic fireman. When we got to the top, the street was alive with people out in the city on a Saturday night. I took her down off my shoulder and planted her upright holding her by the waist. I got Colleen to take several deep breaths and she kept saying "I'm okay, I'm okay". But every time she tried to take a step her legs buckled, and I had to support her again.

The next challenge was getting her across the busy four lanes of downtown traffic without both of us being killed. When "don't walk" changed to "walk", I had her take another deep breath and glided her across to the other side, feet barely skimming the ground. Once across, we stood on the corner for ten minutes looking for a taxi. I planned to take her home to her place and make sure she was okay and then go home myself.

It was a good plan, but at eleven o'clock on a Saturday night, there were no taxis to be found. I took a long look down Pine Street where I could see the lights from my building about a mile away. It looked a lot further. Adrenalin had counteracted all the expensive vodka I drank and buzz-killing reality set in. The breeze that was so refreshing earlier had abandoned me and the thick Florida night laid a suffocating wet blanket on top of the situation. I knew I may have no choice but to carry this 130-pound writhing octopus the entire way in the stifling midsummer heat.

For the first two blocks, I was able to glide her along with her arm around my shoulders and mine around her waist. But she kept getting weaker and more legless and eventually she couldn't hold on to me anymore. Finally, near the corner of Magnolia and Pine Street, I stood her up against the wall to rest.

"Colleen, I guess you aren't much of a drinker. Has this happened before?"

"What do you mean?" she replied. "I'm okay. I'm just a little tipsy".

"Colleen, you can't walk. You can't even stand up".

"I'm okay I told you!"

And with that, she lurched forward to demonstrate that she could walk. I was able to catch her about one foot before her face hit the sidewalk. I stood her up against the wall again and pressed close enough to whisper in her ear.

"My place isn't very far," I said. I'm going to pick you up like we did going up the stairs. We'll be at my place in ten minutes. We can get you sobered up there, okay?"

She started breathing heavy and grinding up against me. "Okay Captain" she whispered. "You're in charge".

With that, I dropped down, bent her by the waist over my shoulder, and headed home down Pine Street. We passed half a dozen bars and restaurants along the way. I'm sure it was a sight to behold. That big bald dude carrying that hot blonde over his shoulder through the middle of downtown. I could hear hoots and hollers from a couple of places. I'm certain somebody took a picture of the spectacle.

Once past the business district, we were all alone moving alongside Jasmine Park in silence under the ancient oak trees. We were less than fifty yards from my place when Colleen started squirming around and demanding, "put me down ... put me down ... I can walk from here!" I did as she asked, and she immediately stumbled headlong into a huge garden of muddy bromeliads just off the sidewalk. She rolled around and tried to get up three times before I waded in and helped her out. She was caked from stem to stern with black mud. I couldn't help but laugh, she was such a mess.

Colleen was not amused. "Look at my pants!" she screeched. "These are $200 linen pants and their ruined."

With that, she started to cry, lost her balance again, and flopped down hard on her rear end back in the mud.

"Oh no you don't", I said, as I snatched her up, put her back on my shoulder, and finished the trek to my place. Fortunately, I lived in an electronically secured building with no doorman or other human I had to encounter on the way up to my apartment. I opened the door and walked Colleen inside.

I sat her on a big bar chair in my kitchen while I fetched a bathrobe and some Woolite laundry soap from the bathroom. For some reason, I had it in my head that saving those white linen pants was a priority. I would have Colleen put on my robe, take off the muddy pants, and I could hand scrub them while a fresh pot of coffee was brewing. My plan got scuttled when I returned to find Colleen stripped down to her white lace bra and panties standing in my living room with her muddy pants in her hand.

"Well okay," I said. "I guess there's no need to be shy and ..."

When I reached for the pants, she grabbed my arm and dragged me backwards and down on top of her on the sofa. She was all arms and legs grinding on me, sticking her tongue in my mouth, and scratching my neck. When I tried to get off her, she grabbed my head and tried to shove my face down between her legs.

"Come on" she hissed. "I want it".

I pushed up off of her to get some breathing room. It was the first time I had gotten a good look at her face in the light since this ordeal started back at the bar. She was out of her mind, heaving and panting like a wolverine in heat, pupils big as dimes. It was clear to me she was more than just drunk.

"Come on, give it to me" she demanded, as she rammed her hand down her panties and started playing with herself.

So, there I was. On my knees beside my leather sofa with this gorgeous half-naked woman out of her mind, frantically masturbating and demanding that I "give it to her now".

I had one of those moments like you see in old cartoons where an angel and a devil appear on your shoulders. The devil looked and sounded like my buddy Steve. "Fuck her", he barked. "Fuck her before she passes out". The angel looked disturbingly like my mother. She didn't say anything. She just gave me that look that blends shame and disappointment into one emotion. I knew there was no chance that I was going to do anything but the right thing.

"I've got to take a shower ... I'm all sweaty ... I stink", I said as I got up and moved towards the bathroom. Colleen seemed not to notice. Her eyes rolled back in their sockets as she diddled away and began to moan. I took the muddy pants into the kitchen and started preparing a sink full of water to soak them in. I watched her from a distance, and she eventually quit wriggling and moaning; eyes closed and mouth open.

I guess she either finished or passed out ... or both. As I went to work scrubbing the mud out of her white linen pants I had to chuckle.

"What a night," I said to the room. And, looking over at Colleen, "What a beautiful mess!"

The next day was Sunday and I got up with the sun like I always do. I milled around quietly tidying up my place while the coffee brewed. I crept downstairs and got the Sunday paper, brought it out to my balcony, and began my Sunday morning ritual.

The night before I had scooped Colleen's sleeping carcass off the couch, fitted her with a big t-shirt, and put her in my bed. I slept in the guest room. I figured she would wake up, find her way out to the balcony, and join me for coffee while we had a good laugh over the crazy first date.

As I sipped coffee and read an article in the Travel Section about Malaysia, I was feeling quite chivalrous. I'd been the perfect gentleman. I was sure Colleen would appreciate that. I was sure she'd be a little embarrassed about last night. I was sure we'd have a good laugh about it. I was sure this would be a quirky but solid launch for a meaningful relationship. I'd done the right thing and surely, I would be rewarded.

Colleen suddenly appeared on the balcony wrapped tightly in my big white bathrobe. Standing in the doorway, green eyes blazing, "Where are my clothes" she barked.

My romantic fantasy immediately evaporated. With those four simple words, she reached inside my brain and flipped a switch that took me from *Cloud Nine* to *Defense Condition One.*

My internal Secretary of Defense suddenly called a meeting to formulate the immediate response to the angry shot just fired across my bow. Should I back her off with an incredulous "Excuse me?" Should I ignore her obvious hostility and come on all lovey-dovey with a "good morning darling, how are you feeling?" The decision was made in a split second, and I opted for an odd combination of nonchalance and literal interpretation.

"They're in the laundry room. Your pants may be a little damp as I didn't want to put them in the dryer".

"What happened last night? How did I get undressed? Why did you wash my clothes?"

I stuck with my approach. I poured her a cup of coffee from the tray next to my chair and motioned for her to sit down opposite me.

"You had too much to drink. I couldn't find a taxi. You fell down in the mud. I brought you here and you fell asleep".

She didn't take the coffee. She didn't sit down. She stared at me unblinkingly and didn't say a word.

"Let me guess", I said. "You don't remember any of that, right?"

"No! All I know is I woke up this morning with a blasting headache and no clothes. I remember we ate dinner and then walked around the lake".

"You don't remember going to Tanqueray's?"

"What's Tanqueray's?"

"If you'll sit down and have some coffee, I'll give you a play-by-play account of the whole crazy night".

"I don't want to sit down. I want to go home".

She stood there rigid, nostrils flaring and impossible to read. I couldn't tell if she was enraged or scared or confused or all of the above. I took a big gulp of my coffee and got up.

"Okay then. I'll drive you home. Your clothes are in the laundry room. If they're damp, I can give you something to wear".

She spun around and headed into the room where I pointed and closed the door. In less than a minute she came out wearing her clothes from the night before, damp pants and all.

"Did you fuck me?" she said accusingly.

"No Colleen. Nothing like that happened. I told you already. You passed out and I put you in my bed. I slept in there".

She walked to the doorway of the guest bedroom to investigate the scene.

"You made the bed already?"

"I always make my bed in the morning. Blame my mother. When I come back, I'll no doubt make the bed you slept in. What's your point?"

She gave me another nasty look and snapped, "Ok, let's go".

After she gave me the directions, not another word came out of her. I slowed down near the park and pointed out the spot where she had fallen and rolled around in the mud. You could see all the plants uprooted and mashed down. She wouldn't even acknowledge what I said. When we got to her house, she continued looking straight ahead and hissed, "Thanks for the ride", flung the door open and leaped from the car.

As I backed out of the driveway and slowly drove down her street, I could feel the rage starting to boil. There was no need for placating tones now. There was no need to hold it in. I was in the solitude of my own car.

"Thanks for the ride?" I screamed to myself. *"How about thanks for carrying my gangly drunk ass for ten blocks in 90-degree heat! Thanks for scrubbing the mud out of my precious linen pants at 2 in the morning! Thanks for not banging me like a screen door in a hurricane! How about some thanks for that you nutty bitch?"*

Letting it out didn't feel as good as I thought it would. It just made me madder. When I got home, I made myself a stiff Bloody Mary and called Kim, my partner's wife who set this whole thing in motion.

"Hey Lando" she crooned in her smooth Alabama accent. "How'd it go last night?"

I took a deep breath and let her have it. Every detail. Every nook and cranny of the story. In one long profanity-laden rant she got a spectacularly clear picture of "how it went".

"Oh my," she said. "I'm sorry things went south. I hope she's okay."

"What the fuck do you mean you hope *she's* ok? I took care of her drunk ass. You know me, Kim. I'm big daddy Lando, the great protector. I got her home, cleaned her up, and tucked her into bed like she was my three-year-old niece. Other than a vicious hangover, she couldn't be more okay."

"Did you fuck her?"

"I just told you the whole story. Did you think I left that part out? No, I didn't fuck her. What kind of question is that?"

"Sorry", she said. "I know you are a gentleman. I didn't mean to insinuate you did anything. It's just a question. I don't quite know what else to say about all this".

"How well do you know her?" I asked.

"I don't know her well at all. She works at the office of my sister Kelly's therapist. They became friends and we met at a barbecue. She seems like a really cool chic. I thought you guys would hit it off, and, well ... I'm so sorry. Don't worry. If you need me to vouch for your character, you know I've got your back".

I could tell she wanted to get off the line and out of this conversation as quickly as possible. If the date had been a rousing success, we'd have had to talk for an hour and make plans for a weekend somewhere all "coupled up". Now that the hook-up was a disaster, she couldn't wait to distance herself from it.

"Ok Kimbo, I know you meant well. It's not your fault" I said and hung up the phone.

I spent the rest of the morning and early afternoon escaping the whole ordeal by surfing the internet and looking at new places to travel. As I disappeared down rabbit hole after rabbit hole of travel fantasies, I imagined establishing a home located in a city with a good airport. That way I could explore dozens of cool places within only a few hours. Singapore, Hong Kong, Manila ... my fantasy cities.

I loved to hear names of exotic cities announced when I was at the airport. "Cathay Pacific flight 119 bound for Jakarta is now boarding at gate 7. Now arriving at gate 3, Dragon Air Flight 141 from Kuala Lumpur". I'd have loved to be stepping off a plane at any of those airports.

Around 6 PM I headed to the gym to take out my frustration on an unsuspecting elliptical stepper. For the next hour or so I played the whole evening back in my head at least ten times. Where did I go wrong? Why is she so angry? What should I have done? Am I the asshole here?

I went home, ate some dinner, and laid in my bed staring at the ceiling. I thought about calling Colleen but wasn't sure what to say. I knew I would never get to sleep until I had some kind of relief. I knew I needed to talk to *my* therapist. I needed to see my Uncle Butch.

Now, Butch Barnes isn't actually my uncle. He's a friend of my father that I've known nearly all my life. Butch is an old Vietnam veteran with a stable of successful businesses in town. He's got a bail bonds business, a private investigation company, a Harley Davidson dealership, two self-storage facilities, and three topless bars. When I got out of the military, he gave me my first job and introduced me to some girls. His superpower is seeing through anybody's bullshit, and he is an incredible judge of character. And, when it comes to doling out wisdom, the Dali Lama has nothing on Uncle Butch.

I rang him up and he said we could meet at one of his bars around 10 PM. I got there early and was chatting with an old acquaintance when Butch came in. He is an enormous bear of a man with a long-braided ponytail and bushy beard. "Youngblood!" he bellowed and administered a spine-crushing hug. He grabbed me a beer from behind the bar and we headed to his office in the back.

Just as I had earlier with Kim, I regaled him with the entire story, blow-by-blow. When Butch listens, you can tell he was a private investigator. He doesn't ask questions. He lets you spill out the story the way you want to. He watches your face and body language. He listens to your tone. Then he asks questions. When I was done with the story, he pursed his lips and asked, "Gotta picture?" I showed him one from Saturday night that the waiter had taken of Colleen and me with my phone.

"Ooooweeee youngblood, that looks top-shelf. She's a little high-end for you ain't she?"

"I'm trying to get off the strippers Butch. Looking for something a little more real".

"Did you fuck her?"

"No, I told you what happened. Banging some girl who is whacked out of her mind isn't my style Butch, come on now".

"I would a fucked her"

"Butch, be serious. I need your advice".

"I am serious boy. That's what she wanted. She took a cab to your place because she didn't plan on going home. Then she proceeded to get out of control, and she figured you would seize the moment. I'll bet when she stripped down, she was wearing some fancy lingerie, wasn't she? She's mad because you didn't take the bait. Now she's gotta get a new plan to get what she wants".

"What she wants? What does she want? Money?"

He took another look at the picture and added, "Your money, your time, your soul ... whatever you got, that bitch will take it. She has seen your world and she wants in. She planned to get you on the back foot from the beginning and to have you properly posed in the "apology position". An ass-kissing, southern-gentleman-white-knight dickhead like yourself is irresistible to a woman like that. An easy mark".

"So, you're saying she planned this whole event? I've been set up?"

"Not exactly. This is the kind of woman who creates chaos then feeds on it. She shakes up your scene, fucks up your plans, and maintains a steady position as the center of attention. All your time, money, and attention need to be focused on her. The moment it isn't, she'll shake shit up some more. She has an intention and a technique, but not a specific plan of action. Chances are she's scheming right now on how to take what happened, or did not happen, and keep it working for her. Look at you. You're all shook up over this shit and you did nothing wrong. That's exactly what I mean. You're obsessing over how to satisfy her right now. This little oxygen thief is your classic "chaotic cunt". Believe me boy, I've seen my share".

While I wasn't happy with his analysis, it validated why I'd come to Butch in the first place.

"What should I do?" I asked.

"What are you most afraid of? What is it that has you quaking in your boots right now?"

"I'm afraid she's going to say I raped her. I'm afraid she's going to file a complaint with the police and tell some crazy story. Half of the neighborhood saw me carrying that drunk bitch through downtown. Nobody's going to believe I didn't fuck her. That's the kind of thing that could burn my life down Butch. I'm not prepared for that".

"That's why I said you should have fucked her. Saying you had consensual sex is a much more believable defense than saying you were a boy scout. Look at you with your fancy car and bachelor crib ... of course, you fucked her!".

I closed my eyes and shook my head trying to get some focus. Butch could see I needed help.

"First off, don't contact her. Let her come at you with her new plan. Once she sees that the "angry bitch" routine doesn't bring you running, she'll switch to a new tactic. You need to find out what her main motivation is, then you can make *your* plan. Second, get this "finding a soulmate" horseshit out of your head. That ship has sailed for you youngblood. You're forty-something and single with a pocket full of money. There's a way to conduct yourself and this ain't it. Get back on the strippers. They're simple creatures with simple needs. Bitches like this one from Saturday night are soul assassins. Let me know if you need my help. You know I'm always here for family".

"You've been a fountain of wisdom as usual Butch. What would I do without you?"

I endured another bear hug and left the bar feeling better but not relieved. When I got home there was a message on my house phone.

"Hi, it's Colleen. We need to talk".

I waited until the next day and called while she was at work.

"Look, I'm sorry for being so short with you yesterday," she said. "I was in a bit of shock. That kind of thing has never happened to me before. I just want to know what happened".

"I understand Colleen, but I told you what happened. Don't you believe me?"

"Well, it's not that. I just can't remember, so I don't know for sure. I've never blacked out before and it is kind of freaking me out. I hope you understand. I just need to know what happened for sure."

"Colleen, there were dozens of eyewitnesses that saw me carry you home. We can go downtown, start at Tanqueray's, and work our way toward my place talking to people. I'll bet someone took a picture. It was quite a scene. Would that do it for you?"

"Well, no. I'm mostly concerned with what happened inside your apartment. When it was just you and me. I have to be sure about what happened. I'm not on birth control. What if I'm pregnant?"

That question shut down my ability to speak momentarily. Before I could croak out a response, she said, "My boss is calling me ... gotta go". And she hung up the phone.

I went back to the gym and stomped the guts out of that poor elliptical stepper again. "Pregnant?" What the fuck was this all about? I thought about what Uncle Butch had said. What was her motivation? What was her plan? She won't call me a liar, but she won't say she believes me. And now she throws out the "P" word. What the fuck is she after?

About 7 PM she called me back.

"Hey, sorry to leave you hanging but it got really busy. I have some great news! I think I found a solution to our problem".

I sat down and poured myself a big-ass bourbon and soda. "I'm all ears," I said.

"Well, I had a long talk with my therapist today. He said it is possible that I've experienced some kind of emotional trauma and I have blocked the whole experience out as a defense mechanism".

She let that hang in the air for a moment for me to get a grip on. A big smile came over my face as I heard Uncle Butch's voice in my head. *"You need to find out what her main motivation is, then you can make a plan".*

"Go on", I said "I'm listening".

"My therapist said there is a special kind of treatment that is like a medically induced hypnosis. It can be used to help victims recover blocked memories. It's called Recovered Memory Therapy or RMT. This treatment is being used to help people recall things that happened to them and get closure on certain events in their lives. It all sounds kind of scary, but I really want to be sure about what happened. I don't want to always wonder about it. I think this new treatment could be the answer".

"That sounds interesting Colleen. Please, tell me more".

"Well, the closest place I could try this treatment is in Atlanta under the supervision of an associate of my therapist. It takes three days, and it is kind of expensive. $10,000. Do you think that's a lot?

I was so glad this conversation was over the phone because there is no way I could have kept a straight face while she spun this bullshit tale. She went on for ten minutes about years of research and miraculous results. Every few minutes I'd encourage her with an "oh really" or "wow, that's impressive". Then she went for the close.

"They are terribly busy, but I might be able to get in at the end of next week. My therapist says the sooner after the traumatic experience I take the treatment, the more likely it is to work. I'll need a deposit by this Friday. Can you help me please?"

I let it hang there for a few seconds and told her that I had to go to out of town in the morning for a business meeting but would call her back when I returned. We could discuss it some more then. I could hear her fidget. She wanted to close the deal right then I could tell.

In my most sincere and reassuring voice, I said, "Don't worry honey, I'll call you tomorrow night. We'll figure this out together".

For once the whole I'm-a-gentleman-and-man-of-my-word thing worked in my favor and she took my promise as legitimate. Now I knew her plan. I had a plan too. And my plan had nothing to do with her plan.

That night I stood on the balcony of my condo sipping whisky and watching fireflies blink on and off around the park. This place I lived was the epitome of swinging-dick bachelorism ... that dream pad all young men fantasize about from the time they build their first treehouse.

I'd worked hard to be where I was; to get this place, to get that beach condo, that fancy car, and just about everything else I ever wanted. Last week, I thought the only thing I needed was a woman to share it all with. That elusive soulmate that would make my life complete. That's the dream I'd chased all my life. That's the American dream.

But in this moment of clarity, I realized that I didn't really want that life. Living to achieve status and meet some archetypical "Joe America" model wasn't *my* dream. I realized I was not the guy with shit on his shoe. I did not have to conform to a lifestyle that did not suit me. I realized that there is more than one way to live a life.

Right there, on that steamy summer night, I knew what I needed ... what I sincerely wanted ... what I should have seen was my destiny two years earlier.

I took a shower, laid in the bed, and turned on a recording I'd made of the waves sloshing against the shore on the island of Phuket a year before. Something about the rhythm of those waves synchronizes my breathing and heartbeat to a peaceful frequency I don't feel anywhere else. At one point I could hear the faint sound of the Thai national anthem playing in the background and I remembered that was the day I learned they play it all over the country on loudspeakers at 8 a.m. That was my last thought before drifting off into a peaceful dreamless sleep.

On Tuesday morning I woke up charged with purpose. I packed my big suitcase, secured my laptop in its shock-proof backpack, and set out with a list of errands.

I stopped by my realtor's office and signed contracts to put both of my condos on the market for sale "fully furnished". I dropped off my car at the Jaguar dealership and told the manager to sell it at the next auto auction.

In the taxi on the way to the airport, I dismantled my mobile phone and threw it out the window into a ditch.

Twenty-four hours later I landed in Bangkok.

Maid for Trouble

Part 1 - The Mole

Expats in Thailand are always bragging about their maids. *"My maid Kung is a great cook; she washes my car and cuts my hair"* ... *"My maid Oy painted the house, dug a well and had her uncle finance my new truck"* ... *"My maid Nut killed a cobra in the back yard"*, and on and on. Mostly I hear it from people who've never had a maid before.

I've had a maid before. In the US I had two. In my city condo the maid was actually a brother and sister team. All I really remember about them was that she was fat, he was gay, and they didn't just clean my place, they sanitized it. The maid I used at my beach place was an ex-biker chic named Dixie (no, really, her name was Dixie). She had a silver tooth, a beat-up station wagon and held strong convictions about punctuality and the power of bleach. They were both expensive, but worth every dime. They didn't interfere in my affairs. They didn't pour out sad stories about their personal lives. They didn't become members of my family. They showed up on a regular schedule and cleaned my living quarters ... period. Apparently, the word "maid" means something different in Thailand.

My early months in Bangkok were spent in serviced apartments. Serviced apartments were new to me. They looked like hotels, and in fact offer most hotel services. The main differences being the rooms are designed for long-stay businessmen and their families. The maids will come at any interval you desire. They even had a laundry facility if you had the free time and energy to wash your own clothes.

The maids in all the serviced apartments I stayed hovered a little too much. They seemed to always be in my room and my business. Once I went to Koh Samui for three days and returned to being locked out of my room and all my stuff downstairs being "stored" in the manager's office. *"We think you go America",* was her excuse. Even though I'd paid to the end of the month, for some reason the maids decided that I had abandoned the room and all my personal effects to run off back to the US, never to be heard from again. The lack of privacy prompted me to start looking for a more permanent living arrangement.

At that point I made some strategically bad moves. A friend recommended a property agent to help me in my home search. The agent squired me around town in her big old Mercedes for two weeks looking at apartments. Her name was Joop, and she looked like Minnie Mouse with a boob-job. Naturally, we started dating. I finally ended up in this high-end stuffy-ass mega building on Wireless Road mostly to impress her. She was more than thrilled to orchestrate every aspect of my moving-in and living arrangements including, of course, the hiring of a maid.

A week after I moved in this short, fat, black-as-tar Thai woman showed up and started cleaning. She spoke not one word of English and when confronted with my rudimentary Thai could only stare in disbelief. I was able to teach her how to use an

electric steam iron and a sponge mop. For some
reason, I'm quite proud of that.

She wasn't a particularly good maid, so I complained
to Joop. She responded with a long sad tale about this
maid being her cousin who lost her husband in a
gruesome farming accident. She painted a picture of a
poor single mother just doing what she can to feed her
two young children. The woman continued to work
for me as I am a sucker for a single mom story.

A few months later Joop and I weren't getting along
so well. The green-eyed monster of jealousy made the
scene and suddenly she was one of those psychic
detectives. She seemed to know my every move. She
knew when I left the apartment, what time I came
home and when I might have had "visitors". I knew
the Thai girl intelligence network was good, but this
was bordering on clairvoyance.

Then one day Joop confronted me all wild-eyed and
full of jealous rage. She burst through my front door
wailing like a police siren with three long brown curly
hairs trapped between her thumb and forefinger.
"These aren't mine" she barked ... *"Look at my hair ...
these aren't mine ... who is this whore?* She stood
there righteous and accusing, the offending hairs
shoved in my face like a big stinky finger.

I examined 'exhibit A" and sure enough, those didn't
look like Joop's hairs. I also noticed that clinging to
the hairs was other debris like small pieces of lint and
dirt. It didn't make sense because the maid had come
that morning and there wasn't any stuff like that on
my floor now. These hairs were kind of matted
together with all this other stuff as if she had dug

them out of the trash bin. But she had come straight in the door with the offending hairs already in her possession.

That's when I realized I'd been had. Evidently the maid swept up my floor and delivered the evidence of last evening's midnight visitor to Joop, throwing me directly under the bus. I was gob smacked and stone-cold busted.

After Joop bilingually berated me for half an hour, she ran out of steam and went home leaving me to wallow in guilt. So, I did what any self-respecting cad would do in such a situation. I changed the locks, got a new phone number, and ran off to Phuket for two weeks.

While stretched out under an umbrella on Nai Harn beach I put it all together. The maid was the mole. She had telegraphed my every move. She was a big fat fly on my wall, broadcasting every indiscretion directly to my possessive girlfriend. Her country bumpkin demeanor had lulled me into a false sense of superiority.

I felt violated and betrayed. But, I had just learned my first important lesson in Thailand ... always hire your own maids.

Part 2 - Boss Lady

The trip to Phuket led to moving down there. After I found a condo near the beach, I knew the maid decision would be coming soon. The low-rise building where I lived used an independent cleaning service run by a rough talking southern Thai woman named Koy. Every morning I would see her arrive with her big Isuzu pick-up truck packed to the gunnels with eager young up-country girls from Isan. They would descend on several apartments at a time and did everything from scrubbing floors to ironing shirts. For the next few months, I was in domestic heaven. They would come when I wasn't there and leave the place looking like a model home. I hoped it would last forever.

For several weeks in a row, I had the same lead cleaner named Saa. Saa was a mousey looking country girl with mis-matched clothes and a horrendous overbite. What she lacked in looks she made up with pure domestic skill. She was in and out within an hour and always left me some kind of fruit in the fridge.

This was my first experience with the 'compassionate maid" syndrome. Thai women, especially those from Isan, can't understand why a man my age would choose to live alone. She thought I must have some dark sadness in my life that could be soothed with a little TLC, so she took it upon herself to "take care". She brought me food. She left me menus and business cards from restaurants and salons and massage places she thought I should try. One day I came home, and she had taken out all my shoes and cleaned them thoroughly. I should note, this is also a great way to ensure job security. I quickly advanced from "using" her to clean my place to "depending" on all the little things she did.

One day Saa showed up in obvious distress. Her head was down. Her eyes were red. She moved like an old lady. I asked her what was wrong ... another strategic mistake on my part. It was pretty simple really. She had become pregnant. Her husband was ecstatic, but her boss Koy was not. She was fired. That day would be her last.

Filled with righteous indignation, I immediately informed Koy that I wouldn't need her services and hired Saa directly to clean my place twice a week. I also recommended Saa to a friend of mine who instantly hired her. I felt downright chivalrous. I'd helped a struggling Thai family make ends meet. I was unfamiliar with the whole "White Knight" thing, but I liked the feeling it produced. Saa worked up to one week before the she gave birth. After she had the baby, she was back to work in two weeks.

Over the next year and a half, I helped Saa build her cleaning business to a point where she employed other girls and was able to buy her own pick-up truck. When I built my own little housing development, Saa and her crew kept all four houses looking move-in ready.

Sometimes I would see Koy, the boss from the old cleaning service, around our end of the island and she was always very genial to me. She would ask how my business was and if I still employed Saa. She was all greasy-smiley, rank with ulterior motive. It was creepy.

One day Saa came to collect her monthly pay displaying the same drained look I'd seen two years earlier. Naturally, I had to know what was up. Head down, in a creaky voice she told me a heart-breaking story. She and her husband had been saving her money and living on his salary derived from painting houses. They planned to move back to their village near Sisaket in the northeast where they could build a house. Her business was "very good", and she had ten girls in her employ. My apartment was actually the only place she personally cleaned anymore. "I am boss lady" she said.

With her newly found wealth and freedom came boredom. She ended up in an illegal gambling den every day. "I play card" is how she put it. It sounded so innocent, just playing cards with some friends.

"I am very lucky at first" she offered, but within a few months, Saa lost so much money she had to sell her work truck to pay her debts. When her husband found out, he took the baby and left her. "He says I'm sick" she pleaded, "Khun Lando, do you think I'm sick?"

I listened to Saa bawl and bawl and tell me the story over and over again. Every time she told it; more came out. She had been invited to play cards by her old employer Koy. Koy had befriended her and stroked Saa's ego saying how proud she was of her business success. Koy called her "little sister". She introduced Saa to a group of women who played and drank and gambled on a daily basis. To Saa they all seemed to be rich. They all seemed to be "boss ladies".

Koy told her she only played a couple times a week. In reality, it was Koy who owned the gambling operation, and the house bank which made usurious loans to the not-so-lucky members of the club. It was Koy that had taken Saa's new work truck as payment for gambling debts. It was also Koy that informed Saa's husband of her nefarious activities.

This was beyond just snuffing out the competition. This was personal. Koy wrecked Saa's life like it was a game she wanted to win.

For sure I've felt sorrier for someone, but I can't remember when. Partly because I felt somehow to blame and mostly because I just wanted her to stop crying, I gave Saa 20,000 baht and told her to take some time off.

I never saw the bucktooth girl from Sisaket again.

Part 3 – The Somtam Queen of Soi Sixteen

After three monsoon seasons, I exchanged all my beach stuff in Phuket for city stuff and moved back to Bangkok. My new endeavors had me busy enough to employ a part time assistant named Ampa. She is a crusty old Chinese-Thai schoolteacher. Without her, my life in Thailand would surely have been less rewarding. When I finally got settled into my new condo, in a building I actually liked, I set her about the task of hiring a maid. I told her my requirements for employment.

"I want them to come twice a week, preferably when I'm not here" I said. I instructed her about my pet peeves, the cleaning products I preferred and laundry requirements. Through it all she nodded thoughtfully and even made notes. I realized those were some demanding parameters for my future domestic aid, but I told her we had time to look.

In a week she called me. "Have maid come now" she said.

I asked her what time and she simply said, "When you go out". I could have asked more questions, but for reasons peculiar to Thailand, I did not.

I went to the gym and ran some errands. When I came back the place was so clean it looked freshly painted. When I opened my fridge a big bag of fresh papaya salad (somtam) was neatly wrapped up in plastic along with some grilled chicken (gai yang). Somtam is like the Thai national food. A spicy salad of green papaya, garlic, lime, tomato, lots of chilies and various other ingredients including the beautiful fresh blue crab in the portion left by my new maid. I liked whoever she was already. Once again, I was wallowing in domestic bliss.

For the next three weeks my apartment seemed self-cleaning. Any time I left the building, I would return to a fresh smelling place with some kind of food in the fridge. Sometimes I'd only be gone 45 minutes. Keep in mind that I'm not exactly a creature of habit in Bangkok. Out late some nights, home the next ... up with the chickens most days but pulling the shades until noon on others. No matter how mercurial my schedule, this new maid seemed to have no problem. She was a phantom and it started to freak me out.

When I called my assistant Ampa to ask about the new maid's uncanny ability to predict my presence, she said, "Are you home now?"

I confirmed that I was indeed in my apartment and she instructed "Go to the window and look down".

After I had gotten into position she asked, "What you see on the corner?". I focused eight floors down on the corner of my small alley and the larger Soi 16. It was lunchtime and dozens of office workers from the skyscraper across the street were clamoring around a street-food vendor with two carts going full blast. Everyone called the proprietor of this mobile restaurant "Noi-Noi, the Somtam Queen of Soi 16". I can attest, she does indeed make the best somtam I have ever tasted. And, from the size of the crowds around her carts in the morning and at noon, Thai people thought so too.

"I see the Somtam Lady" I told Ampa.

She clucked with satisfaction for a moment and corrected me, "No, you see your maid!" "Noi-Noi is your maid now."

Suddenly, it all made sense. The somtam lady was on that corner from 6 AM to 8 PM every day of the week. There is no way for me to leave my building without her or her family seeing me. When I leave, she and her niece would come clean my place. It's extra money they can earn while being on the job at the food cart. Whoever said Thais aren't multi-tasking or problem solvers isn't paying attention.

Noi became part of the family, or I should say I became part of hers. Every day I would sip coffee on my balcony and watch Noi, her husband and her niece arrive just at sunrise to set up the food carts. Even in the failing light I could see Noi's short thick silhouette doing all the heavy lifting while her sorry-ass husband watched and smoked.

Noi pounded the somtam in a giant clay mortar and pestle contraption. Somtam is also knows as Papaya Pok-Pok because of the distinct sound of the wooden pestle bashing rhythmically into the sides of the mortar ... pok ... pok ... pok. Her husband tended two grills, slowly basting chicken, and catfish. The niece handled all the money and phone-in orders. At least four days a week I ate food from this roadside café and sometimes I even paid for it. For two years Noi was usually the first person I spoke to every day.

When I bought three other condos in the building and filled them with renters, Noi serviced all of them as part of my contract with the tenants. It made my tenants happy and was a great way to keep an eye on my units to make sure they were properly maintained. (Yes, I had learned to use the maid as a mole.)

One day she came to me wringing her hands with something obviously on her mind. I suspected she might want a raise, and I was kind of right. Noi wanted to borrow money to buy another super deluxe food cart to set up on the opposite side of the street where she could have several roadside tables and stools. This would be a significant expansion of her business and would cost 45,000 baht. I asked for time think about it.

The next two nights I wrestled with her request. My experience had been that when you loan a friend or family money, it's the surest way to get rid of them. Not to mention that my previous experience with enriching my maid's earning ability had not worked out so well. And from what I had seen, even well-intentioned Thai folks tend to be less than reliable when it comes to re-paying loans ... especially to "rich" farangs. I declined her request through my assistant Ampa to save everyone face.

The next day Noi quit cleaning any of my condos. She told Ampa she was too busy. For several days I did not see her. About a week later I saw her and a handful of helpers setting up the super deluxe food cart, complete with tables and a dozen stools.

Apparently, I wasn't the only person she hit up for a loan. When I spoke to her, she ignored me. Her niece just smiled sheepishly and tried to look busy. Her husband stared off into space, turning catfish on the grill. I was no longer in the family. I was orphaned.

And, once again, I had no maid.

Part 4 - Durian Face

After a few years of soaking up toxins in Bangkok, I decided to move back to the beach. And, having acquired a real girlfriend, I was keen to take a stab at playing house. My girlfriend Mina and I moved to a big condo on the beach two and a half hours from Bangkok near Sattahip.

I offered to hire a maid, but Mina insisted she could handle the big rambling condo. And, in fact she kept the place spotless. A few months into our cohabitation, Mina found a good job and was soon doing the 9 to 5 thing, 6 days per week. She asked me if we could hire a maid. I told her I would leave the interview process up to her.

Mina's boss and his family live in the condo upstairs and we borrowed their maid Jai two days per week. Jai was a young, pleasantly plump Isan girl with a smile that could light up Las Vegas. She was just nice to have around.

One day I forgot Jai's name and asked Mina what the name of our maid was. Mina looked confused and said she didn't know who I meant.

I insisted, "The maid honey ... the girl with the big butt." Jai never cleaned our house again. Apparently, I'm not supposed to notice the maid's posterior.

Later that week Mina informed me that we had a new maid who would come when I was at the gym. Sure enough, my home once again appeared to be self-cleaning. Only on a few occasions did I ever actually see our new maid. She was skinny and dark with a fake diamond on one of her front teeth ... the sure sign of a Pattaya girl. Mina told me she was the former wife of one of the factory workers from her company. I never did know her name.

One night Mina came home, we had dinner and as was our habit, we drank wine on the balcony under the stars. Without provocation, my beautiful, sweet girlfriend looked at me and said, "I fired that fucking maid".

"What?" I heard myself say. I'm not sure if I was stunned about the maid or by my princess suddenly developing a potty-mouth. I'd known Mina nearly six years, and we had lived together more than half of those years. Never, and I mean never, had I heard her use foul words in any language.

"Why? What did she do?" I asked.

"She wants to fuck you ... you want to fuck her ... I can see" she hissed.

I pleaded "Mina, that's ridiculous, I haven't spoken to that girl more than three times since she's been working for us. What the hell makes you think there is something between me and that skinny-ass Pattaya girl?"

Nothing I said would convince her of my innocence. The maid and I were getting it on and that was that. She stormed into the bedroom and began putting on the show of packing her clothes.

Alone I sat on my terrace, staring up at the stars and asking what I had done to deserve this abuse. Nothing is worse than to be a womanizer getting accused of being a womanizer when you aren't womanizing. Confusion turned to indignant rage. So, I decided to do what my father would do to clear up such an obvious misunderstanding. I got everybody in one room.

Mina was shocked when I entered the bedroom and started helping her pack the rest of her clothes. Her surprise turned to horror when I produced her cell phone and demanded she call the maid to come right that moment. Thais being a non-confrontational lot, she made several excuses why she couldn't call before I finally forced the issue by dialing the number myself.

When the maid arrived that night, her demeanor was subservient and timid. She could see that Mina and I were already whipped into a frenzy. For sure she wished she had never come. I started the three-way conversation using my low-grade Thai. Within seconds I had to physically separate the two. I've seen Thai girls fight before. You can't let them get close enough grab each other's hair or you'll never stop the carnage. We repeated this angry dance several times ... me asking questions ... Mina and the maid answering simultaneously ... the exchange becoming overheated ... me playing referee.

Slowly I started to understand. The recently divorced maid had taken on housekeeping as a profession to make ends meet. She had never been a maid before. When she saw the lifestyle enjoyed by me and Mina, she set her mind to getting a foreign boyfriend of her own. Unfortunately for her, she made mention of her new direction while drunk and in the presence of several of the ladies that work for Mina's company. And, she didn't just say she would get a rich foreign boyfriend ... she said she would get me! According to Mina, she had told anyone within earshot that Mina didn't take care of me like she would, and it would be easy to steal me away.

Naturally, the combination of a territorial intrusion and the loss of face with her peers sent my princess over the edge. So, she had fired the maid and come home to kick me a few times just in case I was guilty of something. While I understood, it still stung that I was being battered for something I had no part in. I was living a nice comfortable existence with my beautiful Thai girlfriend in my condo by the sea. As we say in the US, "minding my own business". In a flash I was being accused and abused with foul-mouthed tirades and physical threats.

The maid denied she was guilty of any chicanery. Mina called her a liar and a whore. Finally, I grew a spine and took action.

I cut the heated exchange off mid-accusation. I dismissed the maid very politely, collected her key and thanked her for her time. Mina gloated over her apparent victory. As the maid walked to the lift Mina couldn't resist releasing one last burst of insulting threats down the corridor. Both in Thai and in English (I suppose for my benefit) she screamed, *"You come back I give you durian face!"* (For those who are unfamiliar with durian ... it is a fruit that looks like a rugby ball covered in pyramid shaped spikes. To be sure, getting a durian slammed into your face would be no fun.)

"Durian face ... you hear me whore? Durian face!" she screamed until the maid was out of sight. I never thought about Mina the same way again.

And I seriously doubt Mina ever thought about me the same way either. I explained to her that this kind of domestic drama is not what I moved to Thailand for. That night I continued to help her pack and sent her to her sister's house. We didn't speak for three months.

It was certainly lonely, but at least I had regained control over my domicile. The whole ordeal with the maid had uncovered a smoldering power struggle between me and Mina that I had not seen before. She had morphed into a person I did not recognize in an instant.

To be accused of infidelity and summarily not believed was something I just couldn't get over. She wouldn't apologize and she wouldn't say she believed me. The spat over the maid was the beginning of the end for Mina and me.

So, there I sat, all alone on the balcony of my beautiful seaside condo thinking about it. Through no fault of my own, I suddenly had no girlfriend.

And also, no maid.

Last week, a friend of mine and a newcomer to Thailand, called to meet for a beer. He had recently moved to Pattaya and was living in a nice big beach condo. He picked my brain about things like getting internet service, getting a driving license, and various relocation-oriented queries.

Almost as an afterthought he threw in, "Hey bro ... do you know where I can find a good maid?"

I just smiled and sipped my beer. "Sorry man ... can't help you there".

The Legend of Bangkok Bill

We never really know who a person was before they came to Thailand. What's more, it is impossible to know how extended exposure will affect someone once they get here. If you plan to come and stay in Thailand for any length of time, my advice is to be prepared for changes, big and small. Some people come here and take on a new identity, shedding old lives like a reptile sheds its skin. Others find out who they really are.

Like I said, be prepared.

Big Bill Durant is a comic book super-hero come to life. He's a walking, talking, He-Man Master of the Universe. I may have met more physically imposing figures, but I can't remember when. I first laid eyes on him in the lobby of Casa Summer Breeze Hotel in Patong Beach on the island of Phuket. When he came down the stairway to the front desk, it was as if the Emperor had entered the room.

Six-foot three, 275 pounds of stacked up California beefcake. Think Arnold Schwarzenegger with a good tan and a thick shock of blonde hair. His shoulders looked like dinner plates and his forearms giant ham hocks. He walked by my table and gave me that *"What's up?"* nod Americans give to each other. Not only was this guy a chiseled giant, but he had the leading-man good looks to go with it. I hated him immediately.

Observing him from afar, he had that condescending cop-like demeanor towards lesser mortals. You just know this guy never played second team or sweated a prom date. Simply by his presence, Big Bill made every man in the room feel … less somehow.

Lester, the hotel owner, told me Bill was a retired prison guard from San Quentin State Penitentiary in California. Apparently, he'd had his skull cracked open in a prison riot and got retired a few years early with full benefits. Now he wanders back and forth from the US to Thailand looking for his special purpose. I put him on my list of "guys I'd like to be for 24 hours". He was one of those ridiculous characters a person sees when they spend any time in Thailand. If you made him up as a character for a book, people would disregard your work as "cartoonish" and unrealistic.

A few months later, I was visiting an acquaintance in Bangkok; another cartoon character American who claims his former occupation to be "snake wrangler". When I arrived at his condo to share a few beers and some catch-up stories, I was introduced to his new roommate, Bill Durant.

Bill remembered seeing me in Phuket and treated me like we'd been friends forever. Within a couple of beers and a few bowls of nice hashish, the blonde giant spilled out most of his life story. He was indeed a retired "Corrections Officer". He had been injured in a bloody jailhouse skirmish. And, for sure he was kind of lost and roaming around Asia. My awe and envy of his physical form soon wore away as his personality morphed from "asshole cop" to "adolescent surf dude". He giggled like a little girl when something was funny, and he's really into fart jokes.

He had just been diving in The Similan Islands and his description of the trip was like a fourth grader talking about what he did last summer. Bill employs generous use of words like, *"Dude!"* and *"Awesome"*. I'm not sure what I expected. He wasn't stupid, just really simple.

I asked him how he had remained a "Corrections Officer" in such a nasty place like San Quentin for eighteen years. He replied, "Dude, I got the job right after I got out of the Army and I was just too lazy to look for another gig." I went home feeling guilty about being happy he was imperfect.

Several weeks after our first meeting, I got a call from Bill inviting me to attend a grand re-opening of a nightclub he had been hired to manage at Nana Plaza in Bangkok. Nana Plaza is one of Bangkok's most well-known adult entertainment venues; a big three-story horseshoe-shaped adult playground with dozens of bars packed with hundreds of working girls. I remember arriving at the club and thinking perhaps Big Bill had found his special purpose. He was the consummate Papasan. With his custom fitted black silk shirt and fiercely gelled hair, he deftly directed DJ's, waitresses, and a whole army of tiny Thai go-go dancers. Bill greeted every customer with a big-ass American handshake and a ten thousand-megawatt smile. He was a king holding court, a man in his natural element. It was a fine thing to behold.

Within six weeks Bill had had sex with all the dancers and most of the bar staff. Friction with the French owner ensued. He got fired, and then he got a new job. Bill called me with another invitation to yet another party at another new venue. This place was bigger, better with a brand-new sound system and laser light show.

By this time, Bill was the prince of Nana Plaza, known by everyone on the street. He had a following. He was a draw all in himself. About once a week I'd meet Bill for dinner before he went to work and exchange stories. His stories were always better than mine.

Bill's day usually started about two in the afternoon. He would rise, eat, and go to the gym. After a few hours of hammering his giant frame into submission, he'd shower, play video games, and make phone calls to arrange the evening's entertainment. At 7 PM he'd head down Sukhumvit Road to eat and go to work. From 8 PM to 2AM he backslapped and drank with customers while directing traffic in his club. Whatever happened between the hours of 2 AM and 8 AM was usually unscripted beyond-the-pale debauchery.

If a doctor were to draw fluid samples from Big Bill at this stage of his Bangkok ascent, he would find some or all of the following ingredients: anabolic steroids, Human Growth Hormone, cocaine, hashish, ketamine, Viagra, Ecstasy, Jack Daniels and a little Valium to take the edge off. If you caught site of Bill at all, it was usually getting into or out of a taxi with no less than three Thai girls. He was a one-man diesel-powered party machine.

Within a few months Big Bill had again slept with all the dancers and most of the bar staff in his new club. Friction with the Belgian owner ensued, and he was once again in search of gainful employment.

One evening in Bangkok, Bill called me around midnight in a panic. Apparently, he'd been in steroid and whisky infused brawl and his opponent was in the hospital in serious condition. According to one eyewitness, *"Bill popped the guy like a grape"*. The big man was frantic, hiding from police and afraid to go home. I calmed him down and had him come to my condo on Soi 16.

"Relax Bill, come to my crib. Nobody knows me or where my place is dude. Don't be that stupid fuck who returns to the scene of the crime".

He came, we drank, and we talked. Normally, expats scatter from the scene of a crime and disavow knowledge of anyone involved. One minute, you're drinking buddies for life. In a flash you're The Lone Ranger.

Harboring Bill in my place and calming him down completed our bonding. In some respects, I felt a little responsible for Bill. He's a fellow American, former military like me, and a guy who has a lot of acquaintances, but no real friends. Another person sticking their neck out to help, with no ulterior motive, was a unique event for Bill.

I recommended he lay low for a while, so he came with me to Phuket where I had a big house in the jungle. He brought a travel companion that was just about the skankiest go-go girl I'd ever seen. She slept during daylight hours and ate during the rest. It took me three weeks to get the rancid smell of her perfume out of my house. During one of her waking moments, I studied the beautiful chain of sunflowers tattooed down the outside of her left leg. She caught me staring and, in startlingly good English, stated, "I got them in Sweden".

Before I could respond, she launched into a story about her ex-husband the Swedish gangster. She had been sitting in a car with him in Stockholm when a rival gang executed him in a drive by assassination. She had been shot three times and her husband killed. It was only then that I realized the center of each sunflower bore the telltale puffy scar tissue of a bullet hole. She repeated her short version of the story, "I got them in Sweden". After three days of sunshine and island life, the big man and his "bullet-ho" got itchy for some excitement and went back to Bangkok.

This is about the time I lost track of Bill. Since I'm up with the chickens and he's kind of a midnight rambler, our paths simply didn't cross. I heard he wasn't working. I heard he was still standing on the accelerator. I heard he owed some people some money.

Over the next few months, I gathered bits and pieces of Bill's Bangkok drama from his former friends, associates, and victims. His appetite for drugs, parties, and all things carnal had become larger than his modest retirement stipend from the California Department of Corrections. He became involved with some local illicit substance suppliers to boost his income. Unknown to Big Bill, he was being drawn into a sting coordinated between Thai authorities, an American Drug Enforcement crew, and their Australian counterparts.

When the noose was tightening, Bill fled Bangkok a couple of hours down the road to the seaside resort city of Pattaya, leaving a trail of broken everything.

Pattaya is the modern-day version of the ancient city of Sodom. In fact, I'm sure citizens of Sodom would blush at the goings on in Pattaya. Running to Pattaya to get out of trouble is the definition of jumping from the frying pan into the fire.

I heard no intelligence reports, so I assumed Bangkok Bill had descended into the neon-netherworld of Pattaya, Thailand's open-air brothel-by-the sea. Many who go this route never come back. Those that do return are usually changed in some profound way. It's just that kind of a place.

A few months later I spotted the big man on the prowl back in Bangkok. I had taken a high perch in a familiar go-go palace called "Angel-Witch" in Nana Plaza. The club was just getting filled up for their famous cabaret show at 10:30. Bill arrived as he usually does, with a grand entrance and an entourage.

The ladies he had in tow on this night were quite a diversion from those I'd seen in his company before. Normally, he liked the quintessential pole polisher, plastered with no less than five tattoos, multiple piercings and of course, the true mark of the breed, the fake diamond on one or more front teeth.

However, on this night, both creatures attached to his bulging biceps sported a little more equipment than usual. Even across a big smoky club I could determine they were exceptionally tall for Thai girls. And they were shamelessly displaying a garish array of surgical augmentations. Most notably, breasts that looked like they came from an auto-body shop rather than a skilled surgeon.

After a flash of disbelief and denial, I came to the inevitable realization that Big Bill had gone over to the dark side. Pattaya had taken another victim. In Thailand, his companions are known as "Katoeys" or "Lady-boys". Polite Thais refer to this sector of society as "the third sex". Where I come from, we call them Drag Queens.

Now, I've seen katoeys that were damned convincing imitations of demure Thai ladies, but that's not what these two were going for. Aggressive and surgically assisted, these "girls" weren't trying to look like Thai women at all. Every night is Halloween for this model of katoey, and they were costumed as Transgender Super-Hookers. In the local vernacular we call them "Fembots".

After much back slapping and California kisses with various members of Bangkok's slimy underclass, Bill finally spotted me observing from my perch. I saw him see me. He saw me see him. He sent over a drink as a diversion and vacated with his Fembots in tow. It hurt me to think he thought I'd be all "judgy" about his new direction. Maybe he wasn't quite sure how he felt about it himself.

At 4 AM my phone flashed an unknown number, but somehow, I knew it was Bill. He was drunk and barking like a seal. Without a "sorry it's been so long" or a "dude I lost my phone" story ... he launched into a half-assed explanation and goodbye.

"Dude, my life here is so fucked. I gotta go back to the States and sort some stuff out man. Leavin' tomorrow. Thanks for being my friend man ... you're the only dude in Bangers I trust." With that statement, whoever's phone he was using ran out of money.

A few weeks later, I got a call from Bill. He was in California, living with his sister and working as a "doorman" at a local strip club. He sounded like a kid who'd lost his puppy. Again, he expressed to me how much he appreciated my friendship. He thanked me for all my sage advice, and I wondered what the hell he was talking about. A guy with Thailand withdrawals can babble for hours. He made no mention of coming back. He sounded as though he had resigned himself to a small mean life there in LA. I never thought I'd see big Bill Durant again.

For the next six months I spent most of my time working on a real estate project in Phuket. Island life is great for a few months, but I was glad to finally get back to busy-as-balls Bangkok. One evening, as I was sipping on some duty-free whiskey and watching the sun melt into the Bangkok skyline, my cell phone vibrated across the table. I had to don my reading glasses to confirm what the caller ID was saying. It was Bill.

"What are you doin' homey?" he giggled. I told him I was enjoying a libation and marveling at the Mango-colored sunset. "I'll be right over", he giggled again, then hung up.

He looked great. By my estimate, he'd trimmed about 40 pounds of beef off his frame and lost the freakish look. His clothes were stylish and new. He'd even shed the big romper-stomper boots he used to wear and now appeared not much taller than me. On his left arm he sported a brand-new chunky Bulgari timepiece. When I pointed to it, he said, "Dude, it's a Vulgari, do ya like it?"

Bill has one of those big kid smiles like he is just about to burst into a giggle-fit at any moment. He seemed to want to tell me something, so I topped up his whisky glass and set myself to receive. He began by apologizing for running out of the club several months ago without saying "hello" or "goodbye". Then he told me about his adventure in Pattaya.

Bill had been tipped off about the impending drug sting in Bangkok and retreated to Pattaya without a baht in his pocket. He hooked up with the two Fembots I'd seen him with at Marine Disco in Pattaya. The "ladies" were kind enough to let him stay at their apartment and sported him around like a trophy. They were paying the bills so he was their boy-toy for a couple of weeks before he got another pension check and could afford a ticket home. "Dude, it was humiliating", he confided. "You really have no idea."

The smile left Bill's face and he seemed to drift off for a moment. I tapped the luxurious timepiece on his arm and commented, "Looks like you've got a new Sugar Daddy now". Taking the tease in stride, his I-know-something-you-don't grin returned ... "Not exactly" he said.

Bill took a deep breath, a long pull on his drink and began, "Dude, do you remember I told you about that deal with my dad?"

When I first met Bill, he told me a sad story about how his father had died a year before. His dad was on medication for heart disease for years but was surviving quite well. When some new super drug hit the market, the doctor switched the medication. Bill's dad died, and so did a bunch of other people. There were lawyers and lawsuits, and a bunch of stuff Bill didn't really understand, but he was relatively sure he would get some money someday.

Now I could hardly keep the silly grin off my face. "How much Bill ... How much did you get?"

He struggled so hard to hold in his laughter that he blew whisky and soda out of his nose. He managed to gurgle out, "Two-point-three. Two-point-three million U-S-D!" Now, both of us were giggling, cackling and even a little chortling.

"Well, I can see what you did with some of it Bill" I said again tapping the Bulgari, "But what about the rest?"

Suddenly serious, he said "Dude, I did what you told me ... I invested it!" My heart sank. I wondered what the hell I told Bill in some skanky bar, in some altered state. He trusted my knowledge of this kind of stuff implicitly and I had no idea if I had told him to buy gold, play the market or hide his cash under his bed.

Sensing my confusion Bill added, "I called that chick, the one in Singapore."

Then it came back to me. During one late night/early morning discussion of what Bill should do with any significant amount of windfall, I had given him the name of Sompit, my friend and contact at Credit Suisse in Singapore. Bill had followed my instructions and she had set him up with an annuity-type account that kept his money safe, i.e., out of his hands, and a nice quarterly income. He was literally set for life.

I was elated. He'd done the right thing with his money. "Bill, that's great news" I said sincerely, "Good for you".

Bill took another long pull on his drink, and with a blushing grin offered, "Oh, that ain't all the news bro ... not by a long shot."

After the "now I'm a millionaire" revelation, I wasn't sure I could stand any more. Big Bill raised his glass in a grandiose toast and proclaimed, "I'm out!"

What he said didn't sink in at first. "What do you mean you're out? Out of the US ... I see that".

Emphatically shaking his head, Bill corrected me, "No dude, I mean I'm totally O-U-T!"

I felt a little thick ... I didn't quite understand so I asked, "Bill, do you mean you're gay?" He sat back, exhaled, and dramatically whispered, "Not exactly".

Reaching into his new Prada wallet, Bill produced a glamour-shot picture of what appeared to be a petite young Thai woman. My jaded eye immediately noticed the choker-style necklace worn by the young "lady" and suspected it was covering a protruding Adam's apple. She was also proudly displaying a matching lady's version of Bill's Bulgari watch.

"Well, I see you've graduated from Fembots to Decoys" I said trying to hide my surprise. "Toning it down are ya?"

Ignoring my jab, he said, "Her name is Kik ... here's the house".

Bill pulled out his phone and thumbed through a half-dozen pictures of a cinder block Thai-style house under construction somewhere upcountry.

It would seem that Bill had fallen in love with a ladyboy and was building her mother a house up-country in Udon Thani. In a matter of six months, Big Bill Durant had gone from living with his sister and working as a bouncer at the "Bottoms Up" club somewhere in Orange County, California to a being millionaire married to a transvestite from rural Thailand.

"Bill how did this happen" I asked. "You were such a lady-killer. What made you change direction?" I was sincere with my question. I've never understood the attraction to lady-boys myself. I always wonder why an uber-heterosexual red-blooded manly man would suddenly take such a radical turn.

"Well dude" Bill explained "I spent 16 years working as a guard in a maximum-security prison. Trust me my man, that is a seriously fucked-up sexual dynamic. I guess it just got to me and I didn't know it until I got here to Thailand."

"So, do you consider yourself gay?" I asked.

"No, no, no ... I don't like dudes" he insisted.

"But you like girls with dicks"

Nodding his head and grinning Bill confirmed my statement with an exaggerated whisper, "Exactly"!

The last time I saw Bill, he invited me to his rented condo in Bangkok. He and Kik were getting ready to move upcountry and he wanted to say goodbye. Kik answered the door and immediately retreated to the bedroom as she did not have her face properly applied for company.

Bill sat in an overstuffed lazy boy in the middle of an otherwise empty living room, playing video games on an enormous flat screen TV. On his lap yapping at each on-screen explosion was a snow-white miniature Chihuahua. "Our baby" he cooed in a silly voice, "Her name is Pinky".

They were all packed to move upcountry. Bill explained that the toxic temptations of Bangkok were too much for both of them, so he and Kik (and Pinky) were moving to the sticks to get away from it all. He described life in her village with wonder and awe.

"Dude, it's like living with The Flintstones", he said. I wished them luck and, on my way, out had to endure a spine crushing hug from Bill and even a peck on the cheek from Kik.

As I walked across the parking lot, Bill came out on the second-floor balcony, waved goodbye with Pinky's little paw and yelled down, "Dude, come visit us in Bedrock … yaba-daba-dooooooo!"

Chicken-fried Freedom

I woke up feeling better than I should. I'm sure it's
that false sense of wellness that comes with either still
being drunk or maybe in that blissful no-man's-land
between hammered and hungover. I don't question it.
Feeling good is feeling good. I am grateful whatever
the circumstance. I take a peek at myself in the
mirror. I look better than I expect as well. That's the
thing about being dehydrated ... you look marvelous.
It's as close as I get to being "shredded" these days.

Shuffling to the kitchen to perform the coffee ritual I
count four empty wine bottles and one champagne on
the dining table. Champagne? Where did that come
from? And ... oh my ... I see salt on the kitchen
counter. That can only mean one thing. Ahhhh yes,
that duty-free tequila appears to have been plundered.
Three souvenir Hard Rock Café shot glasses are
turned upside down in the sink, crusted with salt and
lipstick. I count three different shades. Three ... my
favorite number.

The big round clock I got for opening an account at
Bangkok Bank tells me it's 6:05. I should have opted
for the digital one. At least I'd know if it was AM or
PM. My cellphone is dead ... no help there. I take my
French press and big-ass coffee cup out to the balcony
to wait for the sun to give me a sign.

I must be careful. Especially if I've been on a three-
day birthday rampage. When I wake up in Bangkok at
six-something with a depleted liquor cabinet and a
trash bin full of condoms, I am extremely susceptible

to sunset vertigo. It's a condition where you aren't sure if it is dusk or dawn. One can easily come down with it here in the tropics. This close to the equator the sun pretty much goes up and comes down the same time every day. The only cure is a pot of coffee and time.

If the funky orange glow over the city gets brighter and turns yellow, then it's morning. If it starts to wane and turns purple, then it's time to make dinner plans. On this particular day I am ambivalent about which it is. In fact, I find that I don't give a shit most days.

My little side street in Klong Toei kind of looks the same six AM or six PM. No barking dogs. No food carts. No annoying Thai dudes blowing whistles. It is a fairly peaceful place for being in the middle of a city the size of Bangkok. I sit on my eighth-floor balcony, watching the street like a camouflaged cat, waiting for the sun to give me the signal, AM, or PM? Yellow or purple?

The street looks a little wet so it must have rained last night ... this afternoon ... earlier. In the distance I can hear the distinct "frip, frip, frip" of dog paws picking up and laying down on the damp street. I spot him about fifty meters out, cruising right down the middle of the street. We've got a handful of regular soi dogs around, but I've never seen this one before. He's a young and handsome specimen; one of those ridgeback-dingo looking fellas. He's in a brisk trot with his tongue hanging out the side of his mouth; head on a swivel surveying it all as he passes through a strange new territory.

Pouring my first cup of coffee, I envy his status. I know exactly how that dog feels. New trash cans to turn over. New rear-ends to sniff. New territory to conquer. Just leaving. Just arriving. On the way. Unanchored. The exhilaration of escape. The anticipation of what's next. Life unscripted. He doesn't give a shit if its AM or PM either. I toast my canine brother with my first sip of java. *"Welcome to the neighborhood handsome"*.

Being the "new kid in town" is my favorite status. Nobody knows you. You are who you say you are. A man can conceal a suitcase full of flaws if he wields the proper amount of mystery. I consider myself the consummate stranger. Smile or scowl? Gregarious or aloof? Expat or tourist? It's all up to me. It's a strange thing to be good at.

I'm product of my upbringing. When I was young, my family moved constantly. My father was a pipeline inspector. Our house was a silver Spartan Travel Trailer. I never went to the same school more than six weeks until I was 12 years old. Being the new kid in town sucked back then. When you're a pipeline kid, the new kid in town gets his ass kicked a lot. I just wanted to have a home with some friends. We finally settled in Florida, and I got a good long taste of normal life.

Apparently, I wasn't meant to live like that. I left home young and went into the military where I found myself being the new kid in town in Las Vegas at eighteen years old. It was my first duty assignment. I felt like Alice in Wonderland. Then I was the new kid in town in Athens, Greece at 22. I took to the idea of life outside the US immediately. I was the new kid in places like Frankfurt, Madrid, and Amsterdam. Being young and American with a pocketful of currency is a great foundation for being the new kid in town anywhere on the planet.

By the time I returned to the US, I was ruined for a normal nine-to-five-wife-n-kids life. When I got bored, I changed venues as easily as flipping a TV channel. I moved at least once a year for 12 years. My mother said I had "terminal wanderlust". I just wanted to be that dog trotting down the middle of a strange street. That's how I ended up in Thailand. You don't find streets any stranger than Bangkok's.

Now I've been here twenty years. My brother says I must have found what I was looking for. It doesn't feel that way. I've lived all over Thailand too. This is my fourth stint in Bangkok. I still want to roam. I still want to escape. I still want to be the new kid in town. But every time I go to a new place, I kiss the fucking ground when I land back in Bangkok.

The combination of joss sticks, dog shit and diesel fumes smell like apple pie to me. I can't wait to be sitting on a plastic stool, slurping down noodles, and holding a cold Beer Chang to my neck to cool down. I can't wait to be weaving through traffic on the back of a moto-taxi on my way to wherever the fuck I want to go. I can't wait to see that first bashful smile from some slinky pooying who catches me looking at her on the Skytrain. Bangkok is as close as I will ever come to being "home".

Now it's 6:15 and I'm still not sure. Yellow or purple? Not yet. More coffee.

Besides a general feeling of disorientation, another symptom of sunset vertigo is a rambling mind. I see one roaming dog and I'm thinking about where I want to go next. While in twilight limbo you aren't quite sure how to proceed, so there's plenty of time for self-reflection, self-analysis, and some self-loathing too. My squirming monkey mind wanders down rabbit hole after rabbit hole. Thai people say, *"You think too much"*. Sunset vertigo brings that on in waves. Nothing to do but wait and think.

I mean, Bangkok's just another big stinky city in a banana republic, right? How did I let this place get such a grip on me? I don't feel like this in Phnom Penh, or Saigon, or Manila. Probably because none of those cities are in Thailand. Thailand trumps all other Asian countries for me. But why? It's not the only place with sweet mangos and hot women. What's so special about this fucking place? Why Thailand?

I'll tell you why ... fried chicken for breakfast.

I was raised to believe a person should live as free as possible. My home country bears the ironic nickname, "land of the free". However, when I go back to see my family, I am overwhelmed by the restrictions on my personal freedom. We are surrounded by signs featuring the words "do not", "cannot" and "prohibited". It appears every third person is wearing a uniform and "profiling" me. Restrictions and rules permeate every shred of American existence. All the fun and spontaneity have been legislated out of that country. "Land of the Free" my ass!

Here's an example ... in my home country, we are at the mercy of Food-Nazis. Go into a neighborhood cafe at 8 AM and you'll be given the breakfast menu. You are expected to choose from this limited list without question and without variation. Bacon, eggs, pancakes, French toast, etc. If you're lucky you might see an edgy breakfast burrito on the menu. In all, the average American breakfast menu has about eight items on it. Those are your choices. Love it or leave it.

And should you happen to arrive one minute past the arbitrary cut-off for breakfast, you will be referred to the lunch menu. Ask for a variance on this policy and the service staff will have you believe the cooks suddenly lose the ability to fry an egg past noon. Ask to order from the lunch menu before noon and you may be asked to leave. A "Community Service Officer" is sure to be cruising nearby to apply a choke hold or taser should the opportunity present itself.

Here in Thailand Food-Nazis are not tolerated. Menus are volumes long and everything is pretty much available all the time unless they are out of it. And there are no rigid rules that say what is acceptable for breakfast. Noodles, steaks, pizza, omelets ... if they have it you can order it any time they are open. That's standard operating procedure in Thailand.

When I go to my neighborhood market in the morning, I see Thai people swarming around all the food stalls equally. Some people like the sweet sticky fried bananas or those delicious Thai doughnuts. Many order Khao Thom Moo (rice porridge) with pork. Khao Thom is a popular and effective hangover cure.

But, by far my favorite breakfast dish is crunchy and decadent fried chicken with sweet chili dipping sauce. We are free to choose the parts we like. Thighs, wings, even white-meat chicken tenders are available. If I can find Hat Yai chicken, I feel like I've won the lottery. Hat Yai chicken is a Muslim recipe that magically combines the flavors of fried chicken with onion rings. I challenge anyone to find a more complimentary marriage of flavors.

Where I come from, the only way you could have fried chicken for breakfast was if it were cold and left over from the night before. If you set out to find a big plate of fried chicken wings at 8 AM it would be nearly impossible.

In Thailand fried chicken is available in all its crackling greasy glory any time of day, but especially for breakfast. To me, fried chicken for breakfast represents freedom. Freedom from food judgement. Freedom from food rules. Freedom from some calorie-counting asshole telling me what I should or shouldn't eat.

I wait patiently in the queue at my chicken lady's cart a few mornings each week, surrounded by like-minded individuals. We smile at each other because we share a common affliction. We smile because we have the right to choose. We smile because we know what freedom tastes like. It tastes like fried chicken.

And apparently, we also have the freedom to frolic with women half our age and wake up with sunset vertigo. I can sit on my balcony, drinking coffee and ponder the world feeling no pressure to go anywhere in a hurry. No clock is ticking. Nobody is expecting me. No timecard is waiting to be punched. I am not scheduled to appear anywhere. If I want to go back to bed, I can. If I want to go to the gym, I can because it is open 24 hours. If I want to just sit here and wait for the sunrise or sunset while my mind rambles, I can. And I am.

And, since we're talking about freedom ... Do you know what else you have the freedom to do in Thailand? Pee outside. (Sorry but it had to be said. This kind of goes with fried chicken for breakfast.) Since the dawn of man, we've yearned to answer nature's call while completely engulfed in ... well ... nature. I know of no real man who will disagree ... it's great to pee outside.

Make a list of liberties that should be granted worldwide by some global governing body and none would be more universally and unanimously applauded than peeing outside. A politician campaigning on his intention to grant men the right to pee outside would have a solid platform in any country.

In my country of origin, we limit the practice of this hedonistic ritual to our own backyards. To do so in public would surely lead to the reading of rights and public shaming. Here in Thailand, things are a little more relaxed.

Any visitor to Thailand here more than 30 days has witnessed the taxi driver who just couldn't hold it standing spread-legged letting it fly on some unsuspecting palm tree on the side of the motorway. Unabashed and unashamed, Thai men certainly don't have a problem with such a display so why should I?

In fact, this behavior, literally illegal in my home country, is actually encouraged in Thai culture. Let's say you are cruising down Motorway 7 between Bangkok and Pattaya and your bladder starts reminding you about its limited capacity. You pull over at a big rest stop and park in front of the mini mart near the gas station. Follow the signs bearing the image of a guy who has to pee around the corner and behold, sparkling clean urinals affixed to the outside of the building, framed with immaculately trimmed hedges, and accompanied by the highway sounds in the background. An oasis of form-meeting-function if there ever was one. Organized, sanitized, and encouraged al fresco urination.

A modicum of proper privacy is maintained. Desires to embrace nature are sated in a relatively clean and orderly environment. And no one is offended. I've visited a dozen "first world" countries and never witnessed civil liberties like this. While citizens of my country wring their hands over what to do about transgender people in public restrooms, Thailand lets me pee outside.

Come on sun, what's the verdict? Did I sleep all damn day or just a couple of hours? I really don't care which it is. I don't buy into that "you've gotta have eight hours of sleep" theory. In fact, I'm living proof that it's bullshit. I can't remember the last time I had eight hours of continuous sleep ... unless of course it was last night ... or today ... whichever it is.

I suppose I could put on some pants and go down to the Family Mart on the corner. Between here and there I'm sure to see a sign. If the delivery trucks are there bringing supplies, it would be morning, right? There's no shame in it. Even if they can tell I'm all upside down, nobody is going to snicker. Nobody is going to point their finger and judge me a bad person for being in such a condition. Nobody is going to pigeonhole me as a lowlife sunset vertigo sufferer.

Several years ago, I remember being back in the US and staying out all night. I ended up in this after-hours bottle club drinking myself totally sober. I walked out into the blinding light of a Sunday morning. I saw families on the way to church. People were jogging and walking their dogs. I felt like a vampire, hissing at the daylight, and cowering in the shadows. People stared at me in my black clothes and sunglasses, wreaking of alcohol and cigarette smoke. I felt like slinking back to the leper colony and doing myself in. I would estimate I got judged and sentenced to hell about once every 50 feet.

In Thailand we have this thing called "compassion". The Thai phrase "hen jai" means to "see your heart". Thai people understand how you feel. For sure almost anyone I would pass on my way down to the Family Mart would "hen jai". Everyone has experienced sunset vertigo at some point. It doesn't make you a bad person.

If I'm being honest, I'll take a severe case of sunset vertigo every time as long as it follows a night like I just had. It was the crescendo of a three-day bacchanal ending in a libidinous romp with three upcountry angels named Nid, Lek and Porn.

Hey, that reminds me … you know what else we have in Thailand? Girls named Porn. Not just one, but thousands of beautiful Thai girls named Porn. It's a common nickname. I'm not trying to be nasty. This isn't some tawdry sex-tourist's joke. It's more about my home country's puritan roots and coquettish sense of what is and isn't acceptable.

While visiting family in the US last year, I was shocked to find out how woefully naïve and backwards my own people are. I was invited to a barbeque attended by a fairly representative cross-section of society. Everyone was interested to know about my travels to "the exotic far east".

But every time I uttered the word "Bangkok" I got snickers and uncomfortable grimaces from several of the more uptight listeners. I thought to myself, "Really, you're giggling because the second syllable of Bangkok is pronounced "cock"".

And, when I let loose with the word "ladyboy" … well some of the more sanctimonious ladies had to escort their henpecked hubbies away from the conversation. They just couldn't have him hearing such provocative language.

Inside I had to have a private chuckle. What would these prigs think of the nightly events on Walking Street in Pattaya? How would these bible-thumping soccer moms react if they ever encountered a six-foot ladyboy standing on the corner eating a bag of fried grasshoppers?

Still, some of them badgered me for more "tales of the orient". "What kind of cars do they drive?" "Can you get a decent burger over there?" And then the inevitable question ... "Do you have a girlfriend?" American women are obsessed with outing any man over the age of 40 and living in Thailand as a pedophile/sex-tourist.

"Of course, I have a girlfriend" I answered with an evil grin. And then I displayed a picture of my current ladylove on my smartphone and showed them. "Her name is Porn" I said ... "Isn't she beautiful?" All conversation stopped. To all the men I became a superhero. To all the women I grew a tale and cloven hoof.

As they scurried away, I just kept on grinning. "That's right ... we've got girls named Porn ... that's just how we roll in Bang-COCK!"

So, let's put that down on top of the list of freedoms we have in Thailand. Freedom to date girls named Porn. We in fact have the freedom to have one or more ex-wives named Porn.

We also have the freedom to drink a beer in public at 7 AM on a Tuesday. Freedom to tip or not tip at a restaurant as well as the freedom to haggle over the price of just about anything. And we have the freedom to actually benefit personally from government official corruption. We don't have any of that in the "land of the free".

I don't have a car. I don't wear a watch. I don't watch TV. I don't care who is President. I couldn't tell you who won the last World Series. I put ice in my beer and I'm not ashamed of it.

Thailand has painlessly bent me to its will. Out of the dozen or so countries I've been, Thailand is the only one to change who I am by allowing me to be myself. I couldn't live anywhere else. Thailand has enslaved me ... with freedom.

Oh Jesus ... I've gone down that "freedom" rabbit-hole again haven't I? It is my favorite. Nothing gets the blood flowing like a good old-fashioned freedom rant!

Well, one more cup of coffee and ... aha! What's this? The sky's turning yellow. So, it **is** morning! Great, I didn't lose a day. I hate when that happens.

I smell fried chicken.

Persona non Grata

All governments have a list of people they want to keep out of their country. The process of getting and maintaining the proper visa to stay in the Kingdom of Thailand is shining testament to that fact. The "visa run" is a fact of life for many expatriates living and/or working in Thailand.

Several years ago, I was living on Thailand's eastern seaboard at Ban Ampur Beach. My visa arrangement was only slightly inconvenient. I was required to leave the country every 90 days and reapply for this privilege every year. It seems that no matter how far I planned ahead, now, and again my visa's expiry date would sneak up on me. I didn't feel like the Lone Ranger as an entire cottage industry has sprung up supported by the need of expatriates to obey mercurial Thai immigration laws. On one particular occasion, I had the distinct pleasure of participating in a classic one-day overland-to-Cambodia visa run.

This was the third time I'd used the services of "Five-Star Visa Runs", located in Witherspoon's Pub on Soi Buakhao in South Pattaya. Witherspoon's is 70% pub, 30% restaurant and 100% English. Located in the corner of the pub, a spunky English-speaking Thai woman called Wan anchors the Visa Run desk where she coordinates the paperwork, gives you instructions and collects the money.

For 2400 Thai Baht Five-Star will feed you breakfast, transport you, and up to seven other visa runners, to the Cambodian border, expedite the processing of your passport, bring you back to Pattaya and feed you lunch. The total travel time is about eight hours round trip.

Arriving at Witherspoon's a few minutes after 6 AM, I was greeted, filled with coffee, and fed a tasty bacon and egg sandwich. As clandestinely as possible, I surveyed the crew of mugs I'd be trapped in a travel van with for the next eight hours. They were mostly a quiet bunch; heads down, faces buried in Full English Breakfasts and *The Bangkok Post*. It looked as though we would only be traveling with five.

Around 6:30 a sixth member came blustering through the front door with a cigarette in one hand and an active cell phone in the other. He was a strapping young guy with an elaborate wrap around dragon tattoo escaping from his surf shorts and tank top. He was in a loud and animated conversation with someone on his phone demanding "Get your arse down here mate ... it's six bloody thirty". From the overtly cockney accent, I assumed that he was either English or was talking to an Englishman. He also ordered the Full English Breakfast and alternated between woofing it down and running outside to have high volume mobile phone conversations and cigarettes. I assumed he'd be the life of our little party.

Five-Star Visa Runs uses customized travel vans that seat seven plus the driver. They are equipped with big cushy leather-like seats, a nice LCD screen for movies and wireless headphones. I'd compare it to Business Class on a decent airline. On previous trips I'd slept during most of the time on the road. I nearly negotiated the front seat, but a young Irishman in a Notre Dame Baseball cap beat me to it. After we all piled in, I was relieved to see the seat next to me empty. It was shaping up to be another uneventful road trip.

Just as Wan was giving us some last-minute instructions out in front of Witherspoon's, her eyes suddenly grew big, and she jumped into our van with a frightened yelp. She was nearly run down by a maniac on a raggedy motorbike. The driver of the errant two-wheeler abruptly applied the brakes and parked his conveyance directly in the front door of the pub, blocking both entrance and exit. He sprang off the bike and headed towards us on rubbery legs guided by roadmap eyes. He stopped, held out his arms in a mock crucifix pose and bellowed a greeting to someone in our van, "Ya see ... I toll ya I'd faaaking be heeya!" It became horrifically apparent to all of us that this was the voice on the other end of the big guy's phone and our seventh passenger.

If you were directing a movie, and the script called for an alcoholic dirt-bag Englishman living on the cheap in Thailand, Central Casting would send this guy. He's one of those mouth breathing, chain-smoking drunks, who is probably about 38, but looks 58. He was the drinking buddy of the big kid who had joined us earlier. It was unclear how long they had been "mates", but they acted as though they were lifelong friends. The drunk flopped down in the vacant seat right next to me. I held in an exasperated sigh ... a day can truly change in an instant.

As we weaved our way through early morning market traffic, five of us pretended we were already asleep, and the two drinking buddies cackled and howled like horny hyenas recounting the conquests of the night.

Sometime during the load-up back at the restaurant, the big kid had slipped into the 7-11 and purchased a huge 44-ounce fountain soft drink. I would say it contained about four ounces of Coca Cola and 40 ounces of cheap vodka give or take a few ounces for ice. They passed the noxious concoction back and forth between their seats sniggering like schoolboys. The drunk was hammered and singing the West Ham anthem before we reached the main highway.

The big kid's name is Jon. I know that because his drunken friend, Pat, said his name over and over again while he kicked the back of his seat and demanded another swig of vodka. Mercifully, the driver turned on the movie, Die Hard 4, and young Jon immediately became wrapped up in the violence and machismo, encouraging his friend to do the same. With their headphones on, the volume on their alcohol and testosterone-fueled conversation increased about five notches. They sounded like sea lions barking at each other.

Pat-the-drunk, who probably has the attention span of a three-year-old, soon became bored with the movie and started making friends with the other passengers. I feigned sleep and thanked my old friend Xanax I had the calm to ignore the drunk's advances. He started on the two guys in the back seats.

The sixty-something guy in the rear of the van was a retired American with a Thai wife living in Chachoengsao. He is originally from Seattle, WA. I know this because Pat-the-drunk turned around and asked him the same questions four times in 15 minutes. The same was true for the quiet young Englishman in the rear. He had to tell Pat-the-drunk that he was a schoolteacher from Birmingham on holiday a total of four times. Oddly enough, when Pat related his own background, it was different every time. He was from East London one time and Liverpool the next.

Eventually Big Jon displayed other purchases from the 7-11. Out of his rucksack he produced three large bags of the stinkiest potato snacks I've ever encountered. They smelled like feet and onions. Big Jon offered some to all of us. I continued to play dead. After devouring their snacks, Pat-the-drunk immediately passed out and Big Jon sunk into the movie.

In a few minutes I heard a distinct thumping sound that seemed to be coming from inside the van. I could see from the look on his face that the Seattle guy heard it too. When our eyes followed the sound to its origin, we could see the drunk's head banging against the van window as we hit bumps in the road. The old veteran rolled his eyes and turned up the volume on his headphones.

After about 90 minutes, we reached the first rest stop where we all stretched our legs, relieved ourselves and exchanged polite chit-chat. As you might imagine, most of our conversation revolved around Pat-the-drunk and how many more hours we'd have to endure him.

We could see Big Jon and the drunk inside the mini mart connected to the rest plaza. Big Jon was still wearing his wireless headphones, smoking a cigarette, and gesturing wildly. They were inquiring about more vodka and buying sausages on a stick. After we had reloaded and got back on the road the next 90 minutes, was basically a replay of the first 90 minutes. Pat-the-drunk drank … he blathered on and on … he passed out … his head thumped on the van window. With his wireless headphones firmly in place Big Jon hooted and hollered every time something exploded on the movie screen and occasionally turning around to tell us all how great an actor Bruce Willis is.

We arrived at the Cambodian border before noon along with at least six other vans, and thankfully before the two double-decker luxury buses that tout the combination golf tour/gambling junket/visa run combo package. We exited Thailand, walked across a dodgy looking bridge to Cambodia and handed our passports over to our driver/expediter. Most of us took the chance to stretch, get a drink and basically rejoice in being out of the van. Big Jon and the drunk headed straight to the Duty-Free Quonset hut to fill up on vodka, cigarettes, and fake Viagra.

While sitting around with my fellow van-mates, I got to know a little more about the rest of our crew. We had the afore mentioned retired American with a Thai wife and five kids who had been in-country 15 years. We had two other Englishmen: one a schoolteacher on holiday and extending his visa, the other a business owner in Pattaya with a Thai wife and a brand-new baby. The young Irishman turned out to be a time-share salesman from Bangkok. None of us was looking forward to the return trip with the belligerently drunk Englishman and we all agreed something needed to be done.

But I could see by the look on my compatriots' faces, none of them was prepared to say a word. What's more, I understood their reluctance to act. The drunk himself could be easily dispatched. He weighed no more than 60 kilos, and his body was ravaged by years of alcohol abuse. If he needed to be physically ejected from the van, our Thai driver could have easily handled it.

Big Jon however was a different story. This kid is about 2 meters tall and carries a good 110 kilos of muscle. He seemed amicable enough, but you never know how a guy will react when his friend is threatened, and he is all liquored up. It was then I realized I was the second largest man in the van, which probably explains why they all looked at me like it was my duty to sort out our resident drunk and deal with his potential guardian angel.

The guy from Seattle said that he had heard tell of a company that threw a passenger out of a visa run van in the middle of nowhere for drunken rudeness. We all pulled out our written instructions from Five-Star that clearly states that no one will be allowed in the van drunk and consuming liquor in the van is not permitted. So, in a unanimous show of cowardice, we decided to lay this problem at the feet of our Thai driver. To his credit, our driver was surprisingly proactive, especially for a Thai.

Pat-the-drunk had purchased his own bottle of cheap vodka, removed his shirt, and worked his way through about one third of the contents while waiting outside Cambodian Immigration. When he approached the van to reload with the rest of us, our driver stopped him and said that he could not get on board with an open bottle of liquor. After about ten minutes of unintelligible insults aimed at our driver, Big Jon leaped from the van, grabbed his buddy's bottle of vodka, and flung it into a trashcan. *"Get the faaak in the van ya cunt!"* he barked, diminished patience showing. Pat-the-drunk nearly gashed his head open getting into the van. He continued his tirade on our driver in spitting slurred cockney and bad bar-Thai as we got underway.

After about ten minutes Big Jon reached into his Duty-Free bag, produced his unopened bottle of vodka, cracked it open and handed it to Pat-the-drunk. I could see our driver's head jerk in protest, and he threatened to pull over. Big Jon smoothed his nerves by saying, *"relax mate ... it'll put him to sleep"*. As Big Jon continued to assure the driver everything would be okay, the drunk managed put away half the bottle in four successive chugs. As promised, we soon heard the familiar thump, thump, thump of Pat-the-drunk's head on the van window.

As the drunk sat twisted up in the seat with his head banging on the window, I took stock of what I saw. He was small in stature with a disproportionately large head. His teeth were jagged and yellow as corn. He sported a hodge-podge of bad tattoos which included team symbols for at least three different English football clubs. His skin was almost translucent and was covered with a collection of scratches, burns and scars. His face confirmed he had spent many years of looking at neon lights through the bottom of a bottle. The bags under his eyes were cartoonishly big and black. So many blood vessels on and around his nose had been broken he appeared to have a sunburn. I couldn't help thinking he may have some form of degenerative disease, but nothing like cancer or AIDS. He looks like he has some kind of old-world malady like scurvy or rickets. In Thailand, the government health ministers make cigarette manufacturers post warnings on their products complete with horrifically graphic pictures to drive home their point. They should put a picture of this guy on vodka bottles.

When our scheduled "halfway home" stop arrived, the driver eased the van quietly into the parking lot of the plaza. We all exited the van silently being careful not to wake the snoozing drunken carcass next to me. Most of our group visited the men's room and took inventory of the mini mart. I took the opportunity to engage Big Jon in a conversation. Even though he had been drinking all day, he was still quite lucid and congenial. As it turns out, he's not an Englishman at all. He's from Finland, grew up in Sweden and learned all his English from barflies like Pat-the-Drunk ... hence, the cockney accent. He's 28 and has a Thai wife who lives back in Sweden. He comes to Thailand for months at a time to "play". I rarely ask anyone about their occupation or other sources of support in Thailand. I just smiled and said, *"Good for you my man"*. He was a hard guy not to like. The entire trip he was quite jovial, even if he was a little loud. And he was doing his best to keep his friend under control.

He explained that he had only known Pat-the-drunk for a few months, and most of their time together had been similar to what we had witnessed in the van, only in various a sundry beer bars. Big Jon certainly had a lot more patience than me and I told him so. He apologized for Pat-the-drunk and promised to try and keep him asleep until we got back to Pattaya.

86

Sheepishly we filed back into the van ready for a peaceful two hours or so. Just as we rolled over the last speed bump in the plaza, our drunken passenger's head made one last big "thump" and to our chagrin, Pat-the-drunk woke up and began to howl, *"Wha, wha, wha? I gotta piss ... drivaah, drivaaaaah! I gotta have a piss don't I"!* The whole van, including Big Jon let out a sickened sigh as we stopped and backed up to let the drunk relieve himself. We sat in silence and waited for his return. While staggering back to the van, he vehemently berated of all of us as he tried desperately to zip up his fly and walk at the same time. *"Faaaak all ya cunts! Leave a man sleepin' when he's gotta have a piss!"* He threw himself in the seat beside me made about three more bubbles in his vodka bottle and continued to yank on the back of Big Jon's seat and bend his ear about the virtues of being *"true mates"*.

In a few minutes he settled down and we all thought we'd soon hear the familiar rhythmic thump, thump, thump. Unfortunately, our friend decided that music is really what we needed and began to serenade us, at stadium volume, with various football chanteys. At this point I had two realizations simultaneously. First, it was abundantly clear to me that my Xanax had worn off. Second, I had had enough of Pat-the-drunk.

Keep in mind that I had not spoken to this man the entire trip. I had ignored him in a manner similar to how the Japanese treat foreigners; he just wasn't there. When I could stand no more, I spoke up in a commanding voice, loud enough for all to hear. *"Come on man ... enough is enough!"* Silence gripped the van. Pat-the-drunk was gob smacked.

He stared at me with watery yellow eyes and asked, genuinely shocked, *"Wha ... mate am I bov-er-in you?"*

"You're bothering everyone", I shot back. *"Look Pat, we've all listened to you for six hours ... give us a break man, please."*

For a few moments nobody breathed. Big Jon turned around in his seat and pleaded in a whisper with the drunk to go to sleep and leave everyone alone. I took the opportunity to recompose my stoic demeanor, ignoring their conversation.

The drunk wouldn't leave it alone. He came at me again with the typical drunken outstretched handshake hand and a slurred, "where ya from mate?" My heart sank. He's one of those drunks who is determined to solicit a response, even if it's a punch in the face.

"Don't test me" I hissed, straining hard not to lose control He recoiled at first but when he tried to come at me again, I reached into my past and employed my old drill sergeant's voice, snatched off my sunglasses and blasted him with a menacing, *"I SAID DON'T TEST ME MOTHERFUCKER!"*.

Nobody breathed for two minutes. Now disoriented, he pleaded with his bloodshot eyes to Big Jon for back up, but his old drinking partner had opted to feign interest in watching the credits roll on <u>Blades of Glory</u>, our second movie feature. Pat-the-drunk finally shrank and retreated to his side of the van. Soon the rest of us heard our new favorite song. Thump, thump, thump.

By the time we got back to Pattaya, it had started to rain. It seemed to cool everything, including me, down. At Witherspoon's we all ordered food except for Pat-the-drunk. He wandered around looking for all the stuff that had fallen out of his pockets during the trip. Phone, keys, money ... all scattered between the van and the pub and his raggedy motorbike. After he'd collected himself, he flopped down next to Big Jon and spent ten minutes extolling the virtues of friendship and honor and *"standin' wit yer mates"*.

Being a big fan of irony, I noticed the wall behind him was covered with a pictorial collage tribute to the English football star that drank himself to death, George Best. Pat-the-drunk slurred his way through his guilt trip soliloquy and Big Jon purposefully plowed through a pile of fish and chips, pretending not to hear. When he was finished with his meal, Big Jon sucked down the second half of his beer while placing his hand over the still running mouth of his shit-faced friend.

"I'm gonna talk now mate" he stated calmly and waited for the Pat-the-drunk's lips to stop moving. When the murmuring had ceased, Jon smiled like a man being released from prison and said, "I'm glad that big Yank sorted you out proper mate. It was the bloody highlight of my day. Now PISS OFF!" With that said, he stood up, bid us all a good evening, and strolled out onto Soi Buakhao, cell phone to ear.

It was the first time I had felt sorry for Pat-the-drunk. Everyone at the table felt it. Pat-the-drunk felt it too.

He sat deflated in the booth. He looked like a 50-year-old orphan. We all pretended to ignore his slow painful exit.

While driving home in the rain I noticed how tired I was. Feeling heavy and drained like I had worked hard at something and deserved a good rest, I pondered what I had seen and considered what I may have learned. It's hard to find a silver lining in such a day. Other than the fact that I could stay in Thailand another 90 days, I knew it would take some real mental wrangling to glean any other positive gain from the day's experience. But find a silver lining I did as I realized I'd learned three very important lessons.

In the past, I had read countless articles and editorials regarding Thai visa laws. For some reason I had always taken every change and reinterpretation of these laws to be pointed directly at me. I could never understand why the Thai government would want to give me such an obstacle course to run just to stay in The Kingdom. I spend money, I employee Thai people, I pay taxes, I obey the law, I am observant and sensitive about Thai culture ... I have even gone to school to learn the language. It has always been tough for me to understand why they would want to keep me out. But now I see things differently.

They aren't trying to keep me, or guys like me out. Today I had spent eight hours seated next to who they are trying to keep out. Pat-the-drunk ... Persona non grata ... poster child for stiffer visa laws. Ok, I finally get it.

I also learned the true meaning of the word "alcoholic" on this trip. A lot of people use this term to loosely describe someone who drinks too much. That isn't alcoholism. I saw alcoholism right in my face for eight hours. It's not like I haven't known drunks and alcoholics before. I have just been fortunate enough to have an escape route and usually take it. I was shocked to have the death grip of this horrible disease so graphically illustrated. What an awful way to go.

And I learned a lot about what I would call *"Micropolitics"*. It's my own buzzword for the science of small group behavior.

When you have eight men in a van the behavior of the group is actually quite predictable. When the sober members of the group met to discuss how to handle the undesirables, the policy and plan of action were arrived at in a democratic and pragmatic manner. We all agreed in principle to squelching the loud drunk. We all recognized the possibility of resistance by his Alpha-male guardian. So, the group elected to utilize a two-phase approach.

First, we would demand that the existing authority (our driver) enforce prevailing laws and eject the drunk. When the efforts of that authority proved impotent, Plan B was to elect the next ranking Alpha-male (yours truly) to disarm the enforcer and cull the errant member. I would love to think I was selected because of my diplomatic skill set, but I'm pretty sure it was because of my large frame and proclivity for action.

In the end, the majority got what it wanted. The problem was solved, and no blood was spilled.

If only we could get some nations to work things out like eight guys in a van.

Nothing for Christmas

For years I've bragged about my good luck. I truly felt my life was charmed up until and through 2009. Apparently, life has a way of catching up with a person. This year was the worst of my life.

To begin with, I'd actually had a pretty shitty two years. I'd undergone five surgeries in eighteen months. My investments had yielded pitiful returns. The only good thing in my life was my longtime girlfriend; a woman I considered my wife.

Then 2010 settled in. In February, my friend of twenty years and former business partner blew his brains out in his posh office in Winter Park, Florida. He was family to me. We were a magic team; like two brothers who are polar opposites. The only thing we did more than make money was laugh hysterically at ourselves. We were the epitome of an odd couple nobody could figure out. I didn't know how much I loved him until he was gone.

In August, my mother called me home to help make arrangements for her death. She had been suffering from heart disease and lung cancer for several years. I had cowardly managed her illness and impending death from a distance. She called me home to get her affairs in order. She called me home to say goodbye.

I spent a month back in Orlando helping her do everything from completing her will to sorting and digitizing old family photographs she wanted to give everyone. Every day I made her breakfast, and we did the crossword puzzle; at night we'd watch Jeopardy and cooking shows.

When I left for the airport to come back to Thailand, we hugged in the kitchen, and I knew it would be the last time I'd see my mom. In October, just before my 50th birthday, she died.

Soon after, the remains of my family unit disintegrated. My nut-bag sister-in-law has driven a wedge between my brothers and most of the family must side with one or the other. I've probably been to the last fully attended Braxton Family get- together.

Not long after, my wife and I came undone. She and I have a ten-year history of emotional warfare. I decline to be unduly graphic here. When my friends ask me what happened, my best answer is, *"She just kept pushing my buttons until she hit OFF"*.

I am no stranger to failed romance. But this is the first time I've had to be the adult and say "enough". This is the first time I've been the one to make the painful decision to do what is best for both of us. This is the first time I'm not the asshole. Trust me it's easier to be the asshole.

So, I lost a best friend, my mother and at least one brother is dead to me. I've been sick, making no money and have now split with my wife. If I had a dog, it would surely have been run over by the mail truck.

Now comes the holidays. My mother was the Queen of Christmas. Nobody who has ever experienced a Braxton Family Christmas Spectacular will ever forget it. The country ham, Elvis Christmas music, and the presents ... piles and piles of presents.

Even when I moved halfway around the planet and missed Christmas often, my mom would send me a "care package" filled with cookies, handmade candy, and country ham from Kentucky. Just to have my house smell like her kitchen transported me home.

Normally I follow my mom's lead and buy thoughtful gifts for my family and ship them from Thailand. This year, almost everybody got gift cards. My heart just wasn't in it. I did send personalized cards but felt guilty just sending money.

Last year at Christmas, I was entertaining my best friend on his vacation of a lifetime and giving my girl an engagement ring. This year I didn't even buy a poinsettia or put lights in my potted palm tree like I usually do. The Christmas spirit had abandoned me.

Since I didn't want to be totally alone for the holidays, I planned a trip to visit friends in The Philippines, only three hours away. Even though I'm not religious, the Philippines is a Christian country, and the Christmas revelry is in full swing. My flight would leave on Christmas Day and return on New Year's Day.

On Christmas Eve, I drove from Pattaya to Bangkok. My plan was to spend the night and leave my car at the airport in the morning. No matter how loud I played the music, I could not stop my brain from playing me "The Year in Review". I got the entire blow-by-blow downward spiral of the year 2010 over and over. The two-hour drive from Pattaya gave me the headache that comes from fighting back a blubbering breakdown. When I arrived at 3 PM, I was badly in need of a drink.

I got off the Skytrain at Nana Station and returned like a homing pigeon to my favorite watering hole in all of Bangkok, The Eden Club. It's not really a drinking bar, it's a whorehouse; perhaps the most notorious brothel in all of Asia.

The owner is a Frenchman and a former business associate of mine. I'm the only guy I know allowed to sit in the bar and just drink. Customers think I'm the bouncer. I guess you could say I go there for the atmosphere and the privilege. I drink; I think ... I do my best writing there.

After commiserating with the manager and wishing the girls a happy holiday, I sat in my usual spot near the door, sipping a double Jack-on-the-rocks. This is a place where I could allow myself to playback "The Year in Review" and grope for a silver lining.

Two Jacks later I'd played back each and every shitty thing that happened and managed to blame myself for all of them: collectively and individually. I felt guilty about not being there for my family after my mom's death. I felt guilty for not being there for my friends after my partner's suicide. I felt guilty for not buying my grandchildren Christmas presents. I suffered the crushing shame of "the abandoner". And to top it off, I felt abandoned. Exiled. A leper.

This was not self-pity; this was self-loathing at its finest. I looked at my reflection in the broken television's screen above the bar and asked myself,

"What kind of asshole gets nothing for Christmas?" Not a card, not a call, not an e-mail ... nothing came for me this year. Santa had given me the finger; Rudolph had pissed on my tires. Like Ebenezer Scrooge I sat at the end of a whorehouse bar replaying Christmas' past and present; and seeing no light in Christmas' future.

I asked myself. "How is it that a man can work himself into a position where not a single person cares about him, not even enough to send an email? "I never thought I'd be a guy who gets nothing for Christmas. The more I drank, the more sobering a revelation it became.

The manager of this place is another French guy named Miki who is a dead ringer for Antonio Banderas, only he's the size of a jockey. Dressed like a gay Zorro, with ponytail and diamond on his tooth, he approached me with a rarity in the Eden Club, a free drink.

In his smarmy French accent, he asked me, "Lando, could you please watch the bar, I've got to go upstairs and see about a customer with a heart attack".

His placid demeanor led me to believe this was a task he routinely performed. I accepted his free drink and informed him that I was already watching the bar.

Fifteen minutes later Miki came back and waived me off. "The guy's okay ... false alarm".

Ten minutes later, one of the girls attending Mr. "False Alarm" came down to the bar in a panic. "He's not okay, he can't move", she bawled out. Miki tried his best to shush her, but she pulled the famous Thai-girl-squat. When faced with severe distress, a Thai girl's defense mechanism is dropping down into a squatting position, covering their face with their hands, and crying convulsively. You couldn't pick them up with a forklift.

I know the girl quite well. Seeing her distress, I realized something was really wrong. I asked her how old the guy is, and she said, "young guy".

I asked where he was from and she told me "same you, same you ... America". And she just kept saying over and over again, "he can't move".

I glared at the twitching Frenchman and said, "Miki, we're going upstairs".

On the way up in the elevator, Miki kept chanting, "We've got to get him out of here, he can't die here ... he can't die here". I wanted to bitch-slap him. I could smell the fear on the little weasel.

What I found in room #7 was a heavily tattooed, middle-aged man, in the bed, on his back, naked and staring up at his reflection on the mirrored ceiling. His eyes were vibrating. His entire body appeared to be in a spasm. Hands and toes curled up; arched up on his neck ... every muscle in his body contracted ... like someone had just stuck a cattle-prod up his ass. His color was light gray. He was fighting to voluntarily breathe. Miki barked at the girls and they scattered like cockroaches.

I sat down on the bed next to him and held his hand to check his pulse. Placing my other hand on his heaving chest and trying to sound calm, I asked him "What's going on in there brother?" Hearing an

American voice was like throwing a drowning man a lifesaver off a passing ocean liner. He stared at me with those desperate jiggling eyes. In between three forced breaths he hissed, "Vodka ... Viagra ... a shitload of cocaine".

He said he felt like every inch of his body was trembling. He said he was having rushes like blood pressure was going to explode his veins. He could not voluntarily move any part of his body, but he could squeeze out words. He was short-circuited and vapor locked. I have never seen a person so terrified in my life.

I felt like an actor playing a doctor on TV. I asked him all kinds of questions that sounded medical, but I just wanted to calm him down and keep him breathing. Every few minutes he'd have what looked like a mini seizure. His face would contort, his teeth would grind, and I'd talk him through it, focusing on breathing and staying calm until it passed. These "rushes" gradually got further apart, and his breathing got a little easier. We just kept talking and breathing.

My doctor act seemed to have a calming effect. Somehow, I wove together life experience, movies I'd seen and military training to craft a façade of confidence and knowledge. I was a doctor whose only skill is bedside manner. One thing I knew for sure; a guy in this condition needs to believe he's going to make it. He needed to believe I could help him.

Miki the weasel poked his head in the door to monitor our progress and to make sure my patient would remember to pay his bill. When I revealed to Miki that the man's condition was a result of cocaine overdose, he broke into a new chant ... "He didn't get it here ... he didn't get it here", his shrill voice trailing off as he scurried back to his hole down in the bar.

When you're talking to a guy both of you think is close to death, conversations tend to be pretty candid. I told him, "Look man, you're all seized up with poison, you're trapped on the fifth floor of a whorehouse in Bangkok, and nobody is going to get a doctor. I'm all you've got".

In my heart I knew the spineless Frenchman would block any attempt to bring sirens and paramedics, especially with a drug related incident. "I'm all you've got". I didn't realize the gravity of the situation until I said it out loud.

I told him he didn't have real heart attack symptoms. His pulse was strong and racing no faster than mine; no numbness in his extremities; only minor tightness in his chest. It seemed that if he had a heart attack, it had come and gone. From what he described, and how he looked it seemed like he was in some kind of toxic shock. I have no idea where I formed this expert prognosis, but I began to do what we're trained to do in the military for wounded soldiers who go into shock.

After getting him more comfortable, we began to unlock his spasm-wracked limbs by manually flexing his hands until they worked. Pretty soon he could grip my fingers, so we moved on to his forearms, bending his wrists, flexing, and releasing. Next his toes, his feet, his calves, and so on. He literally had to consciously relax every muscle in his body. His body had to manually override the scrambled signals his brain had been sending.

After a couple of hours, he was back in control of his muscles and his color had turned to pink. Seeing himself return to human form in the overhead mirror convinced him he might walk out of this place after all. When he broke into a sweat and got chills, I told him this was his body spitting out the poison. He believed every word of it.

Another hour with an ice bag on his neck and two girls giving him a foot massage finally got him up and dressed. We got him down to the bar and fed him a big plate of pork fried rice and a banana. Four hours into his ordeal, the guy paid his bill, hugged me like a brother and left.

I felt like I'd been completely in control and totally at the mercy of fate simultaneously. Me and Jack Daniel's spent the rest of the night pretending nothing happened. The next day I flew to Manila.

When in the Philippines, I do all my thinking, drinking, and writing half immersed at the swim-up bar in the Wild Orchid Resort in Angeles City, a decidedly healthier venue than my whorehouse perch in Bangkok.

Halfway into a book I wasn't reading, the brain decided it was time to give "The Year in Review" another look-see. I thought I already knew how it ended. I thought I'd refer to 2010 as "the worse year of my life ... except that part at the end where I saved that dude's life".

As it turns out, the shock to my system on Christmas Eve was like hitting "reset". Watching "The Year-That-Was" roll by, it surprised me to see I was no longer the villain; no longer the "unlovable cad" or the cowardly abandoner. My glass was half-full once again. While a further review of my shittiest year wasn't exactly champagne and puppy dogs, I appeared to be viewing my life-movie through a different set of lenses.

Remembering my old business partner took me back to ten years ago, when I decided to end a successful career in a business that made me soul sick. I sold my fancy houses and cars and moved to Thailand. Every time I see a guy sporting around town in a big BMW, or overhear someone talking about a hot new IPO, I long for the old days. For ten years, self-doubt has been part of my daily diet. "Did I do the right thing, or was I just running away?"

That business and that life sucked my best friend's soul out. Greed and pride consumed him. Somehow, he had worked himself into a place where he reasoned we'd all be better off without him, so he took his own life. That is certainly a worse place to be than just *"a guy who gets nothing for Christmas"*. That could have been me.

No longer do I doubt my decision to change directions ten years ago. Right there in the pool at the Wild Orchid, I laid that little bag of self-doubt down, never to pick it up again. Rarely do I find myself doing the right thing for the right reasons. Ten years ago, I did, but did not know it until now. Confirmation of a life-changing decision ... peace of mind ... I'll take that for Christmas any time.

As I continued to review the year, it appears I had also undergone some guilt replacement. The guilt I felt for managing my mother's death from a distance was replaced with gratitude. She and I made a deal. I came home to help her settle all her affairs properly and she wouldn't haunt me for not attending the "death party" American people call a funeral. Remembering our last month together, we got to properly say goodbye, on our own terms. I know a lot of people who would give up Christmas for life to have that. The last time I saw my mom, we hugged in the kitchen and I told her I loved her. That perfect memory is the eternal Christmas gift.

And to top off this bountiful holiday season, I also got a big old dose of humility. I finally lost at the "hurt you" game. The woman I'd woken up with for seven years and I are long time veterans of this manipulative power struggle. We are Hall of Fame emotional blackmailers. She was tougher than me, so I finally just took my ball and went home. Sometimes you get something you need for Christmas, like socks or underwear. I got a big-ass bag of humility. Never got that for Christmas before. Thanks life!

And there were a couple of gifts I'd completely forgotten about. As a side-effect of visiting my mom, I got to spend more time with my two sons than in the past five years combined.

One night my oldest son Jay and I set out in a driving rainstorm in search of a new Bar-B-Q joint everybody was raving about. We sat in the covered outdoor tables, eating ribs, watching it rain and flirting with the waitresses. I don't ever remember being that glad to see him before.

Me and my youngest son Jonas, walking on Cocoa Beach at night, drinking Red Stripe beer out of quart bottles ... feeding Jonas Jr. chocolate donuts ... carrying my sleeping baby granddaughter to the car after a day at the beach ... you can't buy that at Macy's. Not all gifts come wrapped in fancy paper, I guess.

While I was sincerely grateful for the attitude adjustment, I couldn't quite put my finger on what switch had been flipped. I was thankful for the epiphany, but I wondered how had the bizarre encounter on Christmas Eve affected me so profoundly? What barrier to self-respect had been removed? What hidden path to hope had been illuminated? It's like feeling better from taking a placebo. I don't understand what is happening, but I'll take it.

Things became clearer when I saw my "patient" again.

As I was enjoying the 3-for-1 happy hour at the Roadhouse Saloon in Angeles City, I felt a presence behind me and a warm hand on my back. "Get this guy a double Jack" he told the barmaid ... "He saved my life yesterday". There he stood; Michael Greene, my seized-up patient from the night before. He was healthy as you please ... grinning like a guy who just

kissed the devil on the lips and lived to tell the story.
As it turns out, he lives in Angeles City. He was
probably on the afternoon flight from Bangkok to
Manila.

He seemed completely recovered; we bar-hopped
until 4 AM. I told him about my life, and he told me
about his. Sometime in the middle he asked me,

"What the fuck were you thinking? What in God's
name made you come up to that room? If I died,
you'd have been the scapegoat. You know Thais don't
take the blame for anything. A dead Yank full of blow
in a whorehouse ... somebody has to answer for that.
What were you thinking?"

"That weasel would have let you die" I told him.
"They'd have dumped you in the klong ... just another
death-by-Thailand. Nobody was going to help you
man ... I just couldn't leave you there."

In the middle of a pulsating go-go bar, he hugged my
neck and held on like a little boy which attracted a
tableful of drunk Aussies' attention. Before they had a
chance to make comment, he lifted his drink in a
ceremonious toast. "Mates, raise your glass and toast"
he pointed at me ... "To a man of fucking action". The
Aussies complied and listened intently as he told them
the story in graphic detail.

While I listened to his version of the story, it dawned
on me what switch had been flipped that night. For
more than a year I had been a man who waits. I had
become a person that things happen to. I had become
a passive observer of my own life. I was just sitting
around waiting for more bad shit to happen.

What happened on Christmas Eve reminded me of who I really am ... a person who takes what life deals him and gets on with it. More importantly, a person who doesn't bitch about a situation he can do something about. I had forgotten that I am the guy who jumps in the pool when a kid is drowning. The guy who pulls people out of a burning car. The guy who does something when shit hits the fan; even if it's the wrong thing.

Having the balls to do something ... anything ... is a defining feature of my character. I don't know how or when I forgot that. Listening to this guy tell our story illustrated this fact brilliantly.

When he was finished telling the tale I realized that it was possible that I saved Michael Greene's life on Christmas Eve, but I definitely saved my own. Two men were going down hard that night in the Eden Club, and I think I saved them both. Me, cheesy as it may sound, *"a-man-of-fucking action"*.

For the first time in a long time, I was the hero of my own fucked up fairy tale.

I wondered how I would feel about it when I got home to Thailand. I wondered if it would all seem like a bizarre dream. I wondered if I would be proud of it and tell all my friends. I wondered how people would take it.

I live in Pattaya. There's a lot of bullshit being thrown around in a town like Pattaya. Spend a few weeks and you'd think every Navy Seal, CIA and MI6 agent in the world lived in there. Would anyone believe my "I saved this dude's life" story?

It didn't take long to find out.

I was spending a nice afternoon at my favorite watering hole in Pattaya Beach called Tahitian Queen ... affectionately known as "TQ" among old-timers. Us "cool kids" hang out in the back corner near the DJ. Everyone was in high spirits, swapping stories about what they did for the holidays.

Some guys went out of town with their wives or girlfriends. Some guys went back to their country of origin to be with their family. It seemed like I was the lone sad and single traveler that escaped to the Philippines for the holidays. I wanted to tell my story, but it didn't fit with the others. It would have been like everyone was enjoying a jazz festival and suddenly having a punk band take the stage. Luckily, no one seemed to notice my lack of input.

A few hours into the session, the daytime manager approached me with a free drink and a warm "Happy New Year" greeting. His name is Little Chris and he's a dead ringer for the old '80s fitness guru, Richard Simmons. Chris spent about six years as a dispatcher for the US Army in Afghanistan. He's a happy little fella, but he has seen some horrible shit to be sure. We are old friends, and I was happy to catch up with him.

Somewhere in the middle he casually asked me, "So, anything special happen in the Philippines?" I was really caught off guard. I didn't know how he knew where I had been. My mind spun quickly trying to recall if I'd told anyone. I played it off and said, "Yep, had a great time as usual".

He could see I was confused and assuming a defensive position. Chris smiled and said, "Don't freak out brother", and pulled his mobile phone out of his pocket. He scrolled through a few pages of pictures and settled on one of a bunch of dudes in camo-fatigues in front of a big armored personal carrier. He zoomed in on one particular guy looking tough with his wrap-around shades and MP5 machine gun. "This guy looks familiar?"

I couldn't believe it. It was Michael Greene, the guy I saved at The Eden Club. He zoomed out a little and I could see a younger version of Chris smiling and squatting down in the front of the group for the picture.

"I spent a few years in Afghanistan with this guy" Chris explained. "We call him Tattoo Mike. Some of his crew came through here the week after Christmas. They had been up in Bangkok and lost track of Mike one night. When they finally found him, he told the story of how some big bald dude from Pattaya saved his life when he was all jacked up in a whorehouse. They went to the Eden Club to find out who he was, but the girls only knew his Thai nickname, "Khun Neung". I knew it was you right away."

Chris had sent Mike an email and found out we were partying together in Angeles City. That's how he knew where I was. I was gob smacked. "Fuck me" I said. "Bad news travels fast".

"Bad news my ass dude ... you're a hero! Even if he is a total sack of shit".

"What do you mean" I asked. "The guy's a douchebag?"

"I don't know him that well really, so it isn't for me to say" Chris said. "Ask Loud Kevin. He's known Mike a long time. He can give you the real poop. I'm just a gossipy cunt".

I looked into the far corner of the bar where Loud Kevin usually sits and spied him drinking alone. I don't care for Loud Kevin at all. He's a nasty drunk and he likes to man-handle the girls. He is unaware that I don't like him. He is also unaware that I am the person who gave him the nickname "Loud Kevin".

He talks twice as loud as anyone I've ever met, even before he gets drunk. As it turns out, he spent a lot of his military years working in an armory with a firing range where soldiers practiced their marksmanship. I'm guessing he was too cool to wear the protective earphones provided, so he ended up with hearing problems. That's why he talks so loudly. I didn't know that when I gave him the nickname.

I was curious to know more about the guy whose life I'd saved. All I knew was what he told me. So, I got two fresh beers and carried one over to Loud Kevin.

"Happy New Year Kevin" I said with cheer.

"Yeah, yeah. Same to you dude. Thanks"

"I understand that you know someone I met in Bangkok; a guy named Michael Greene. Is that right?"

"Tattoo Mike? Yeah, I know that douchebag. I'm guessing you're the one who saved his junkie-ass at the EC".

"Fuck me, are there no secrets left in this world?"

"I'll be honest brother ... the only person you did a favor is him. Even his own mother would be relieved if that prick took a dirt nap".

Loud Kevin took a long pull on his beer and gave me a brief synopsis of what he knew of Michael Greene.

They had lived in the same apartment complex in Angeles City for a couple of years. According to Kevin, Tattoo Mike had impregnated three different Filipinas over the period of one year. All three gave birth. He denied all of them and supported none of them. Greene had worked in Afghanistan for various US security contractors. When one of his team members was killed in a firefight, Greene pilfered the guy's locker at their barracks, stealing his watch and some cash. He got run out of Afghanistan and was mainly working in Syria. He couldn't go back to the US because he was wanted for child support in California and a two DUI convictions in Washington state.

Kevin concluded the report with the statement, "He stole a pair of my sneakers at the gym and traded them for a bag of weed". I got the feeling he had more stories to pile on if that wasn't enough.

All the air rushed out of my hero balloon. I felt like I'd interfered with the natural order of things. I'd somehow short-changed karma by saving this asshole's life. I sat there on a barstool with my head hanging low, staring down the neck of my beer.

"Would it have made a difference?" Kevin asked. "If you knew he was a piece of shit before it happened, would you still have saved him?"

I shrugged and nodded my head. "No difference man. He's an American. I couldn't just leave him there".

Loud Kevin smiled and raised his beer up for me to clink a toast. "You see. It ain't about who he is brother. It's about who you are".

The Princess and the Pop Star

So, I'm a tattoo guy. Now, I don't mean I've got "a" tattoo. I in fact have a serious tattoo collection going on. I'd describe it as a work-in-progress "skin tapestry". Back in the US my kids say I'm "inked out". But I think that distinction should be saved for someone who couldn't squeeze even one more tattoo onto their body. I've still got open space I intend to fill. If you don't have a tattoo, it's okay; I'm not a tattoo snob. In my mind there are three kinds of people. People who have tattoos. People who don't have tattoos. People who have tattoos and wish they didn't. Nothing is sadder than a person with a tattoo they don't want.

For the past five years or so I've had one tattoo artist named Tiki. He grew up somewhere between Amsterdam and Christchurch, a nutty mix of Maori and Dutch. He's one of those people you only meet in Thailand. Tiki has a delightfully twisted sense of humor and is also a spectacular artist. I choose him because of his artistic eye and precision application of my tattoos with the old school bamboo method.

Since meeting him, I'm one of those guys who only gets his tattoos "hand-poked" with no fancy machine. It takes a hell of a lot longer, but it feels like a much more natural process, and the lines are flawless. When I consider things that might be in a tattooist's tool kit, I don't immediately think of a micrometer. Tiki uses one to measure distances between lines that are supposed to be straight or look straight. He says he doesn't like using an electric tattoo gun because he hates mistakes. According to Tiki, "It's a lot easier to get things right when you are drawing a picture one pixel at a time". I have no idea what Tiki's real name is. But whatever it is ... "precision" is his middle name.

Before I met Tiki, my tattooist of choice was a Thai guy named Joe. I met Joe the way you should meet your tattoo artist; through a hot girl with bad-ass tattoos. During an afternoon drinking session at my favorite watering hole in Pattaya, I noticed a girl with an incredible tattoo of a demon's face on her back. The artist's attention to detail gave the face such a powerful expression I couldn't stop looking at it. I was looking at the demon and it was looking back at me.

The demon girl said her name was Pom. I bought her a drink and asked who the artist was. Pom was quite evasive and said she couldn't remember. I had a hard time believing she didn't remember a person who inflicted that much pain ... at least 20 hours' worth by my estimation. But that's kind of how Thai people are. They protect information like its gold. I plied her with a few more drinks but still couldn't get a straight answer.

It took me four trips back to the bar until she finally gave up the name. "It's Joe, from Thirteen Crowns" she confided. "His shop is on Pattaya Klang". She sent the artist's contact info to my phone. After all that resistance, she gave up the name so easily that it made me think she must have cleared it with him first. I gave her 500 baht for the information which she thanked me for and added, "Don't make fun of him and the MJ thing". I gave her a blank look and she said, "You'll see ... just be nice, he's my friend". I left the bar with my information and a riddle to solve; what is MJ?

I was all excited the way tattoo guys get when they are ramping up for some new ink. I knew what I wanted. I knew where I wanted it. I just needed to make sure this guy Joe was the right artist. An artist's attitude and personality play a key role in the tattoo process. Think about it ... you are going to sit for several hours with someone you just met and let them hurt you. What's more, the scars are going to be with you for life. The memory of that image on your skin will forever be connected to those few hours with that person. I've got some tattoos from nameless, faceless artists and they mean less to me somehow. The artist is nearly as important as the tattoo itself.

I must have been running my mouth about a new tattoo while drinking at another favorite hangout because the heavily inked Thai bartender asked me, "Where you go for new tattoo?".

"Joe at Thirteen Crowns" I said.

He raised his eyebrows with a surprised look, "Oh, you know Joe? He do for you before?"

I told him it would be my first tattoo with Joe, and I asked, "Is he good? Am I making a mistake?"

"No mistake mister", he said. "Joe is number one".

He brought me a fresh beer and added, "Joe is a little crazy with the MJ thing, but he is the best".

With that he walked away before I could ask the question, "What the fuck is MJ?"

When Joe answered the phone, I was shocked to hear nearly perfect west coast American English. I told him that the girl with the demon on her back recommended him. "Oh, you are Pom's friend? Well then we are brothers already" he chuckled. I liked his attitude immediately, so we made an appointment for the following Sunday.

For the next several days I toyed and tinkered with my new tattoo's design. It would be a stylized Thai-Cambodian dancer. This figure is called an "apsara". In the mythology of the region, they are "celestial dancers" that originally started out as water nymphs. This nymph-from-heaven would be placed near my heart as it symbolizes my former wife, an Isan beauty queen named Mina. The figure has a particularly enchanting face and big ole knockers, just like her.

When I arrived at *Thirteen Crowns* tattoo shop, I was stunned by how immaculate the place was. I've been to other Thai tattoo shops and most of them aren't as hygienic as people from the west are accustomed to. But Joe's shop looked more Hermosa Beach than Pattaya Beach. He even had a cool collection of skateboards mounted on the walls he had hand painted. There was some chilled-out music playing and incense burning. The vibe drew me in instantly. I felt like I was back home in my favorite head shop.

"Hey man! Welcome to Thirteen Crowns" he sang out. Joe appeared from the back of the shop with a huge Starbucks cup and a big-ass smile. He turned out to be a dark-skinned and lanky thirty-something with that wavy hair you see on Thais from the southern provinces. We shook hands American-style and immediately dove into a deep and meaningful tattoo conversation. I showed him some of the examples I printed out from the internet and the modifications I want to make for an original tattoo design. Joe listened attentively even taking down some notes and making little sketches.

In the middle of our conversation, Joe turned and barked out some orders to someone milling around behind a partition at the back of the shop. The language he used didn't sound like any variation of Thai I'd ever heard. In a few moments a plump, white-skinned Asian girl with a pixie haircut appeared with a tall glass of iced coffee for me. She placed the drink on the desk where we sat and disappeared before I could even say "thank you". "That's my wife Yoshi", Joe said. "She's Japanese".

When I was all done spilling out my ideas for the new tattoo, Joe told me to go have lunch somewhere and come back around 3 PM. He said he would draw an original tattoo based on the artwork and ideas I had given him. I was thrilled and the anticipation that comes before the ink flies was building.

I sat in a little shophouse restaurant down the street and worked my way through a half dozen chicken wings and some papaya salad. The chicken was juicy, the somtum spicy as hell and the beer seemed extra cold. I knew I had found the right guy for the job. There is something about getting the right artwork in the hands of the right ink-slinger at just the right time. The whole process leading up to a new tattoo makes life more urgent somehow.

I'd had a couple of shitty years. I had come to second guess myself quite a bit. Life had become a bit of a grind. Now, after a long stretch of personal doldrums I felt like my decision-making process was functioning properly again. I was doing the right things for the right reasons. I didn't exactly have my mojo back, but I felt like I was methodically tracking it down. Tattoos can nail those feelings down and hold them in place. They mark beginnings and ends. They keep memories fresh and clear.

When I returned from lunch, I found Joe's rendition of my apsara was beyond my expectation. He'd captured the perfect facial expression and sense of movement. The overall shape was just right for the location it would go. And the ornate headdress worn by the dancer was meticulously detailed. She looked right at me. "Jesus Joe!" I exclaimed, "Let's get that girl on me!"

Joe turned and barked out some more Japanese and Yoshi magically reappeared, shuffled over and took the drawing to another small table. She pinned the paper down to a board and placed tracing paper over the top to make the tattoo stencil. Once everything was secured, she picked up a pen in each hand, took a deep breath and began to trace the complicated picture onto the tattoo stencil paper using both hands. Her hands worked simultaneously and independently. I couldn't stop watching. To this date it is the most amazing demonstration of manual dexterity I have ever witnessed. She finished the entire tattoo within two minutes without ever picking either of the pens up from the paper. Joe saw me staring, shot me a knowing smile, and said, *"She has many talents"*.

While Joe was positioning the stencil on my chest, I could see Yoshi preparing the tattoo chair and instruments like an apprentice surgeon. The inks were ready ... the tattoo gun was sanitized, and Joe's giant Starbucks cup was filled to the brim with ice coffee. Once I approved the position of the tattoo, Yoshi led me to the chair and Joe selected some music on his computer. The endorphin rush that comes with the knowledge pain is on the way hit me and I embraced it like I'd done so many times before. The heartbeat quickening, nipples hardening and that taste of electric adrenaline dancing on the back of my tongue. I cannot explain why I crave this feeling.

Joe revved up his tattoo gun a few times and began applying ink with no undue fanfare. Like most good tattooists, he made a couple of inkless passes to test my threshold of pain. Most people have an unrealistic idea about how they are with pain. While I'm a big ole sissy when it comes to seeing blood and such, my tattoo pain threshold is pretty good. Sometimes I fall asleep in the chair. Satisfied that I wasn't a "flincher", Joe took a long pull on his ice coffee, adjusted his chair height, and began to apply my apsara.

Some tattooists prefer to work in silence. Some talk too much. Joe is one of those guys who interviews you while he works. He looked me in the eye, pointed to the apsara and said "So, tell me about this woman". For the next two hours, Joe and Yoshi heard the saga of Lando and Mina.

I talked about how we had met twelve years ago in Bangkok. She was running a bar near Washington Square with two of her childhood friends from Buriram. I went to meet a friend there to play pool and fell in love with Mina the first time I laid eyes on her. She had it all; that long sheet of black hair, skin like toasted cinnamon and that flashing little girl smile. She's the first Thai girl I ever met with dimples.

Her girlfriends explained to me that in their village Mina's beauty was legendary. She was Miss Loy Kratong, and her mother was Miss Loy Kratong, roughly the equivalent of homecoming queen or prom queen back in my home country. Loy Kratong is an annual celebration that falls on the first full moon of the twelfth month of the lunar year and pays tribute to the water spirits. I called Mina my *full moon princess*. Looking at her was like drowning in moonlight. To this day I don't have to see the full moon to know it is there. I can feel it. I can feel her.

Mina was as charming as she was beautiful. She had a knack for saying the cleverest things in the most hilarious ways. Most Thais will clam up if they don't know how to say something in English. Not Mina. If she didn't know exactly what to say, she'd make use of the words she knew. She didn't know the words "tank-top" or "singlet", so she would say "shirt-no arm". A handkerchief was a "small towel". She thought "Harry Potter" and "helicopter" were the same words. When I corrected her, she said, "Yes, yes ... farang in the sky. Oooooh ... big magic!" She was linguistically fearless, and it made for some side-splitting conversations.

A beautiful Thai girl you can talk to ... now there's a unique find if ever there was one. The combination of her beauty and quick sense of humor hooked me like a big dumb fish. My grandmother would have said, "the boy's nose was wide open".

The romance burned white-hot for a few months, but I wasn't ready for *"big love"* at the time. I was too busy being a Bangkok bachelor. I didn't want this relationship to fall into my normal pattern where I put up a grand show of fidelity only to reveal my true identity, a heartless and horny cad. I wanted to keep the memory pristine. So, I let Mina go like a prize blue marlin ... *"strictly catch-and-release"* I told my friends. I preferred that she miss me rather than hate me. What's more, I'm sure Mina had a long line of suitors waiting just offstage. She wasn't done playing yet either. We secretly stayed in touch through several other relationships and finally got back together. We both thought we were ready for *"big love"*. Nothing is hotter than an old love affair rekindled.

Mina and I decided to escape belching, hissing Bangkok and started our new life together on the golden sands of Ban Ampur Beach about twenty minutes down the eastern seaboard from Pattaya. I had purchased a big bare-shell condo there a few years earlier. I blew the place out and designed it especially for her. We called it "Green Heaven" because the color of the walls matched the Gulf of Thailand slapping at the shore thirteen floors below. For the next five years, it was heaven. Just me and my full moon princess floating above the beach on our custom-made cloud.

I could see Yoshi loved this story. At first, I couldn't tell if she understood English or not. But as she assisted Joe, filling up his inkwells and freshening his coffee, I could see her cheeks flush and her eyes light up with my fairytale love story. "So, what happened to her" Joe asked. "Are you still together?"

Then I told the rest of the story. After five years of pure bliss, things started to change with Mina. She would get uncharacteristically moody and started accusing me of cheating on her. One day she came at me in a rage saying she'd just spoken to her sister Duan. According to Mina, Duan said I had three other wives. The most alarming part of the accusation wasn't about the cheating. Mina's sister Duan had been dead for two years. When I pointed this out to her, Mina locked herself in the bathroom. I could hear her inside sobbing convulsively.

Mina's state of mind deteriorated rapidly over the next few months. She continued having "conversations" with her dead sister and sometimes would speak to me using different voices. At first, I thought she was just joking around, but then it started to get scary. One day she'd be my sweet loving companion. The next, an evil witch spewing poisonous bile, berating me and everyone we knew. Some days she'd lock herself in our bedroom for hours or go *talk to the monks* for days at a time at the temple in Bang Saray. I knew she was sick. She knew she was sick. I finally got her to see a psychotherapist in Bangkok.

"Delusional schizophrenic and possible dissociative identity disorder" is what the doctor said.

Apparently, her father suffered from the same type of mental illness. The doctor gave Mina a bag of pills and sent us back to the beach. She was okay when she was on the medication. But, with no warning she'd stop taking her pills and before you knew it, I was dealing with one or more evil Minas.

"Please, I can't take those pills any more baby" she pleaded. "I have no feeling". The medication basically turned her life into one with no ups or downs ... no thrills ... nothing to look forward to ... just a steady hum of bland normalcy.

Mina roller-coastered on and off her medication for months and eventually became a danger to herself and all those around her. My little princess was only about 95 pounds of mostly tits and hair, but she scared the shit out of me when the different voices started coming out. Six months after her diagnosis, Mina was admitted to a hospital for mental disorders in Bangkok. She was unable to function out in the real world.

For nearly a year, I visited her every weekend. During the week, I sat alone in Green Heaven, burning incense, and praying to whatever deity would listen to please bring her back to me. I don't ever remember missing anyone that badly before.

One weekend I went up to Bangkok to see Mina and she was gone. The hospital had discharged her without telling me. "You are not her family" the administrator said with racist scorn. "She went home to be with her **real** family". Apparently, Mina's brother-in-law had come down to Bangkok earlier in the week and checked her out of the hospital. She was up-country in Buriram at her mom's house. I called and called. I contacted everyone we ever knew to see if they'd heard from her. After three desperate and sleepless nights, I got the call from one of her friends. Mina was dead. She had hanged herself at her mom's house.

Yoshi let out a little "yelp" when I told this part of the story and tears shot down her cheeks as she rapidly retreated to the bathroom. I felt bad for ruining the fairytale for her. Then again, she should have known that tattoo stories involving a loved one rarely end happy. For every unicorn and rainbow tattoo there are ten of dead friends, family members or pets. We want to wash away the pain with more pain, but we don't want to forget. "Sorry dude", I said to Joe. "But you did ask".

Joe held up the mirror to show me the finished line work on my apsara. She looked fantastic! Joe shook his head slowly and made a long *"m-m-mmm"* sound, "Girl with tits like that always brings the pain my brother".

We took a break so Joe could switch to the tattoo gun he uses for shading. When I used the bathroom, I could see Yoshi seated at a small desk hidden away in the rear of the shop. It must be her little girl-cave as it was decorated with a combination of Hello Kitty characters and a Keanu Reeves poster. She was deeply buried in something on her little pink laptop. There was a fresh Beer Lao opened and poured into a Star Wars mug.

I returned to Joe and settled back into the tattoo chair for the second installment of my apsara, the all-important shading. This is where good tattoo artists can separate themselves from the hacks. Not everybody gets it right. Joe revved the gun a few times and started in. After a few seconds, a voice in the rear of my consciousness shouted out, "Hey, ask him what's up with this MJ business".

I said, "Hey Joe, everyone I asked about you says I should know about you and MJ. What are they talking about?".

The whining tattoo gun stopped. Joe looked me in the eye and gave a puzzled look. "You don't know about me and MJ?".

I sat there with a clueless look on my face for what seemed like an eternity. Finally, Joe spun around on his chair, turned up the music and went back to work without saying a word.

After being all chatty for two hours, the silence was a little uncomfortable. I wondered if I had offended him somehow. MJ ... MJ ... MJ? I took a deep breath, closed my eyes, and tried to relax. The music Joe turned up got me to feeling a little nostalgic. It was an old R&B album from 1979 called *"Off the Wall"*. Michael Jackson when he still looked like a black guy. It's probably the first music I ever attempted to dance to. The songs took me back to my early days in the military when I was just a young punk running around with my boys thinking I was badass. Michael crooned, *"We're the party people night and day. Livin' crazy that's the only way ... "*, Man, that seemed like a hundred years ago.

After a few deep yoga breaths, I was a bit more relaxed and opened my eyes. And that's when I saw it … a shelf high up on the wall of Joe's shop maybe one foot below the ceiling. It ran around the entire room. Sometimes you see this in Thai buildings because it holds all their buddha images and other religiously significant items. They put it up high out of respect.

But this shelf didn't have any buddhas. This shelf was chockful of one thing … Michael Jackson action figures. Young Michael with a The Jackson Five … Thriller Michael in that signature red and black jacket … Billy Jean Michael with the white sequined glove … "Smooth Criminal" Michael with the white suit and fedora. There must have been fifty of them! MJ! How the fuck did I miss that? There were Michael Jackson concert posters on the walls. Even a picture of Joe posing with the Michael Jackson wax figure at a Madam Tussaud's museum in Pattaya.

I had been so self-absorbed with this tattoo that I totally missed all these obvious clues. Joe could hear me whisper to myself, "Oh, MJ … ohhhhh". He stopped the gun and walked over to plug his phone into a charger. While he was standing there, I finally took notice of *his* tattoos. How had I missed that? He was totally inked-out in Michael Jackson tattoos. In all he probably had 20 images of Michael ranging from age six up to his freakish post-surgery look.

"Oh, now I get it Joe", I said. You're a huge MJ fan, right?"

Joe raised his eyebrows and smiled shyly, "Something like that" he said.

I felt like a jackass for not noticing but intrigued at the same time. For the next half hour, I spilled out every factoid I ever heard about Michael Jackson. I blathered on that Michael and I were the same age and how I used to watch the Jackson Five cartoon on Saturday mornings.

Joe just kept tattooing and saying "uh-huh", never really commenting on anything I said. I hoped he was just concentrating on my tattoo. I hoped he wasn't just some idiot who had a vague idea of who Michael Jackson was and went all-in on his image. I've seen Thais get tattoos of Che' Guevara who don't even know how to say his name. I was beyond curious about why this guy was so obsessed with the image of Michael Jackson. Why would this young Thai dude decide to become a walking monument to the King of Pop?

I could hear myself prattling on like a mindless schoolgirl, so I shut up for a while. After some awkward silence, Joe must have sensed my curiosity and began talking.'

"A few years ago, I went to Japan" he started. "That's where I met Yoshi".

Joe had gone to work in a Thai restaurant in Tokyo. Yoshi's dad was the landlord. Joe and Yoshi took a shine to each other, and she showed him around to the hip places to hangout for young people. Before he knew it, Joe had a big circle of friends. The Japanese adored him because he's tall, slim, Asian-handsome and he has that cool wavy hair. And by all accounts, Joe can really dance.

"I was at this party" Joe said. "Some Michael Jackson music was playing, and I started doing some of his dance moves I saw on videos. Pretty soon everyone was watching me".

According to Joe, some Japanese guys approached him later and asked if he had ever done any "shows". Joe didn't know what they meant, but he soon learned. These guys managed several celebrity impersonators acts that worked all over Japan.

"They had Prince, George Michael, Mariah Carey and a bunch of guys who did Elvis" Joe said.

Within a few months, they helped Joe develop a solid 30-minute act where he danced, lip-synched, and moonwalked to a handful of Michael Jackson's most famous tunes. He worked conventions, weddings, and big birthday parties.

"I got paid a lot" Joe confided. "More than I ever made at the restaurant".

Joe and Yoshi became a serious thing and soon got married. When Joe brought Yoshi back to Thailand for a family visit, she fell in love with the place, so they stayed. Joe had also fallen in love with the art of tattooing after his first Michael Jackson tattoo in Japan and spent the next two years as a tattoo apprentice while performing his act all over Thailand.

Joe's stage name is "*MJ Thai*", and he treats it like an alter-ego. One moment he is jolly Joe the tattoo guy. In the blink of an eye, he turns into crotch-grabbing, moon-walking *MJ Thai*, busting moves all over the stage.

"I'm really kind of shy" Joe confided. "So, I have to become this MJ Thai character to perform".

He opened *Thirteen Crowns Tattoo Shop* with money he earned performing at weddings and parties. *MJ Thai* still does several shows a month.

Now I was the one not saying anything. I had closed my eyes and my mind drifted back to my first tattoo in a sweaty little shop spitting distance from the Acropolis in Athens, Greece. The guy didn't speak a word of English and it took him four hours to finish a tattoo that I later found out many people considered a satanic symbol.

Then I was at this shop in New Orleans on my fortieth birthday called *Electric Ladyland Tattoo*. It used to be a jewelry store with big display windows. I got a 10% discount for being inked in the chair set up in the window so everyone passing by on Esplanade Avenue could see. My tattooist wore contact lenses with horizontal pupils that made him look like a goat and prosthetic fangs for the whole "vampire chic" look that was popular that year.

When Y2K rolled around, I wanted to do something epic. I figured if it were going to be the end of the world, I wanted to be in the most sacred place I could find, so I went to Angkor Wat in Cambodia. Under the inky night sky, I got a tattoo on my chest from a dreadlock wearing Aussie with a tattoo gun connected to a car battery.

And now here I was, getting a tattoo of my dead wife from a Michael Jackson impersonator in Thailand. I had an inward chuckle and whispered to myself. *"You can't make this shit up"*.

"That's why people tried to warn you" Joe said. "They want you to know I have kind of a crazy other life as MJ Thai. Maybe you won't think I'm serious about tattoos. But I have a lot of energy. I can be serious about two things".

I realized Joe thought maybe I regretted coming to his shop. He thought I thought the MJ thing was weird.

But I didn't think it was weird. After so many years in Thailand, nothing seems strange to me. In fact, I thought it was kind of cool. Tattoo artists are people too. Creativity manifests itself in many ways. Besides, I've always been a big Michael Jackson fan. He is an icon of my era. We're the same age and born in the same state. What's more, enigmatic artists like Michael Jackson, David Bowie and Prince have dominated the soundtrack of my life. My kids have seen the Thriller video no less than a thousand times! The MJ story endeared the new tattoo to me nearly as much as the incredible graphic design. I could now proudly proclaim, "I got a tattoo from Michael Jackson", and then tell this kooky story.

Joe stood up, laid down his gun, and said, "Mr. Lando, I think we are finished". When I examined the new tattoo in the mirror I got choked up. He really nailed it. The apsara had attitude, passion, and grace. She was perfect. My Full Moon Princess was alive again!

Joe barked out some more instructions to Yoshi in the back of the shop to which she replied rather sharply. I had no idea what she said, but Joe's demeanor changed immediately. He looked at me wide-eyed and shrugged as if to say, "What's this all about?".

For the next five minutes Joe and Yoshi were behind the partition near Yoshi's desk in what I would call a semi-heated exchange. I didn't need to understand Japanese to know Yoshi was winning. Finally, Joe came out with a roll of cling-wrap tattooists use to protect new tattoos and Yoshi following close behind.

"Uh, Mr. Orlando" Joe stuttered. "Yoshi has some ideas about your tattoo".

Yoshi spoke to me in Japanese and Joe translated. Apparently, she thought my tattoo wasn't finished. She said my apsara looked *"lonely"*. She said the tattoo was just another half-naked girl. She said it didn't tell a story.

"She's a full moon princess with no moon" Joe translated.

"No moon" Yoshi added in English.

Yoshi handed a piece of tattoo stencil paper to Joe with a drawing on it. He held up the paper for me to look. I was astonished to see an incredibly detailed and realistic drawing of a full moon. There were also seven little geometric starbursts scattered opposite the moon that were round in the middle with seven small rays of light emanating from each.

Yoshi explained and Joe translated. "She found this picture of the moon on the internet and then redrew it. It is an actual image of the full moon on Loy Kratong the year Mina died" Joe said.

He left that statement of fact just hanging in the air and watched me mentally wrestle with it. My mouth hung open and hot tears threatened to roll down my cheeks. I couldn't get my head around it. A tattoo shop in Pattaya isn't exactly a place one expects to experience random acts of kindness. Why would this young woman I've never met before from halfway around the world care that much about my sad story? I was gob smacked and overwhelmed with her compassion. We all just stood there in silence for a few moments. Joe's words from four hours earlier rung in my ears, *"She has many talents"*.

"What are the stars?" I asked.

"They represent years" Joe said. "The five stars above the dancer represent happy years. Two stars are below and represent the sad years".

When he placed the stencil over my new tattoo, they framed it perfectly. The moon appeared behind, above and to the right of the dancer with the stars rounding out the left side of the image. Now my Full Moon Princess was dancing under the moon and stars. I sat back down in the tattoo chair without a word and Joe went to work. Yoshi sipped her beer and watched with satisfaction.

Stepping out of the air-conditioned shop into the greasy, salty night, I walked and walked until I got to Beach Road and headed South. I could hear the cling-wrap over my new tattoo rustling under my shirt. I could hear the waves slapping at the shore. I could feel the moon watching me. The endorphins that had been working so diligently before were wearing off and I was immersed in that post-tattoo feeling of peaceful accomplishment. The demons were vanquished ... the princess was saved ... Once again, I was the hero of my own twisted fairy tale.

I stopped at this deserted no-name beer bar on Pattaya Beach Road and ordered a frosty pint. Lost in my own thoughts, I barely noticed the barmaid when she brought my beer.

"Hey mister", she said. "If you want, we can play music for you". From behind the bar, she spun the monitor for their computer-driven music system around for me to see the endless song selection.

"Sure", I said. "Got any MJ?"

A Sure Bet

It had been a while since I was in Bangkok. My old friend Lester invited me up to look at a restaurant he was thinking about buying. It was a good excuse to put on some long pants and do some city stuff. It always gives me a greater appreciation for home when I spend a few days in The Big Smoke and then come back to the beach.

We met at this restaurant called "No Idea" on Sukhumvit Soi 22, across from where the old Washington Square used to be. The sprawling neighborhood between Soi 16 and Soi 24 in Southeast Bangkok is called Klong Toei. It was my backyard and playground for several years. It felt good to be back. The chaotic din of traffic, the piquant aroma of street food. Nothing beats Bangkok for pure atmosphere.

When I got there, Lester was already talking to a group of guys who seemed like they were lubing up for a "one night in Bangkok" experience. There were two Canadians and one American. The American guy's name was Glen and I hated him the minute we met. He was wearing this bright orange Denver Broncos jersey and going on and on about how he couldn't see the football game that morning in his hotel room.

"What kind of shithole, monkey-ass republic is this?", he bellowed "You call this a civilized country when I can't even see **my** Denver Broncos?"

A belligerent, entitled American ... imagine that. He went on and on about "his Broncos" for a good twenty minutes. I wanted to punch him in the throat.

Finally, one of the Canadians asked me how long I had lived in Thailand. At that point, I was celebrating year 16 and they were all quite impressed, except of course Glen the American.

"I don't know why anyone would stay here that long. I saw all I need to see after the first two trips" Glen said. "Bunch of whores and thieving monkeys. Same as Tijuana".

I had already decided to be tolerant of this guy because I didn't know if he or his friends were important to Lester's restaurant deal. So, I just smiled and said, "Tijuana, really?"

"Yeah, I used to go there a lot. But now I'm working a bunch of these oil fields in the middle east, so I come here to piss my money away. You'd think as much money as I spend these monkeys could let me watch MY FUCKING DENVER BRONCOS!" He just kept getting louder and louder ... and he wasn't even drunk yet.

Lester shot me a tight smile. He knows me well and could tell Glen was getting under my skin. I offered to buy the next round of drinks and Lester followed me up to the bar when I ordered.

"Who is that obnoxious prick Lester?

"I don't know him," Lester said. "He came with the Canadians. I know them from Phuket".

"So, are any of these guys crucial to your restaurant deal?"

"Naaa, as it turns out, the restaurant got sold while I was on the plane coming up from Phuket. I'm heading back tomorrow afternoon. I just happened to run into these guys".

I got my change from the bartender, gave Lester an evil grin and said, "Well then. Game on!"

When I got back to the group, I made it a point to grab the stool closest to Glen. When the others got involved in some hockey oriented conversation I seized the chance to buddy up to him.

"So Glen, you're a big Broncos fan I see"

"That's right! I used to be a season ticket holder until I started working overseas. Never missed a home game".

"Well, have you ever been there when the Raiders whip their ass? Like the season opener when Gannon threw for four touchdowns ... or did you see that game in the Black Hole that knocked them out of playoff contention? The Raiders handed your Broncos their ass!"

I proceeded to list just about every game that the Oakland Raiders, hated division rival of "his" Denver Broncos, had beat them in a meaningful game. He tried to banter stat-for-stat, but he soon realized that I was a long-standing member of Raider Nation and could out football him.

Once I had him on the back foot, I started to open him up and see exactly what his problem was. I asked why he had such a hard-on for Thailand. I didn't understand why any red-blooded American male wouldn't think this place was Disneyland for adults.

He had a long list of complaints. He couldn't eat Thai food because it was too spicy. He didn't like Thai people because they were always smiling at him and he thought they wanted something. They didn't carry his favorite brand of tequila in the bars. He couldn't find Corona beer. And from what I could gather, he was one of those guys who thinks everything in a developing country should be dirt cheap. Food, liquor, transportation, and especially sex.

He was the proverbial "Cheap Charlie" with an imperialistic attitude towards any country not called America. He thought people should beg to get one of his almighty US dollars. I've invented a word for this kind of person; "bellignorant", a combination of belligerent and ignorant. The US seems to produce an inordinate number of them.

The sample size of his entertainment experience in Bangkok was limited to go-go bars in Soi Cowboy, Nana Plaza, and Patpong. "They're all the same," he said. "Just loud-ass techno music in a roomful of skinny tattooed whores". Even with his limited sampling, he had managed to form negative opinions on absolutely everything.

When I asked if he had seen any live music, Glen said, "All I've seen is a bunch of Filipino cruise ship bands playing Hotel California. I like rock-n-fucking-roll. Can't find that here".

When asked if he'd ever tried any Royal Thai Cuisine, he said "What's the difference? It's all the same, rice and chillis, I can't eat that shit".

When I asked if he'd ever been to any upscale or private clubs he said, "I ain't payin' for that kind of shit".

Finally, he turned to me and said, "Look man, I can see you are trying to help me out. I can see you have lived here for a long time and you like it. I'm telling you, I've been here more than five times and I've seen it all. At least enough to know that for me, it's a pile of monkey shit, okay?"

"Then why do you keep coming back?, I said. "If it sucks so bad, why are you here?"

"Because these assholes like it," he said, as he pointed to his Canadian friends.. "They come to golf and whore. They like this shithole and I keep waiting for it to be a good time but it hasn't happened yet".

Glen may have thought these Canadians were his friends, but they seemed happy I was talking to him so they didn't have to. He was as rigid and narrow-minded a person as I have ever met. I ordered another round of drinks and let the silence between Glen and I get borderline uncomfortable.

"Alright, then Glen from Denver," I said. "Do you like to gamble?"

He puffed up and bleated, "I play Texas Hold'em online every weekend. Fuck yeah, I like to gamble!"

"Good," I said. "Here is what I have in mind". "I'll bet you one thousand Thai baht that I can walk you out that door and take you to a place that features a kind of entertainment that you have never seen before, and you will enjoy it."

He shook his head like a four-year-old fighting sleep. "Naw man, I've seen the ping pong shows, the pussy-smoke-cigarette show, hell I've even seen the "frog show". I don't need to see any more of that shit".

"No, you dumb hick" I snapped back. "I'm not talking about silly sex-parlor tricks. This is a city of 12 million people. Why do you think Bangkok is legendary? Because of some country girl learned how to smoke a cigarette with her pussy? Open your mind hillbilly, there's a big beautiful world out on those streets and you're missing it".

Glen clammed up and seemed to be awaiting my proposition, so I said, "I'll bet you that I can take you to a half dozen places walking distance from where we stand and you'll see shit you not only haven't seen before but didn't even know existed. For every instance I make you admit that *I* get one thousand Thai baht. Every time I show you something you've already seen or don't enjoy, *you* get one thousand Thai baht".

The gauntlet was firmly thrown down. I stuck out my hand to shake on it. By now the other members of the group had stopped their conversations and were monitoring ours. One of the Cannucks urged him on, "Go ahead Glen, whaddya got to lose? You either have a great time or you'll make some money. You can't lose!"

The other three men stood silent and Glen could feel the peer pressure mounting. Finally, he thrust out his hand and barked, "Okay fucker, let's see what you got!"

Lester bought us all one more round and we toasted to "one night in Bangkok". On our way out the door of the pub Lester patted Glen on the back and with a knowing grin said, "Good luck tonight mate". Glen and I walked out onto Soi 22 and turned left towards Sukhumvit Road.

Before we had taken twenty steps, Glen piped up with "Hey, I hope we don't have different definitions of "walking distance". It's hot as balls out here and I'm wearing this thick jersey. Don't get me all sweaty".

"Well Princess, do you want to go change into something more appropriate? Perhaps a tennis skirt? We've walked half a block and you're already bitching. Is it your time of the month? Is that what this is all about?"

Glen could tell right away I wasn't going to suffer any whining and was reconsidering the whole venture. Before he had a chance to balk, I spun him around and said, "Look, we're already here at our first stop".

He found himself staring into a black mirror reflection of his face on the door of a nondescript two-story building. He took a step back to read the letters on the wall above his head. "*Titanium*. What's this place?" Glen asked. I pushed the door open and invited him inside.

A flock of attractive young Thai ladies dressed in traditional Vietnamese Ao Dai appeared in two lines to greet and escort us to a seat. I could see Glen having trouble focusing with the drastic lighting change from outside to this windowless cave of a bar. With a hostess on each side guiding us along, we shuffled through the dim purple neon maze to the middle of the bar on the farthest wall.

"Wow, this place looks like something out of a movie!" Glen exclaimed. "What goes on here?'

"This is **Titanium** Glen. It has been around as long as I've lived in Thailand and it is a legendary hangout for ex-pats, locals, and tourists. They have the most well-stocked bar in Bangkok including your precious imported tequila and Corona beer. They also have the most dangerous bartenders in town, so be careful and don't get into any drink challenges. They also have a sub-zero room upstairs with an Ice Bar where you can select from a dizzying array of imported vodkas and play Russian Roulette with your liver."

Glen took a look around bobbing his head up and down to the chilled house music playing. "Nice place man, but I've seen the ice bar thing before. This ain't nothing new. I don't see any tequila behind the bar other than that shit with the plastic hat on the bottle".

I could see he was going to try and be a hard-ass. I called the bartender over and we exchanged pleasantries in Thai. I asked him to show us his premium tequila selection and he started pulling bottles out from under the bar with no liquor tax stamps on them. In all, he gave us a choice of nine genuine Mexican tequilas from Cuervo 1800 up to Gran Patron. We settled on two chilled shots of Tres Generations and chased them with ice-cold Coronas.

"Alright", Glen said. "So are you going to tell me when I'm supposed to be amazed and give you a thousand baht?"

I looked at my watch as I saw a mousey looking Thai girl come in the door in sunglasses carrying a guitar case. "I'd say in about 30 minutes Glen. Relax, enjoy your beer".

For the next half hour, I dug into Glen some more. He had an unusual upbringing. His parents were some kind of Christian missionaries in the Philippines for ten years. Glen spent much of his early childhood traveling around to different provinces with his parents spreading the gospel or some such nonsense. When he was about 10 or 11 years old, they moved back to Denver where his parents split up and got divorced. Glen's dad remarried right away and started a new family. Glen lived with his mom, her two older sisters, and three cousins. He was the youngest person in the house and the only male.

After high school, Glen got accepted to a university in Vancouver and got dual degrees in geology and some kind of engineering. He went to work for a company that manufactures drilling equipment for oilfields all over the world. And now, 20 years later, he was the guy they sent to oversee installations and guarantee the warranty on their equipment. He had never been married. "Not even close", he proclaimed proudly. He made over $300,000 a year and saved all his money. He didn't even own a house or a car.

There was a sad naivety to this guy. He was that kid whose mom only let him ride his bike on the sidewalk wearing a helmet. He'd never caused any trouble.

He'd always followed the rules. He'd never taken his parents' car for a joy-ride. He'd never banged a girl without a condom. He'd never tried any drugs stronger than marijuana. He'd never faced any fears or conquered any inner demons. He played it safe and secretly admired guys who didn't. His bellicose blustering was a smokescreen for the fact that he was kind of a pussy, and deep down knew it. All that noise was just him trying to fit in and be part of something.

He had taken my bet because he was happy to have someone to talk to. He had no intention of having a wild and dangerous night. He just didn't want to sit alone in that hotel room. I won't say I began to like him, but I didn't want to punch him in the throat anymore.

Facing me, Glen's back was to the stage, so he couldn't see the band getting set up. While we were talking, the bar began to fill up with its normal hodge-podge of clientele. Japanese businessmen who lived in the area ... young middle-class Thais out for a night on the town ... tourists from the massive hotels that clustered in and around Khlong Toei ... and old fart expatriates like me. We don't come here for the stiff drinks or the hot hostesses. We come to hear the band.

Right at 9 PM, the house music trailed off, and the lights went even dimmer. A sultry female voice came over the loudspeakers to announce, "Welcome ladies and gentlemen to *Titanium*. We know why you're here. We know what you've been waiting for. And now we're gonna give it to ya!"

And with that, the stage exploded with light and a guitar roared to life like a chainsaw, tearing into the riff at the start of the old Rare Earth tune, "I Just Want to Celebrate". Glen nearly jumped onto my lap. When he turned around, he witnessed what was going to lose him the first round of our bet. It was **Unicorn**, an all-girl, all-Thai, rock band; legends in Bangkok. The look on his face was as if he had literally seen a unicorn running through the middle of the bar.

Unicorn isn't just a girl singer, but a six-piece band with guitars, keyboards, drums, and sometimes a horn section. All Thai girls! The whole bar got up and grooved as they ripped through a myriad of classic rock tunes from artists like Tina Turner, The Rolling Stones, Led Zepplin, even Queen, and U2. Glen stood through the whole set with his face lit up and his mouth wide open. They ended the set with a rousing sing-along version of Joan Jett's "I Love Rock-n-Roll" and Glen was blowing his lungs out singing along. When the band finally took a break we ordered another round of tequila and Glen said, "Fuck me man! That's what I'm talking about! Rock-n-fucking-roll! Those chicks are hot!"

We toasted to "girl power" and did our second shots of the night. When we sat the shot glasses down on the bar, Glen said, "Alright dude", reached in his pocket and pulled out a thousand baht note, and stuck it in my shirt pocket. "You got me. I have never seen anything like that before and I did not expect to see it here. Well played sir."

I plucked the bill from my pocket and gave it back to him. "Hang on to your money slick, I'm not the kind of guy who won't give you a chance to even up. Let's move on to the next stop".

Glen chattered non-stop as we crossed Sukhumvit Road and headed towards the higher-numbered streets. When we got to the corner of Soi 33 I had to interrupt him and introduce our next venue.

"Alright Glen, this is Soi 33, also known as the Art Bar District". I started to give him a brief history and a rundown on what happens on this famous street, but he cut me off and said, "Yeah, yeah. I been here before. Bunch of whores in evening gowns slurping expensive lady drinks. They all wanna be wined and dined and paid a fortune for some pussy".

I took a deep breath and gave Glen an exasperated look, then walked down the street ahead of him without saying a word. When we got to the busiest part I stopped and took in the ambiance. Soi 33 has always been a fertile playground for me. There were maybe a dozen big bars named after famous artists. Renoir, Degas, Dali ... all tarted up to look like posh watering holes with sexy sirens clad in their best evening wear.

It is a favorite venue for ex-pats and businessmen who aren't into the pulsating go-go bar pay-for-play scene. The intended illusion is that these places are a more dignified way to get laid like an old-fashioned "pick-up joint" or singles bar. The girls are a little older, speak better English, and are more presentable than standard go-go girls should you want to take them somewhere. The bars appear to be more upscale and have a wider selection of premium wines and liquors. A couple of them actually have cigar rooms. But, make no mistake, they are just fancy storefronts for hookers. A kinder-gentler form of prostitution; and considerably more expensive.

Glen was resisting the leash like an old bulldog who doesn't want to go for a walk. "I been here before man, I told you". "Just dressed up whores with fewer tattoos".

"Well then, you'll get your money back won't you?" I said.

Standing in the middle of Soi 33 I said, "So Glen, how many of these bars have you been to?" He started naming them, "Renoir, Degas, Dali and that big one called Napoleon". "So, you've never been to Van Gogh?" Glen rolled his eyes, "I don't know man … they all look the same".

I stepped onto the sidewalk and started up the steps to Van Gogh Club, "Come on Glen from Denver, set yourself to "receive".

Entering Van Gogh Club, it certainly seemed like all the other "art bars" on the street. The front of the place has a large open area that looks like a dance floor. The ceiling is two floors high with a big disco ball hanging down over it. There's a balcony that is open to a second floor and we could hear the sound of billiard balls clacking together and people laughing up there. Down the left side of the first floor is a long bar that stretches to the back of the building. Replicas of Van Gogh paintings hang in gilded frames on every wall with Vincent's haunting self-portrait leering out at us from the balcony.

A chubby little barmaid waddled over to us in a too-tight mini-skirt and a beret. She seemed to know me but I did not recognize her. We seated ourselves strategically at the high tables protruding from the wall between the main room and the long bar. From there we would be able to survey the place without having to roam around.

When the barmaid asked, "What you drink?", I only said two words. "Khun Fon?" She nodded in affirmation and scurried down the long hallway and through a beaded curtain.

Glen was taking in the atmosphere of the place, bobbing his head to an old KC and the Sunshine Band tune playing upstairs and ogling a rather curvy pooying who was preening in the mirror. The high-grade tequila and girl-power rock show at *Titanium* had altered his mood significantly. But, I could sense his skepticism about this place.

"Yeah man, I don't know if I've been here before, but I can see it is the same as the others. The girls are a little older. The customers look like ex-pats, not tourists. But, it's still just whores in fancy clothes. I've seen this shit before".

"Well Glen," I said, "Things aren't always what they seem. Some of these places have unique features you may not have experienced". And, right on cue, the mayhem began. A long protracted howl echoed down the hallway. "Khun Landooooo! Landoooo my darling where have you been?"

Sashaying down the hallway was none other than Fon, the flamboyant and notorious Papasan at Vincent Van

Gogh Club. Fon is a Thai man about five feet tall, of indeterminable age, and whose sense of fashion registers somewhere between Prince and Elton John. On this evening he sported a pair of banana yellow bellbottom pants and a flowing silk floral blouse that was blinding shades of orange and green. His blue-black hair was meticulously swept to one side Justin Beiber style and his sparkling purple lip gloss seemed to pull the whole 70's hot-hippie-disco look together. Fon clomped down the hallway towards us in white platform heels with his arms outstretched and blowing kisses all the way. Glen looked mortified.

Fon hugged me like a long-lost lover and chattered away in his exaggerated girly voice. "Oh my gawd Khun Lando, so long since I see you. Where you go? What you do? Who is dis guy?" He turned his attention to Glen so quickly it startled him.

Glen extended his hand and said, "I'm Glen. I'm from Denver". Fon switched to his man voice to shake hands and offered, "I'm Fon. I'm from Thailand". Then he broke back into his crazy girl voice, told us some dirty jokes, and brought two shots of premium tequila from the bar.

When Fon went to the back for a few minutes, Glen said, "Who the fuck is that guy? How do you know him?"

I said. "That guy is probably the most notorious pimp in Bangkok. I'd say he has at least 100 girls in his stable and he never forgets a customer."

Then Glen asked, "Is that how he knows you? As a customer"

"Glen, Fon introduced me to my first Thai wife. Her sister worked here and he played matchmaker. That's something else he does. He sources wives for lonely foreigners. Don't let that clown act fool you. That dude's a businessman".

When Fon returned, we chatted in Thai for a while about people we had in common. Glen took the opportunity to scan the room. Since Fon had come out, about five times as many girls were circulating in our part of the club. I could tell Glen was catching a good tequila buzz and eyeing up several of Fon's friendly ladies.

Just as suddenly as before, Fon turned his attention to Glen. "So Mr. Denver, you want to take some ladies? I have many to choose from. I can see you like big tits and ass, am I right?" Glen nearly swallowed his tongue and fumbled for an answer. I couldn't hold in a chuckle because I knew what was coming.

Fon took Glen by the arm and escorted him to the center of the dance floor. He snapped his fingers and two girls rolled out a big overstuffed leather chair. Fon parked Glen in the chair, stepped back, and said, "Ok Mr. Denver, it's showtime!"

With a quick clap of his hands, the lights went down, a laser light hit the disco ball, and James Brown's "Sex Machine" burst out of the sound system. Fon, who is an excellent dancer, busted a couple of patented James Brown moves and bellowed, "Alright ladies, let's get down". Girls started flowing from everywhere onto the dancefloor. In an instant there were at least 30 girls, all dressed in stylish street clothes, giggling and grooving and humping each other all over the place.

Fon started signaling girls to dance directly in front of Glen in groups of two and three. While they wriggled and teased Fon would say their names and their special talents. "This is Missy, she has big natural tits and can really suck a dick. She like girls too. This is Candy, she looks very sweet, but is super nasty ... maybe she squirts for you. Ooooh, this is Jenny, she a three-holer!"

The show went on and on, Fon dancing with the girls and getting more and more descriptive as he went. Glen sat frozen with a big silly smile on his face. I could tell, he had no idea what to do. As the music wound down, Fon selected two extremely curvy girls to escort Glen back to our table to drink with us.

I chose Van Gogh Club because of what Glen had objected to about the go-go bar girls. He made it clear that he didn't like skinny girls and also had an issue with tattoos. At this club, there were plenty of girls with curvy bodies, few tattoos, and all speaking English. I also figured what Glen truly needed was to get laid. His attitude wreaked of pent-up sexual tension. I thought surely a trip to the hotel with one or more of Fon's finest would be the attitude adjustment he needed.

But, to my dismay, Glen wasn't feeling it. He suddenly became quite timid, smiling like an idiot, and standing frozen between two beautifully buxom Thai girls. Fon's girls aren't overly aggressive and grabby. They don't ply the customers for drinks and grope them in the bar. They aren't pushy about being chosen for anything further than a nice conversation. In this place, men come for companionship and a few laughs. If there is sex to be had, the customer usually makes the move. Glen either didn't understand the concept, didn't know what to do, or didn't like his companions.

Every ten minutes or so, Fon would swing back around to check on us and try to close Glen on a couple of girls. Glen just kept grinning like a moron and saying, "no thanks, I'm ok for now". One of Glen's companions named Bella finally took his hand and placed it on her ample rear end. "You like my butt" she giggled. Glen just kept grinning and nodded yes. And there he sat, frozen, with his hand glued to Bella's butt, because she had put it there.

I took a bathroom break and when I came out Fon was waiting for me with a shot at the end of the bar. We clinked glasses, shot the tequila down and Fon said, "What wrong with dis guy? He like lady or not?"

I told Fon I wasn't sure. He seemed to like how they looked and was enjoying their company, but something about him was off. "He doesn't seem to know what to do," I said. "It's like he's waiting for orders".

Fon and I leaned on the bar watching Glen, with his hand still glued to Bella's butt. Then Fon said, "Maybe he needs a teacher. Maybe he wants to go to school". I let that thought sink in for a few seconds and my devious brain began to form a new plan.

I paid our bill with Fon, collected Glen at the door, and reentered the heady Soi 33 atmosphere at about 11:30.

Standing in front of Van Gogh Club I said, "See Glen, I told you I'd give you a chance to win your money back, and clearly you had already seen a place like that before. My bad. Now we are even".

Glen shook his head, "Naw man, I've never seen a place with that many hot Thai chicks before. And that Papasan ... well it was worth a thousand baht just to meet him. He fished out 2,000 baht from his pocket and offered it to me.

"Not so fast my friend. I've got one more place to show you. No bet this time. Just a place I think you'll enjoy. If you dig it, pay me then. If you don't like it, we are even".

Glen protested and said he was tired. I countered with the fact the place I had in mind was only 50 meters down the street. And I employed the oldest line in the party-boy handbook, "Come on man, just one drink". To which Glen dutifully replied, "Alright dude, just one drink".

I don't know when this whole adventure turned from a gentleman's bet into a treasure hunt for Glen. I didn't really like him, but I was inexplicably determined to find him some kind of sexual adventure. I mean, it is Bangkok ... if you can't scratch your itch here, it may not be scratchable. Going to Bangkok and not having some kind of sex is like going to Paris and not seeing the Eiffel Tower. I just felt like Glen had never had the full Bangkok experience.

He followed me in silence deeper into Soi 33 until we came to a building with no sign, no lights, and only a single door that looked like it came right out of a medieval dungeon. I pushed the green glowing button on the wall to ring the bell inside. Soon, the small window at eye level slid open and two thickly mascaraed eyes looked out at us through the iron bars. "Khun Neung for Pang," I said. The window slammed shut and the door opened.

I motioned for Glen to enter first. I didn't want him to have a chance to escape what I was walking him into. We stopped a few steps in to let our eyes adjust to the darkness. We were standing at one end of a long corridor with a bar on one side and a wall full of white cathedral candles on the other. There must have been two hundred candles of all different sizes flickering and dripping wax down onto the floor. They looked like they had been there for centuries.

Music moaned through hidden speakers, dark minor tones somewhere between chanting monks and jazz noir. The aroma of musk and opium incense filled our nostrils. Two tiny Thai girls, one in black leather garters and the other in a red latex catsuit escorted us down the spooky corridor to the end of the bar.

Glen's eyes were as big as pie plates. He followed the girls without a word. I ordered some beers and shots. Glen just continued to survey the place slowly, scanning from left to right. The bar was on a raised floor and we could look down onto the main floor to see some tables and some booths on the far wall. The place was so dimly lit, we couldn't see any other customers, but we could hear some murmuring every now and then. Out of the darkness girls wearing all manner of sadomasochistic attire and cosplay outfits would appear and disappear with drinks and empty glasses. Finally, Glen took a long pull on his beer and said, "Dude, what the fuck is this place?"

I held out my hand like a game show presenter and spanned the whole room. "Welcome to **Demonia** Glen, a place free from judgment where just about any itch can get scratched."

Glen leaned in and whispered, "Is this one of those S&M bars?" he asked.

"What do you mean Glen? Spaniards and Mexicans? I don't see any".

"No dude, you know what I mean. Slave and Master shit. Guys come here to get their ass spanked or to find a slave girl. You know what I mean".

"Well, I would call this place a fetish bar. For sure, there is a lot of female domination going on, as well as some guys who like the slave girl thing. But, there is also a lot of cosplay. Remember, this is the old Japanese quarter of Bangkok, and those boys love their costumes".

Glen sat upright on his barstool and scanned the room again, mouthing the words "female domination" silently. When his eyes finally came around to meet mine, he opened his mouth to say something and stopped mid-thought. His eyes opened wide and I could see his pupils dilate. I looked behind him in a mirror and I could see what he saw coming up behind me.

It was Madame Pang, the big boss in this den of demons. Alabaster skin, wild raven hair, and untamable curves all trussed up in a black leather dominatrix outfit. She looked like something out of an x-rated graphic novel. I didn't turn around, but let her sneak up behind me. Pang wrapped her arms around my neck and planted a dozen black lipstick kisses on top of my bald head. I looked like a cat had walked on my head with muddy feet. She spun me around and planted another one right on my lips, backed off, and then grabbed the back of my head and went in again for a long deep tongue lashing.

When she finally let me come up for air her girlish smile disappeared and I got her kabuki mask glare. Nostrils flaring she barked, "Where have you been Khun Neung? You don't call me. You don't come to see me. Did you forget about me? I hear your wife died ... can I have you now?" Then the dimples and impish grin returned. Classic Pang, an angel and a demon residing in one scorching hot package.

She went behind the bar to get some cold towels to wipe the lipstick off my head and reappeared with a riding crop that matched her outfit perfectly. Scowling again she held it up to my face and said, "I should beat your ass with this, you hear me?" "Yes, mistress" I chuckled.

She stepped out away from me to take a look at Glen who was sitting silently with his mouth hanging open. Pang extended the riding crop and used it to close Glen's mouth. She kept it under his chin and forced him to hold his head up higher and turn to the side. Suddenly her smile returned and she crooned, "What did you bring me? What is this?"

"Madame Pang, this is Glen, he's from Denver".

Still holding his chin up Pang said, "I don't care where it's from, why is it here?"

I placed my hand on Pang's arm so she would lower the riding crop to let Glen speak.

"I'm, I'm not sure" Glen stammered. "I came with him".

Pang brought the crop down in a quick and accurate stroke right on Glen's crotch with a distinct "pop". He jerked and yelped like he'd been electrocuted.

"Wrong answer" Pang barked. Then smiling sweetly she said, "You came here to buy Madame Pang a drink, isn't that right?"

For the first time since we came in, Glen showed a toothy smile, "Yes, yes Madame Pang, that's why I came".

Pang barked out some drink orders to the bartender. Glen and I continued on beer and tequila, and she had her traditional double Johnny Black with a splash. We clinked glasses and had a three-way conversation where I explained to Glen that Pang and I had been a thing when I first came to Thailand. She and I cackled with laughter as we reminisced about people we knew and things we used to do. She explained to Glen she called me Khun Neung. "Neung means the number one in Thai," she said. "This asshole was my first true love. So I give him the name "Neung"".

Glen listened with wrapt attention and didn't move a muscle. He didn't dare as Pang was holding him down on the barstool with the riding crop still placed firmly on his crotch. Whenever Glen interjected a comment, she'd give him a look that said, "Why are you talking? Did I say you could talk?". And then, without warning, Pang would turn to Glen with a smile and include him in our conversation. I could see his mind swimming.

The girl in the catsuit appeared and whispered something into Pang's ear. Pang excused herself saying she had to "arrange a party". As soon as she was out of earshot, Glen stood up to stretch his legs and exhale for the first time in 20 minutes. "Where the fuck did you meet her? How long were you together? Is this the kind of shit you are into?" I could tell he was intrigued and terrified.

I explained to Glen that I had met Pang years ago when she was the main attraction at the cabaret show at Angel Witch in Nana Plaza. She started as a high energy go-go girl, but soon graduated to performing all kinds of acrobatic stunts on stage. I'd seen her climb up a pole in the middle of the stage, hover 15 meters above it, and drop to the floor in a split. As the show grew larger and more grandiose, Pang morphed into this dominatrix character. She'd appear on stage in wild costumes looking like the daughter of the devil himself, mercilessly spanking supplicants to ear-bleeding metal music and paralyzing the audience with her vicious stare.

Glen repeated his question, "So, is that what you are into?"

"No, not really. When we were together, she'd come to my place, scrub off her makeup, and turn into a sweet little cuddle-bunny. We'd watch movies and make pizza together. She has a great sense of humor and she's up for anything. The Madame Pang thing is an act. She'll be whoever you need her to be. Pang's an actress at her core. Although, over the past decade or so, she's built her brand as a dominatrix and I'm sure she's quite good at it. But I never think of her that way. The time we spent together is etched in my memory as some of the wildest and most carefree of my life. She is one of my favorite people in the world".

I let Glen sit and absorb my answer for a moment and added, "The question is Glen, is this the kind of thing *you* are into?"

He shook his head and gave me a nervous smile meant to cover his confusion. "Na, man. I don't think I could let some chick spank me. This shit is for real freaks."

I saw Pang coming back down the long bar towards us. She had changed outfits into something even sexier than before, with leather chaps, a bustier made of little chains, and a nazi officer's cap. I got up to find the restroom but before leaving I whispered in Glen's ear "Everybody gets their freak on sometime Glen". As I walked by Pang making her approach, she stared straight ahead towards Glen and made a kissing sound when I passed, and then she slapped me hard on the ass with her riding crop.

While on my way to the men's room I saw three girls dressed as vampires mauling a big fat guy in a private booth. I couldn't see his face because one of the girls was straddling it. The other two were taking turns blowing him and stomping on his bare feet with stiletto high heels. This must have been the "party" Pang was arranging. I'd forgotten how freaky this place could get. I took my time in the bathroom, checking my phone and splashing water on my face. I wanted Pang to have some one-on-one time with Glen.

When I returned Glen had resumed his seated position and Pang was standing over him looking down from her spike-heeled perch holding him in place with the riding crop on his crotch again. I could see some black lipstick on Glen's ear and neck. There was a pair of chrome handcuffs on the bar near his drink.

"Am I interrupting something?" I asked, pointing to the handcuffs.

"Um, no, no, no, Madame's just messing around" Glen stuttered. Then he looked down at his watch and dramatically announced, "Dude, it's getting late. I'm thinking we should go".

Pang looked at me unblinkingly, waited a moment, then she lifted the riding crop from Glen's privates. "Up to you," she said, putting her nose in the air and giving a little shrug; like a cat bored of playing with a mouse.

While Pang got our bill together Glen stood up and gathered himself. He was drunk and flushed and battling what looked like an uncomfortable erection. We walked down the dark corridor towards the dungeon door with Glen scurrying ahead of us as if he couldn't wait to get out. Pang opened the door and Glen shot out onto the street waiting with his back to us under the street light.

I turned and gave Pang a big bear hug and she whispered in my ear, "Thank you for the present. It is so ... so fresh".

I held her at arm's length to get one more look and said, "I'll bet you a thousand baht it comes back here tomorrow".

Pang cackled ... "Baby, I'll bet you a thousand baht it comes back tonight".

Lights out in Bangkok

Six years ago, I started down a career path I never expected. I became a teacher. If you would have told me in 2014 that I would be a professor at a major university in Thailand less than twelve months later, I'd have laughed in your face and asked for some of whatever you were smoking.

The whole thing came about as a result of two things: poverty and boredom. How and why I became strapped for cash is a story for another place and time. But the boredom had been a problem for a while. I'd reached the point most expats do when they no longer desire to run and play like a tourist. I'd seen all the temples. I'd been to all the beaches. I'd engaged in all the sport sex I could stand. And, while I was happy to be writing for several local magazines and websites, I'd really run out of things to say and was tired of talking up goods and services offered by the magazines' advertisers. I was bored and broke and a little bit lonely.

Out of the blue I got an email from someone I'd met about eighteen months earlier. A guy named Tim Otterbach contacted me and asked if I was interested in teaching. Tim is one of those "been around the world ten times" expats with a girl in every port and story for every barstool. We'd met at the gym in Pattaya. Tim had read several of my magazine articles and hit me up for advice on how to get into writing. We became casual acquaintances and exchanged some emails, but I hadn't heard from him in quite some time. Now here he was, offering me a job teaching English.

I must admit, it is something I had considered. Considered and dismissed that is. I researched the process, and I knew I'd have to take a course to teach English as a second language, get certified and a whole bunch of other rigmarole like getting a work permit and finding a school to hire me. To be honest, I just couldn't see myself in a short sleeve shirt and tie teaching phonics to a room full of jabbering children. So, I dismissed the notion completely.

But that's not the kind of gig Tim was offering. He had gone through the ESL training, gotten certified and through a serendipitous turn of events, ended up being the director of the English program at King Mongkut's Institute of Technology in Bangkok. KMIT is a huge university with over 25,000 students.

Tim's job was to hire and manage native English-speaking teachers for a variety of classes offered at the school. "I could use a smart guy with good old American work ethic" he said. So, we scheduled a meeting in Bangkok a week later.

I met with Tim at his little condo in Bangkok and got the run-down on the job. The school was launching a huge program to teach TOEIC courses. TOEIC stands for "Teaching of English for International Commerce". If someone applies for a job that requires communicating in English, they take this test to rank their abilities. A front desk clerk at the Sheraton needs about a 6.5. An air hostess for Delta needs about an 8. An air traffic controller needs a 10. My job would be to teach two-week long crash courses in improving the TOEIC test scores of KMIT students. It was the only thing I had going, so I decided to follow this teaching thing and see where it went.

First, I had to organize and complete an ESL certification. There are several different kinds (I won't bore you with the details) and I chose a TEFL (Teaching English as a Foreign Language) course near where I lived in Pattaya. The course cost about $1,000 and lasted five weeks.

When I showed up to the school it appeared that I would be going through the whole course solo as the only people in the classroom were me and the instructor. My teacher's name is Gabe, an American from New York, a couple of years younger than me. We hit it off right away. Just as I was about to revel in the attention of a one-on-one experience, we were joined by another student. His name was Joe, another fifty-something from Holland. I hated him right away. So, it was just the three of us for the next five weeks.

The course flew by quickly and I really learned quite a bit. Part of the TEFL program is several hours of actual teaching in a classroom. So, we had some "field trips" to fulfill the classroom hours required to complete the course.

First, we gave practice lessons to a group of students enrolled at Juthamart hairdressing school in South Pattaya. It was hot, sweaty, and exactly what you'd expect a hair-dresser school in skanky old Pattaya to be like. We had about fifteen students that included a handful of bargirls being financed by their "sponsors", a six-foot-tall ladyboy from Laos named Candy and two big hairy Iraqi men using their education visas to the fullest.

Because ladyboys must be the center of attention at all times, Candy sat right up front and immediately began her attempt to dominate the classroom. She saw the sweat rolling down my neck and said, "Are you hot teacher? We can take a shower together".

After the class erupted in laughter, I spoke in a disappointed tone to her in Thai. "I am your teacher not your customer at the bar Candy. What you said isn't polite." With that short burst of rudimentary Thai, I took control of the classroom and Candy behaved for the remainder of the lesson.

We had to come up with our own lesson plan, so I combined a little role play with a listening exercise. I had my colleague, Joe from Holland, come in pretending to be a customer in a salon. I had Candy the ladyboy act as a shop employee and ask him what kind of haircut he wanted. Joe used keywords like "short", "long", "sides" and "a little off the top". I had the rest of the class listen and draw what they thought the haircut should look like.

The results were hilarious, and I soon had them all in the palm of my hand. By the end they were fluent with ten new words that formed a lexical set specifically for hairdressers.

When we had to teach a classroom full of forty ten-year-old kids, I was secretly mortified. Forty sets of hungry little eyes staring at the big farang. I felt naked. My first move was to ask the kids who in the class spoke the best English. They all pointed to a mousey little girl with a pair of bright pink cat-eye glasses named Pueng. I pulled a chair up in front of the class and said, "Pueng, come up here. You are the assistant teacher". Between this precocious little Thai muffin and me, we conducted an excellent class on past tense verbs versus present tense.

After getting our certificates, our instructor Gabe took us to lunch and pulled me aside and asked, "Okay, so you know you have a knack for this right?".

I hadn't really thought about it, so I played it off. "Ahhh ... you're a great teacher Gabe, that's all". But the truth is, I was shocked. Shocked by how easy it was. Shocked by how responsive my students had been. Shocked by how much I liked it.

Gabe said, "Lando, teaching is kind of like dancing; you only enjoy it if you're good at it, and you're only good at it if you enjoy it". I was happy to find a new gig. It was the first real thrill I'd felt in a long, long, long-ass time.

Once certified, I packed my bags and headed for Bangkok. Tim hooked me up with a place to stay through another teacher. He was an old Aussie that was taking a job in Burma and I took over his lease. It was a sterile little people box in a mega-tower on On-Nut Road. It wasn't exactly home-sweet-home, but the university is out by Suvarnabhumi International Airport and this was the most convenient part of town to live for commuting. Every afternoon I caught bus #1013 to Lat Krabang. It took 45 minutes and cost 16 baht. And just like that I was living the life of an English teacher in Bangkok.

The university was a lot different than I expected. It is a spread-out rambling affair with a jumbled-up combination of buildings and sports fields and agricultural parks. It reminded me a little of the university in my hometown; a school that started out as a smallish technical college that just kept adding on over the years until it was huge.

I was actually employed by a private company called New Education World. They had the contract to teach all the English language courses. Tim was my supervisor, but the boss was this little dragon lady named Nidnoy. She was a miserable old spinster who secretly hated all of us farang. Before every TOEIC round started, corporate would send down our regional boss, a young gay-as-fuck Brit named Stuart. He was about two meters tall, really skinny, and sported flaming red hair. I nicknamed him "The Flamingo". I figured out right away that if I just showed up on time, was dressed reasonably well and didn't complain, my teaching career would run pretty smoothly.

The students were great. Every night I'd have a classroom of 30 to 70 eager kids ranging from freshman to postgraduates. Everybody had taken the TOEIC exam and wanted to improve their scores. Some of them were quite bright. Some of them were dumber than a bag of hammers. I got better and better at it with each class.

I started teaching other classes offered by New Education World during the day as well. I taught four-skills English to small groups. I taught IELTS which is similar to TOEIC but for entry into an

English language university like in the US, UK, or Australia. I taught English for corporate clients like Honda and Ford.

And then they found out I was a writer.

The government of Thailand kind of knows their education system is a mess, so they have made some moves to improve it. One thing they did was mandate incoming freshman in certain majors take "Academic Writing" courses. "Academic Writing" means learning how to write term papers, book reports, theses, etc. One day the crusty old witch Nidnoy came to me all smiley and oozing with ulterior motive. She handed me an Academic Writing textbook and asked if I thought I could teach it. Before you know it, I was an actual professor at the school teaching two classes of twenty freshman twice a week for a nine-week semester. I'd gone from a newly minted TEFL grad to college professor in a matter of four months. It was head-spinning.

In my writing classes I got to know the students a lot better and had to keep fairly meticulous records on their attendance and participation. I also had to read and grade all their papers. I started to realize why teachers bitch so much about low pay. For every hour you teach there is probably another hour of work you don't get paid for in preparation and paperwork. I was learning what being a real teacher is all about.

My students covered a wide array of personalities. This nerdy genius named Prince sat in the front row of my first class wearing big Clark Kent glasses and his watch over the sleeve of his shirt. During breaks we'd talk, and he taught me everything I ever wanted to know about YouTube, The Cloud and artificial intelligence. I had this wreck of a kid named Reggie that only woke up to take tests ... which he somehow aced. I had one girl whose nickname was "Font" because when she came up to write something on the white board the letters were so uniform and flawless it looked like she had her own font. I had the lazy fat kid. I had the flirty girls trying to Lolita me into a better grade. For me, it was exactly what being a college professor should be like.

But my reaction to it was not what I expected. I didn't expect to know these kids personally and care about them. I found myself giving advice like an uncle or a grandpa. They came to me to talk about all kinds of life challenges, and I took it quite seriously. When one of my students was in a motorbike accident, I had to stop myself from rushing to the hospital. When one of my IELTS student's boyfriend beat her up, I wanted to go whip his ass. I didn't expect this kind of personal interaction and I did not expect to have any attachment to these kids. Somewhere along the line I had come to believe I was emotionally unavailable. I wasn't quite sure how to feel when I found out it wasn't true.

I moved into a more comfortable apartment in On Nut and settled into a pretty regular schedule. A couple of days a week I'd go in at 9 AM and teach my morning writing class, have lunch in the big student-faculty canteen, and teach my afternoon class starting at around 1 PM. Other days I'd come in around 4 PM and teach TOEIC for five hours. Various other classes were sprinkled in intermittently and my income averaged a nice livable wage. Life was rather good for old Professor Orlando.

During the first part of October, I'd signed on to teach some more TOEIC classes that ran from 4 PM to 7:30 PM. The program had been wildly successful, and we had a dozen teachers with an average of fifty or so students per classroom. I was feeling surprisingly good about my career and financial turnaround. I've lived in Bangkok four times before, but this was the first time I didn't feel like a tourist. I was a real Bangkokian doing Bangkokian stuff.

In mid-October, my birthday arrived, and I had a great agenda all mapped out. I'd head to work about 3 PM, taking a change of clothes with me so I could leave my teacher stuff in my locker. I'd teach my TOEIC course, change clothes and jump on the Skytrain's airport link to downtown Bangkok via Lat Krabang station. From there, Bangkok was my oyster. I could jump off anywhere in my old stomping grounds to eat, drink and get down! Happy Birthday to me! It's the first time I remember being excited about a birthday in a long time.

I had a huge class that night of about eighty-five students. I hate to use the microphone to teach, so I walked around the classroom using my theatrical voice to make sure everyone can hear me. It keeps everyone, including me, interested but it can be a little exhausting. After the first break I started to get a second wind because I knew "birthday time" was only ninety minutes away. I drove hard through the last couple of lesson modules and finished right at 7:25. The whole class let out a sigh and students streamed out of both doors of the room. With my books collected I headed down the big indoor-outdoor corridor towards the parking lot.

As soon as I broke the plane of the door, I could sense something was wrong. There was none of the normal din created by chattering students. No joviality ... no laughter ... just a haunting emptiness. I could see small groups of students huddled together glued to their mobile phones. I could see students sobbing uncontrollably and hugging each other. I didn't have to ask anyone what was going on. I already knew. There is only one event that could affect all these students so drastically and immediately. The king was dead. I always knew this day would come. I just didn't expect it to happen on my birthday.

I never took the notion of royalty from any country serious. I'm an American ... we scoff at such arcane silliness. But, after living in Thailand the first year I began to understand what the royal family means to Thais. It's not silly, it's part of their social fabric and their culture. You don't have to believe in it ... they believe in it. And that makes it real.

The royal family are beings above the rest of us humans with near godlike status. Now, I'm not sure all of them deserve such adulation, but Thailand's last king, Rama IX certainly did. He was a truly exceptional human being. Over the years I'd come to respect and understand the power this man wielded and the influence he had on every individual in a nation of nearly 70 million people. There is no reason to make a list of his accomplishments. One look at the crippling anguish on the faces of my students is all it took to understand how valuable King Bhumiphol Adulyadej had been to his people. Imagine a day where everyone in the country lost their father at the same time. The grief and sense of loss was overwhelming.

I sat down on a bench next to a big koi pond that flanked our building. For the next twenty minutes or so I just watched. The only sound that could be heard was the soft murmuring of people sobbing and consoling each other. I am not Thai. I did not have the right to be part of it and I've been in Thailand long enough to know that. Lights in the rooms of all the buildings around me started to go out, and no new lights were turned on. Within half an hour I was in total darkness. Even the streetlights went out.

All the air was sucked out of my birthday plans. I grabbed a taxi in front of the school and took the long ride all the way back to On Nut alone. Bangkok looked deserted. At 8:30 on a weeknight on a major thoroughfare through some of the most populated parts of a city with twelve million people and I don't remember seeing anyone. The whole city had a sick jaundiced glow. Nothing was bright. Nothing was vibrant. An eerie cloak of silence draped Bangkok like a death shroud.

When I got to On Nut, I walked down a small cut-thru street that is home to a bustling little street food market. Normally there are at least forty vendors selling everything from papaya salad to cotton candy. All the carts and stalls were closed up but one. The old Muslim lady that makes fried chicken was the only stall open. I grabbed a bag of chicken and sticky rice, then shuffled home in the darkness.

I walked through my apartment without turning on the lights. Opening my last beer, I sat on the balcony eating fried chicken looking out over an entire city that was weeping.

October 13th would never be the same again.

World Class People Watcher

People are always asking me, "What do you do in Thailand?" Well, there's a lot of things to do in Thailand, and I've done most of them. But, without a doubt, the ancient art of people-watching is still my favorite pastime. The people-watching in Thailand is the Gold Standard of the sport.

Great people-watching consists of two elements: the watcher and the watched. The group being watched should be as diverse as possible in a setting where they are either totally comfortable or completely lost. Either way is interesting. The watcher should be a person who knows how to be alone in a roomful of strangers and a keen observer of details. I consider myself to be a world class people-watcher.

I've spent time on Bourbon Street, Wall Street, and the Sunset Strip and none of these places even remotely compares to the pure entertainment value of what I see in Thailand.

Session 1 - Guaranteed Handsome

Manicures, pedicures, facials, and other assorted body-scaping services are dirt cheap here in Thailand. My bi-weekly trip to Estee' Salon sets me back a whopping $15 for the best simultaneous mani-pedi a person can get. I usually fall asleep during the process, but sometimes the people-watching is just too good to ignore.

Estee' is a big popular salon on Pattaya Beach's
Second Road. On this high-season Saturday all ten
chairs were full of snowbirds from a variety of
countries. Expat Madams were in getting a cut-n-
color or touching up their acrylic nails. A big Russian
biker came in a leather vest and cut-off jeans outfit
that made him look like one of The Village People. He
had an appointment for some kind of "waxing".
Sitting in the corner, sipping my Americano, getting
my hooves trimmed and watching Pattaya's
psychedelic human aquarium ... you simply cannot
buy this kind of entertainment.

The star of today's matinee walked through the door
like he was walking into a saloon, not a salon. A
lanky, closer-to-sixty-than-fifty looking American
pushed through the double glass doors and timidly
approached the cashier.

With a baritone Texas drawl, he inquired, "'S'cuse me,
ya'll cut hair?"

He drew a blank stare from both of the girls at the
counter. After three more attempts at verbal
communication and a little sign language, one of the
more outgoing staff caught his drift, grabbed him by
the arm and said, "Yes, cut hair on head, cut hair on
face ... more handsome sure".

In his wrinkled-up cargo shorts and mismatched
Hawaiian shirt, the man shuffled zombie-like behind
her to the barber chair. He sat stoic staring at his
reflection in the mirror as if waiting for the
executioner.

My two attendants and I took stock of Tex from our
corner vantage point. His hair was shoulder length
and unkempt. His big Yosemite Sam mustache was
comical. And the baggage under his eyes would
exceed the carry-on weight limit on most airlines. My
manicurist raised her eyebrows and said, "For sure
this man in the right place".

Then, as happens so often in Thailand, just what the
doctor ordered magically appeared. Bounding out of
the back like a big playful puppy came Lek, a twenty-
year-old Thai girl poured into Jennifer Lopez's body.
In a giggly-jiggly little girl voice she announced to Tex
that she would be his *"sty-rist"*. He looked mortified.

Lek speaks just enough English to be hilarious. I've
been to restaurants where the waiters are also opera
singers, but Lek turned Estee' into some kind of
novelty salon where you get your hair cut by a
comedian.

Within 60 seconds Tex was completely under Lek's
spell. She effortlessly drew the man out of his crusty
shell, and soon everyone in the salon learned that he
actually was from Texas, divorced, almost retired and
visiting his brother who lived in Thailand. Since his
mother had died and his kids moved to other towns,
his brother invited him to come on an extended
holiday. He arrived two days ago. "The people seem
n-i-i-i-ce" he drawled.

Lek talked Tex into a much shorter cut than I'm sure
he had envisioned. My guess is he just wanted to sit
in the chair and be fussed over a little longer. I'd bet
it's the first time he has seen his ears in three decades.
He even let her chop about an inch and a half off that

giant cookie duster hanging under his nose. She finished him up with a straight razor shave and a little eyebrow trim.

When she was done, Lek exclaimed, "Oh mister Clooney ... Sorry I don't recognize you before ... please can I have your autograph?"

The other stylists and salon staff applauded and wolf-whistled with approval. Tex chuckled and you could see that he had dimples and a nice smile. Young Lek had shaved ten years off the gangly old coot; even his clothes seemed less wrinkled.

Feeling a kind of magic connection to Lek, and not knowing what to do next, Tex reflexively gave her a big tip and his business card. Lek giggled, wrote her name on the back of the card, and handed it back. "When you want handsome ... come see Lek ... guarantee handsome okay?"

Tex grinned bashfully and acknowledged everyone in the salon on his way out. As if he knew I was watching, he shook his head and held up the card with Lek's name on it. "Guaranteed handsome ... you can't beat that".

Welcome to Thailand Tex.

Session 2 – The Human Aquarium

There was this place everyone in Bangkok knows on the corner of Sukhumvit Road and Soi 5. The actual name was "The Soi 5 Food Center"; a boring name that belies the fascinating human interaction that took place therein.

The whole corner looked like a heavily populated coral reef pushed up onto land with all kinds of interesting creatures appearing from holes and dark crevices.

Massage hawkers, tuk-tuk drivers and roving packs of burka clad Arab women bartering for all the knock-off Louis Vuitton crap they can carry. White men in business suits, euro-trash tourists, African hookers; I even met an elderly Englishman in town for "gender reassignment" surgery. Don't tell that guy you can't teach an old dog new tricks.

On a particular Thursday night, I showed up at Soi 5 late and grabbed my favorite seat at a dining table attached to the wall just inside the bar. It's a perfect spot because it features a clear view of the indoor-outdoor bar spilling out to Soi 5 and the long glass windows in the restaurant that face Sukhumvit Road. Since it was later in the evening, the clientele in the bar seemed to be a little more well-lubricated than I'm used to.

Four individuals were drinking at the bar. On the far left facing in was a sixty-something, chain-smoking old Aussie. He was frail and weathered with some kind of malformation in his wrists. His hands turned outward at 45-degree angles from his forearms. He seemed to have complete function in his hands, just no ability to straighten out his wrists. He used his freakish flippers to light one cigarette after another while chewing the ear of the doughy Englishman on his right.

I assumed the man was English because he was wearing a complete Manchester United Football Club uniform; not just a shirt mind you, but a complete bright red replica home uniform ... accented with yellow rubber flip-flops. I never once saw his face, but I could detect the muffled rolling diatribe of a thoroughly pissed Cockney rhythmically drinking and gabbing his way through the evening. The old Aussie had struck up a football-based conversation and they yammered away like long lost brothers.

On the opposite end of the bar was a rather odd pair. A tall, good-looking Thai man dressed in khakis and a Hawaiian print shirt was talking with an old white guy who was almost short enough to be a dwarf. This guy was the only person at the bar who was standing, and he was still shorter than everyone sitting on a stool. A thick shock of blinding white hair was slicked straight back to show the world he wasn't afraid to take whatever came at him right in the face. His bulbous red nose appeared to dip below his upper lip when he smiled. He looked like a drunken old proboscis monkey. It was he who decided to mingle conversations with the pair at the other end of the bar.

"Whaddya from England"? He squawked at the two football fans. "I've got a friend from London, ya' know where that is"? "My friend, he's from Buckingham Palace, that's in England ain't it"?

Because he stepped out from the bar, looked right at them, and raised his voice, the Old Aussie and the footballer knew the belligerent dwarf was talking to them. Old Aussie engaged the intruder with a placating tone and informed him that, yes, his friend was indeed from England.

The sawed-off little man continued, "Yeah, I been all over England ... London, Manchester, Chelsea ...", and he went on for nearly ten minutes, naming every city with a population of 10 or more people in most of the United Kingdom. For some towns he even stopped to tell a bit of WWII history and named famous people who hailed from them.

Old Aussie and the footballer were both amazed and terrified. Did they dare mention one of them was from Australia? The old man sensed their uneasiness and broke the spell with "I'm Red from Dayton ... Dayton, Ohio, ya know where that is? It's in the USA". He smiled with his dangling nose and offered his stubby hand in friendship.

The guy in the Man U outfit shook his hand with gusto. I was secretly repulsed by the site of the old Aussie's deformed flipper reaching across the bar to do the same.

Once introductions were over, Red-from-Dayton bleated on, "This is my friend Tommy ... he's from Thailand ... he's a singer down in Pattaya ... ya know where Pattaya is?"

The handsome Thai had been leaning his back against the bar, smiling, and monitoring the conversation in silence. I was happy to see the Thai avoid the trauma of shaking Old Aussie's afflicted fin. Tommy offered the traditional Thai wai instead. Everyone did their best imitation of the polite gesture and the Thai staff all gagged back their laughter.

"Ask him how old he is ... ask him!" Red insisted. He dramatically slapped down a thousand baht note on the bar and declared he'd take all bets if Old Aussie could guess Thai Tommy's age within 5 years.

Old Aussie didn't take out any money, but he carefully considered the taller than average, well-manicured Thai man in front of him and said, "36 mate ... not a day over 40". Red from Dayton erupted with a victorious cackle and mocked, "Yer only a couple a decades off Guv-nah!" Reaching for his ID, like he was used to doing it, Thai Tommy smiled and said, "Actually, I'm 60".

Incredulous, Old Aussie and Mr. Manchester inspected the ID as if they were treasury agents on the hunt for counterfeits. The number they had been given simply did not match the face it was supposed to belong to. Thai Tommy smiled with satisfaction.

"Why would he freakin' lie about being 60 you bloody morons?" Red chided. "That must be an English thing".

Again, Old Aussie offered his twisted limb for the Thai to shake hands, "Well done mate, well done". This time, Thai Tommy couldn't avoid the bent flipper and graciously gave it a little squeeze.

The four-way conversation then broke down into a survey of age. Red-from-Dayton was 84; Mr. Manchester whose face I never saw was 56; Old Aussie never revealed his age but examined his own reflection in the mirrored column next to his stool as if to say, "That guy's sixty? What the hell happened to me?"

In an effort to change the subject and gain some control over the conversation, Old Aussie pressed Thai Tommy for some music. "Well sing us a song then sixty-year-old Tommy. Red says you're a singer ... let's have it".

Thai Tommy graciously declined ... Old Aussie kept asking every five minutes, and Thai Tommy patiently declined again and again.

At random intervals, Red-from-Dayton would blurt out, "It's a freakin' shame he won't sing, 'cause I'm tellin' ya limey pricks this boy can freakin' sing!"

Finally, Tommy gave in. "Well, I don't know what to sing for you guys" Tommy defended, "Why don't one of you start me off?"

Mr. Manchester must have announced he could carry a tune as all eyes turned to him. Because his back was to me the entire time, I could never understand a word the chunky footballer was mumbling. Then, I heard him clear his throat and over the din of the street and the bar I heard a clear, entirely in tune, tenor voice singing the old Rod Stewart hit, "I am Sailing".

He wasn't half bad, but unfortunately, he only remembered about half of the first verse, so he started it again. When he got as far as he could go on his second run, Thai Tommy leaned in and finished it for him.

In a perfectly raspy, unaccented performer's voice, Thai Tommy finished all three verses. He sounded like Neil Diamond. He sang it with passion, style, and perfect pitch. He sang it right to Old Aussie and Mr. Manchester. The whole bar and half the restaurant fell silent under his spell.

When he finished, holding out that last note with just a touch of vibrato, applause erupted from the bar and outside in the street. Old Aussie slapped his fins together and bellowed *"Bravo ...bravo"*. Tommy accepted the adulation like he was used to getting it, then graciously waied and excused himself from the scene.

Mr. Manchester's shoulders shrugged as he mumbled an apology about not singing as good as Thai Tommy. Old Aussie lit a new cigarette off of an old one and replied, "Mate, I don't do anything as good as that man sings". Red-from-Dayton beamed with satisfaction, he was a man who loved to be right.

Everyone sat silent for a moment, stunned by the impromptu performance. As the bar and the street came back into focus, the remaining three drinkers noticed a pack of four young bar girls making their way down the vendor-encrusted sidewalk. Old Aussie and the Englishman woofed and hooted at them, producing the desired giggling response. The girls smiled and dramatically blew kisses, but never slowed their pace.

Old Aussie slapped the bar with his left flipper and said, "Awww, we almost had 'em mates! We almost had them little fish in the boat! I think that chubby one fancied you Red!"

Red-from-Dayton was not amused. "First ya want music, now yer huntin' pussy? Jesus, do I have to do everything around here?" And with that statement, Red walked out of the bar and down Sukhumvit Road in an apparent huff.

Old Aussie and Mr. Manchester didn't even have a chance to discuss what that was all about when Red returned with a new friend. "This is Ayeesha ... you pricks buy her a drink!" Standing before them was a six-foot-tall African hooker. Red had found her in front of the Starbucks just a block away. She looked like Michael Jordan in a miniskirt.

"Now this is what a real woman looks like boys ... not those giggling monkeys you was barking at ... for sure you'll get yer money's worth with this girl".

Old Aussie and Mr. Manchester froze, mortified by this spectacle. Ayeesha stood on display patiently, smiling whenever they had the courage to raise their eyes to her level.

Red insisted, "Buy the lady a drink you tight-ass tea-drinkin' bastards!" Instead, Old Aussie excused himself to the men's room while Mr. Manchester feigned an urgent phone call he just had to take outside on the street.

Red-from-Dayton stood victorious and cackling in the middle of the bar. "I knew you boys was fags, come on Ayeesha, I'll buy you a drink honey ... where you from, Angola?"

As it turns out, she was.

Session 3 - Saturday Night Anywhere

It made my girlfriend's evening when I called and told her we should go out for dinner. It's her last workday of the week and some Saturday night seafood sounded good.

We live walking distance from a little fishing village on the Gulf of Thailand called Ban Ampur. There are a cluster of waterfront seafood restaurants that all have one thing in common; the food you eat in them comes from boats bobbing in the water right in front of you. "Fresh" is the main ingredient in Thai food.

In Thailand, where restaurants outnumber people, deciding where to eat can be challenging. Most of the places in the Ban Ampur Seafood District are the same business model; big-ass family-style. The only way to separate them is to discern the specialties of the house. You end up choosing a place to eat based on a favorite dish that one place makes better than all the rest. On this night we were on the hunt for our favorite, Black Pepper Crab.

Good Black Pepper Crab means Sri Nuan, a mega-restaurant that can easily hold 500 people. Saturday night at Sri Nuan means being in loud, noisy, crowded, and frenetic Thai seafood joint with battalion-size families marching in and setting up camp.

We drank most of a bottle of wine at home before venturing down the beach. You really have to prepare yourself for the sensory assault you're walking into. It's like being in a huge aquarium full of aggressive fish. I find it best to embrace it, plant myself right in the middle and hit "record".

Sri Nuan is a concrete and tile megalith; a faded green, two-story colonial style building with terracotta tiles covering the over-sized roof. The inner dining room can host 300 people at long picnic-style tables seating parties of 10 to 20 each. An outer dining room on a wide covered porch seats another 100 or so at big round tables. Recently they've added open-air seating on the grass and sand that goes all the way down to the water.

All the seafood is displayed in live tanks and concrete holding pens full of circulating water and all manner of sea creatures. One would have to be a marine biologist to identify all the species available for consumption. My girlfriend and I wandered up and down the display like we were at Sea World.

Finally, we settled on sitting outside under the stars. We had an excellent view of the little harbor and the biggest outdoor sports screen I've ever seen showing Rafael Nadal whipping the daylights out of someone at the French Open. There must have been 100 people congregating around the concrete tables scattered over the sand and grass.

Suddenly, my Thai Princess put her nose to the wind and declared, "Tilac, foon toc lao". Loosely translated; "Sweetheart, it's going to rain now". In an uncharacteristic "take-charge" move, she transported us inside before we ordered. We captured one of the only small tables left in a strategic location with a waiter that understood the meaning of the word "tip".

Within in minutes we were enjoying frosty beers and had food on the way. I praised my girl for her tactical restaurant prowess, and she expressed her admiration for the smooth 100-baht teaser slipped to our waiter.

As forecast, the sky ripped open, and the restaurant became smaller by about a third. Rain-soaked families scrambled to move food, shoes, grandmothers, and baby strollers under the giant hat-shaped tile roof. Service and consumption resumed within three minutes. Dislocated tribes soon put down roots again and restarted their respective parties. We were way ahead of them thanks to my sweetheart ...the weather girl.

Equally predictable was the seating of a large family directly across from us at a table for 15 or so people. They arrived in groups of three and four, some wet from being seated outside and some just arriving with dripping umbrellas. Immediately visible was a classic character at most Chinese Thai family get-togethers, The Drunken Director.

This forty-something Thai woman, wore the telltale puffy "birdhouse" of hair favored by upper-middle class ladies. Stomping flat-footed up to the head of the table with a tumbler full of Johnny Walker Red and ice, she immediately began barking orders to waiters, rearranging the seating, and dragging chairs from other tables. All this she did without her glass ever once touching the table.

After they'd all been seated, then rearranged by The Drunken Director, then seated again, we could begin to delineate who was who in this ever-so-typical Thai family. The Drunken Director was seated near the head of the table by her husband; another common feature of the Thai entourage ... "The-Quiet-Guy-Who-Pays". Dressed from head to toe in Lacoste golf clothes and sporting a really sweet Omega watch, this guy didn't have a hair out of place. He thoughtfully listened, drank beer, and checked his phone every ten minutes. He did a good job of pretending to listen to his whisky swilling wife pontificating to her younger twin sisters seated to her right. They openly ignored her, carrying on a conversation with each other instead of listening. The Quiet-Guy-Who-Pays was jealous of their immunity, I could tell.

Seated to the quiet guy's left was no one. A space left empty by a teenage son who was busy outside on the terrace in an animated private conversation with someone on his pink cell phone. His shirt was also hot pink as were his old-school Converse high-tops. His skintight black jeans matched his eyeliner. My girlfriend dubbed him "The Pink Panther". By the time he sashayed in and took his place at the table, the family was well into its first course. I could see that for him, it didn't matter if all the shrimp were eaten ... he was a vegetarian. He was the only person the Quiet-Guy-Who-Pays talked to all night.

Watching one of these big families consume food in large quantities can be a gruesome sight. The Drunken Director didn't have the patience to wait for food to be passed, so she got up and walked around the table, drink in hand, to reach over everyone and grab handfuls of food. She'd stand there chewing with her mouth open and talking at the same time. The others ignored her. They were busy eating, or talking or on their phones, or smoking, or all of the above. Big plates of food hit the table and carcasses came out. Depleted Heineken bottles congregated on the metal drink cart displayed like battlefield trophies. This garish theater of gluttony seemed to be repeated at every table in my line of sight.

Breaking the spell of this carnivorous carnival was the only real child of the bunch and obviously the baby of the family. She was a cute little pig-tailed muffin, with pink silk ribbons in her hair and a "Hello Kitty" T-shirt to match her stylish older brother. However, she didn't turn to The Pink Panther when the four Pepsis she consumed started her doing the "pee-pee dance".

It was her older, university-age, brother with the boy-band hair and two cell phones that came to her rescue. In all, he patiently escorted baby sister to the little girl's room once for every cola consumed. He entertained the squirmy toddler throughout the entire evening, the consummate big brother.

The table was a beehive of activity. People getting up and sitting down; other groups joining for a drink and a nibble; the action never stopped. One thing remained constant: the cotton-haired old lady anchoring the far corner. Her hair was like a long-bristled brush, snow white and growing straight up in kind of an exaggerated flat-top. She wore a blue Chinese Nankeen print garment that could best be described as a housecoat. The twins, I'm assuming her daughters, took up positions on each side of her. They deftly cracked crabs, shelled shrimp, and deboned fish, keeping the old lady's plate piled high and beer glass full.

With a maelstrom swirling around her, the elderly elf steadily and deliberately devoured an alarming amount of sea harvest. She only stopped to sit back and have shells and bones taken away. Once a fresh plate was in front of her, she picked up her utensils and went to work. She wasted no energy talking. She had come to eat.

After two hours of full-contact consumption, the Quiet-Guy-Who-Pays summoned the waiter and produced his Platinum Card. The signal was sent out table-wide that the party was over ... at least the free part anyway. Members began to peel off every few minutes, each walking by Quiet-Guy-Who-Pays and acknowledging him with a touch on the shoulder or the passing sniff of a Thai kiss from the younger girls.

Boy Band Brother appeared to have a hot date and excused himself, ear to phone. The Pink Panther was back outside, rejoining his private conversation, twirling car keys around his finger. Apparently, he had somewhere to be as well.

The Drunken Director was already in the car passed out on the passenger seat. The twins wrestled Old Cotton Top away from the table and into to the backseat. The sugar-fueled pig-tailed princess leapt into the car and wiggled on her sleeping mother's lap.

Behind the wheel, Quiet Guy ensured all members were on board and appropriately buckled in, and then slowly rolled out of the parking lot, stopping briefly to tip the car attendant 50 Baht.

The big silver Mercedes was riding low, as full as their bellies. It could have been Saturday night anywhere.

One of Them

A funny thing about living in a tropical paradise is, you still need to get away sometimes. Most expats are terminally restless by nature. Once or twice a year, we need to see different stuff and talk to different people. Some guys go back to their country of origin. Some guys go somewhere else exotic. I take the middle path. I go somewhere exotic that reminds me of my home country.

I come from Florida where we have palm trees, beaches and it is hot as balls most of the time, just like Thailand. So, I don't miss the weather or the landscape. I miss talking to other Americans. I miss people understanding old Bugs Bunny and Star Trek references. I miss people who understand that "football" is a game played with an oblong ball by gigantic humans fitted with body armor. I miss tuning into a radio station I've listened to for decades and hearing songs that are as old as me. For me, "home" isn't a place but a sense of belonging.

So, how can I get a little bit of "home" without spending 26 hours in a flying tube? Easy, I go to Angeles City in the Philippines.

Angeles City was home to Clark Air Base, one of the largest US military installations ever outside the US. As it is with most overseas US military bases, a unique community sprung up around the base, mixing American "culture" with native sensibility. In the case of Angeles City, that included a huge red-light party zone known as Fields Avenue. It consists of bars, pubs, and restaurants of all descriptions catering to every whim and decadent desire of oversexed and overpaid servicemen fortunate enough to get an assignment to Clark.

In the early 1990s, two events rocked Angeles City right off its rails. The government of The Philippines refused to renew the lease on the base, so the Americans pulled out taking nearly every ounce of economic support from the region with it. And, in June 1991, volcanic Mt. Pinatubo erupted, plunging the whole area into darkness and ash. Nobody expected Angeles City to survive such a vicious one-two-punch.

But it did survive and in fact came back pretty damn strong. Thousands of servicemen, many with Filipina wives, retire and call Angeles City home. The old party zone on Fields Avenue arose from the ashes and began to expand. To this day, travelers from all over the world go to Angeles City for the wild, wild west feel, the cheap booze and of course, the busloads of young province girls that come to work the bars.

I live in Pattaya, Thailand, the modern-day city of Sodom. Like Angeles City, it was a playground for US servicemen during the Vietnam War. But Pattaya has morphed into a legitimate thriving seaside resort town despite its smarmy reputation. Angeles City remains frozen in time. For me, going to Angeles City is as close as I will ever get to time travel. The skanky bars. The greasy food. The friendly girls that can kick your ass playing pool. Angeles City ... where day-drinking is a religion and barhopping is a sport.

Normally, I go to AC whenever I feel like it. It is only a three-hour flight from Bangkok and there isn't really a "high season". It's pretty much fun all the time. But I found myself conveniently possessing a legitimate reason to go.

I had been writing for a couple of real estate magazines in Thailand and was asked to accompany a group of property agents to Angeles City to explore the real estate business there. Jack Seymour, an Englishman who owned and operated a realty company in Pattaya, had expanded to Angeles City. He wanted to extend the range of his brokers based in Thailand to include AC. I was to be the imbedded journalist on the trip. My job would be to chronicle the whole event, publish articles in magazines and fill the company's website with content.

If the truth be told, hanging out with a bunch of greenhorn English property monkeys was not exactly my idea of a good time, but they paid for the ticket and the hotel. And, by my calculation, the job only threatened to take up half of my time, so I'd have plenty of opportunity to do what I wanted.

A couple of days before the trip, I came up with a brilliant idea. Since I was already getting a free plane ride and hotel room, I decided to go for a trifecta and get a free ride to the airport. Normally, it costs around 1,200 baht to get from my front door to Suvarnabhumi International Airport in Bangkok. So,

I came up with a fiendishly cunning plan to get that paid for by another employer.

For the past six months, I'd been writing dozens of stories and website content for a big property developer called the New Nordic Group. They had projects all over southeast Asia and I was their go-to journalist. I pitched their marketing director, (Anita-the-boss's-daughter) on a new feature article about their eclectic fleet of cars used to transport VIP customers to and from different projects. New Nordic would pick up prospective investors in cool cars and squire them around. They had two 1950's vintage convertible Cadillac sedans, a 1975 Rolls Royce Silver Shadow, and an Aston Martin Vanquish just to name a few.

My idea was to write an article about the fleet from the perspective of a VIP customer.

"I'll have to take a ride in one of your cars Anita", I said.

She chuckled, "I knew that was coming. Where do you want to go?"

Anita agreed to get me to and from the airport for my trip to the Philippines. Trifecta complete! I wouldn't have to pay for a thing. In fact, I would get paid for the ride after I published my story.

On the morning of the trip, I got up at 6:30 and took a taxi to New Nordic's headquarters on Pratumnak Hill in Pattaya. I had no idea what kind of car I would be riding in. The taxi let me off in front of the main building and as I walked up the driveway, a young Thai guy dressed in a three-piece suit and a chauffer's cap approached me from the parking garage. "Mr. Braxton?" he asked. I nodded my head, and he took my suitcase and backpack. "Wait here please".

I assumed that I would be riding in one of their newer vehicles like the Range Rover or big Mercedes-Benz since the airport is almost two hours away and an old Cadillac might be less reliable for distances. I was secretly hoping for the Aston Martin, but the car that emerged from the underground parking garage was something else out of a spy novel. A snow white 2015 Rolls Royce Ghost floated to a stop in front of me and the chauffer magically appeared to open the rear passenger door. All I can remember saying is, "Oh my".

I slipped inside like a hundred-dollar bill sliding into a brand-new wallet. I should have been overwhelmed. I should have felt silly and out of place. I should have felt guilty, like I'd done nothing to deserve riding in such a luxurious vehicle. Instead, a feeling of comfort and wellness like I'd never experienced came over me. I felt invincible and untouchable. I plugged my phone into the Bose docking station on the arm rest and put on the cushy headphones that matched the ice-colored leather interior.

Since you can't hear the engine or sense any bumps in the road, riding in the Ghost doesn't give you a sensation of moving. Instead, you feel like the outside world is coming towards you. As we peaked the top of the hill and got the panoramic view of Pattaya Bay I had a premonition that this would be the beginning of a memorable journey. If going to Angeles City is time travel, then I was in the perfect vehicle to get anywhere in the multiverse.

When we ramped up onto Motorway 7 heading for Bangkok, the driver shifted to the right lane and never got out of it. Every other driver on the road just seemed to sense this twelve-cylinder predator bearing down on them and got the hell out of our way.

Fumbling with my phone to choose just the right music to accompany the experience, I had to ask myself what genre of fantasy I was living. Am I a rock star perhaps, heading to a big gig? Na, rock stars ride in cheesy stretch limos with titty-dancers hanging out of the sunroof. Am I a foreign dignitary or diplomat? Na, they usually ride in blacked-out SUVs that have those little flags on the bumpers.

Finally, I found my playlist full of ear-bleeding alternative rock and my fantasy gelled. Hurtling down the road at 150 KPH in a white Rolls Royce listening to *Corrosion of Conformity*; I was a Bond Villain. Goldfinger, Scaramanga, and Blofeld all rolled into one! My private jet was fueled and waiting in Bangkok to sweep me away to Angeles City. *"Once I reach my lair, Bond will never find me! Mwah ha ha ha!"*

When the car floated to a stop in front of the international terminal and the driver opened the door, my fantasy continued a little longer when a group of Japanese tourists all started snapping my picture. I don't know who they thought I was, but I showed them my best super villain strut. With my wrap-around Ray Bans and my Bangkok tailored shirt ... compared to me, Goldfinger is a wussy.

Three hours later, I descended the airstairs onto the tarmac at Clark International Airport in Angeles City and it was clear that my fantasy was over. The permanently hazy sky, the sound of roosters crowing, the smell of burning plastic. Ah yes, the Philippines. It looks like Asia but feels like Mexico.

The rattletrap old van from The Wild Orchid Resort was quite a downgrade from my white Rolls in Thailand, but I was glad to arrive at my destination, nonetheless. Something about landing at an American air base and heading to see some old friends felt like a homecoming.

I checked into to the Wild Orchid Resort and counted that I was called "sir" 17 times before my suitcase ever hit the floor of my poolside room. The Wild Orchid is a rambling four-story pink monstrosity with two pools, an open-air restaurant, and the most ass-kissing staff you'll find anywhere. On a good day, the Wild Orchid might score a three-star ranking, but I prefer it to any of the newer, swankier places in town. The rooms are big, the AC cold, and you could survive for 30 days out of a Wild Orchid minibar. It's packed with all the old American junk food I never see in Thailand like Cracker Jacks, Cheetohs, and Snickers bars. The little fridge is jammed full of ice-cold San Miguel beers in those stubby little brown bottles. I popped one open without checking to see if it was an appropriate hour to start drinking. I was officially in AC mode.

After a quick shower, I donned my AC uniform. Jeans shorts, flip flops and a tank top emblazoned with a beer logo. I topped it off with my black Oakland Raiders cap and headed towards Fields Avenue. Most of the bars had been open for three hours already.

The entire avenue was closed to vehicle traffic and clustered with big tents and display booths. It was the annual "Bike Week" celebration. Now, I've been to some "Bike Weeks" that were serious events held to pay homage to the all-mighty motorcycle and it's corollary lifestyles. Where I'm from in Daytona Beach, the event is internationally known, and people travel from all over the world to see it. Even where I live in Thailand, "Bike Week" is celebrated in Phuket and Pattaya on a grand scale. The bikes are beautiful and some of them quite expensive.

In Angeles City, it isn't so fancy. The bikes lining each side of the avenue were mostly monuments to Filipino ingenuity and welding skill. They could best be described as "rat bikes". Odds and ends and pieces precariously fastened together and painted garish colors ... lots of flames. There were also lots of novelty vehicles with sidecars and dozens of "trikes". Members of local motorcycle clubs had set up tents selling t-shirts, beer, and food. Filipinos never miss a chance to have a party.

Many other local businesses had set up tents hawking everything from real estate to solar panels. I was supposed to meet Jack Seymour at the tent for his real estate company, but the afternoon heat was wilting and winding through the tent city to find him seemed like a sweaty proposition. So, I popped into Voodoo

Lounge for another San Miguel to cool down. I crisscrossed Fields Avenue three or four times that afternoon, changing venues after each beer. Warming up my barhop muscles I suppose.

I didn't start on the tequila until I got to Gecko's.

Gecko's is your classic Filipino girly-bar-in-a-hallway set up. There's a bar at the front of a long narrow room with a stage stretched down one side facing booths and tables along the opposite wall. All the walls are mirrored to make the place seem less claustrophobic.

The fat little mamasan named May gave me a big hug and said "Maurice, where have you been?" On my first trip to AC ten years earlier, I called myself "Maurice" (my father's name). At least once a day, someone in AC will remember me as "Maurice".

I said, "I've been working for money to come spend in your bar Mama May". I squeezed her big rear end and added, "Oh no, are you sick? You are losing weight!" She punched me in the gut, pointed to a seat on the wall and replied, "Sit down asshole ... have some tequila".

I parked myself behind a small round table on the wall and surveyed the daytime "talent" on stage. At that time of day, the girls working as "hostesses" in the bars on Fields Avenue can be a little underwhelming. Especially if you come from Thailand where the girls are well-groomed, well-trained, and uninhibited. These Filipinas seemed as country as a chicken coop. Standing glassy-eyed in a line on the stage, shuffling back and forth with no particular rhythm, wearing big granny panties sticking out under their matching polka-dot bikinis. They look like exactly what they are; the prettiest girl in a poor family that came from a thousand islands away to have sex with foreigners for money.

I'm one of those guys who enjoys being alone in a room full of people. I want to observe but not engage. Bars like Gecko's are perfect for that. My sex tourist years ended long ago. I have no intention of getting my ball in play at Gecko's Bar in the middle of the afternoon. I just like the atmosphere. The mamasan knows that. The servers too. I bought a few lady-drinks for my waitress and tolerated a half-ass neck massage from Mama May. But mostly, I was just decompressing in my own little bubble.

My lone wolf bubble was suddenly invaded by three chattering American Navy boys bursting through the door. I say "boys" because they all looked twelve years old. I was barely legal age when I went in the Air Force, but I never looked at young as these kids. It was easy to tell they were squids because of the diversity of the trio. There was a tall skinny, whiter-than-white redhead kid splattered with big orange freckles. He looked like a baby giraffe. There was a nerdy black kid with thick glasses and a mouthful of braces. The leader of the pack was a good-looking blonde boy with a fresh US Navy tattoo on his forearm. He opened his mouth and southern Alabama came pouring out. I'm fairly sure I'm the only person in the bar that could completely understand what he was saying.

And, he was saying a lot. Apparently, he had been to the Philippines before and was leading a familiarization tour for his shipmates. They'd gotten some shore leave from their ship docked down in Subic Bay and hightailed it up to AC for some whoring and drinking. As they mindlessly yammered away, I surveyed my beer and figured I had about ten more minutes of this to endure before I paid my bill and hopped on to the next venue.

Bama Boy immediately started ordering shots and ogling the girls. He grabbed the hand of one of the girls on stage and said, "Hey baby, you wanna do a body-shot?" She helplessly looked to the mamasan who smiled and shook her head yes. The timid young girl was led down off the stage and over to the trio of horny hyenas.

The blonde kid bought the girl some sort of pink-colored lady drink and explained to his shipmates what the "body shot" was all about. According to him, for a special fee the waitress would bring a shot of tequila, salt and lime and he could use the girl's body to assist in consuming the shot. A tray with enough gear for two shots arrived. The baby giraffe and the nerdy black kid eagerly awaited the ritual and chanted "body shot ... body shot".

It was clear that the young dancer was new to this game as she needed one of the waitresses to coach her through it in Tagalog, the language of her province. She leaned back and flattened out as Bama Boy made a shiny trail of lime juice from her belly button up to her breasts. He then sprinkled margarita salt along the trail and dropped down on his knees and started licking it off, beginning at her navel. The girl lay motionless staring at the ceiling as the waitress coached her through the experience. Baby giraffe and the nerd continued to breathlessly chant, "body shot, body shot". Once the good-looking kid reached her breasts, he gave each nipple a few flicks with his tongue, stood up, and downed the shot of tequila waiting nearby. He sucked on a lime and triumphantly beat his chest like King Kong. His cohorts cheered like he'd just broken some world record.

The young Filipina sat up and cleaned herself with a baby-wipe. But it wasn't over yet. Bama Boy grabbed the girl's hand and said, "Now you do me". He yanked his t-shirt up over his head to expose his bare chest and belly and repeated his demand, "You do me". He leaned back against the wall and awaited "his turn".

The waitress/coach explained to the girl what he wanted. The poor girl looked terrified but shook her head in the affirmative and began performing the same ritual on the blonde kid. She carefully made a trail of lime juice from his navel up his belly to his hairless chest. She sprinkled the salt just as he had done. Bama Boy's cohorts fell silent, holding their breath in anticipation. The girl dropped down on her knees and began licking the salt trail slowly up the boy's body. He murmured lurid comments like "yeah baby, that's how I like it ... do it ... do it".

When she got up to his chest, she gave each nipple a quick flick with her tongue just as he had and stood up. Her coach then handed her the full shot of tequila with the lime and gave instructions. The girl shot the tequila, sucked the lime, and held her hand over her mouth. Her eyes welled up with tears. Her nostrils flared as she labored to breathe. She removed her hand and projectile vomited directly into Bama Boy's face. She wretched, then, the remaining contents of her stomach rushed forward in a second blast with such force; it made an audible "splash" when it hit his chest. The pretty boy from Mobile was covered in tequila, lime juice, and partially digested chicken adobo. The girl sprinted down the bar and disappeared through a little door under the stairwell.

I stood up and headed for the exit, stepping over baby giraffe and the nerd who were literally rolling on the floor with laughter. I handed Mama May a thousand peso note and told her to keep the change. Trying to contain a giggle fit, she pulled back the entry curtain, opened the door and light from the street caused me to squint and lower my Ray Bans. I couldn't believe the sun was still blasting away. I had no idea what time it was.

Behind me I could hear Bama Boy screaming, "What the fuck man ... bitch puked on me ... what the fuck?"

Oddly enough, my mindset had switched to food search mode and I was shuffling along Fields Avenue considering my dinner options. I stopped at a cross-street to decide and right in front of me was a tent with two huge flatscreen TVs hooked up touting different real estate developments in and around Angeles City. I stepped back to see the sign on the tent, and it was JS Realty, my friend Jack Seymour's outfit. I'd found it after all!

I stepped into the tent out of the sun and watched a few minutes of a video featuring sweeping drone shots of Subic Bay, teams of Filipino construction workers and 3D renderings of houses and apartments. A smooth and sultry voice came from behind me asking, "Is there something I can interest you in sir?" My brain lined up a half dozen smart-ass answers as I slowly turned towards the voice. But when I saw where it came from, I suddenly lost the ability to make a sound.

Standing in front of me was the most beautiful woman I will probably ever see in my lifetime. I opened my mouth, and nothing came out.

"Are you okay?" she asked.

"No" I croaked. "I am stunned. You are stunning. I have been stunned." She smiled and it was like flashbulbs going off. I thought I might have an epileptic fit.

"What a sweet thing to say" she replied. "Here let me get you some water ... it's hot out here".

She handed me a cold bottle of water from a cooler, and I held it up to the side of my head to cool down. I was happy to hide behind my sunglasses. I couldn't look at her directly without feeling naked. I looked around the tent like I was checking it out, but I was really just avoiding her gaze.

"I'm looking for Jack Seymour" I said.

"Oh, Jack went home already", she said. "It's too hot out here for him. Are you a friend of Jack's?"

"Sort of" I said. "I know him from Thailand. I'm here with a group of people".

"Well, you're not English, so you must be the American journalist Jack told me about. Your reputation precedes you."

"God, I hope not" I said. "I'm Orlando from Pattaya."

She held out her flawlessly manicured hand and said, "I'm Minerva from Pampanga. You can call me M".

"Minerva? So, you are the Roman goddess of wisdom?"

"Ah, an educated man. I'm impressed"

"I'm not sure if one mythology class in junior college qualifies as education, but as long as you're impressed, I'll take it. Let me guess, you've got sisters named Diana and Venus."

"No, just an older sister named Juno ... she's a bitch just like in Roman mythology".

We bantered on like this for a few minutes and I started to feel more at ease with this goddess. She was quick-witted, nimble-minded, and when she laughed it was a low chuckle that was a little naughty.

I was staring into her mirrored sunglasses now as if I were trying to make eye contact. All I could see was my own reflection and I noticed I was swaying a little, like my body was sensing the rotation of the earth. *"Fuck, I'm drunk"* I thought. *"If I'm so hammered*

that I'm swaying, for sure I'm babbling like an idiot".
I figured I'd better make a graceful exit and try a
smoother approach another day.

As I struggled to excuse myself, M asked, "Where are
you off to Mr. Orlando?"

"Well M, you may not believe this, but I've been
barhopping all afternoon and I think it would be a
good idea to eat something. Any recommendations."

"Oh, there are many good places to eat around here.
But I do recommend you change your shirt before you
go in anywhere".

M reached out and grabbed my elbow to turn me
sideways. She pointed to a big splash of vomit
glistening on the side of my tank top. She crinkled up
her nose and said, "I think this might put some people
off".

"Would it make any difference if I told you it's not my
puke?" I asked.

"It's Angeles City Mr. Orlando. It's hard to make it
through a day without getting something on you".

I backed out of the tent giving M a very sincere Thai
wai and pledged to be in better shape the next time I
saw her.

I walked around the corner and opened the bottle of
water M had given me. I held out the vomit smeared
side of my shirt and attempted to rinse it off. It was
then I realized I was at what I call "the turnstile of
darkness". It's at the end of a day-drinking session
where you have a choice to go home and get some rest

or walk through the turnstile and enter the dark side. You pay later.

I've been through the turnstile on many occasions. Waiting on the other side is a blurred memory of drinking too much, talking too loud and possibly waking up with a stranger. And more often than not, it leads to a vicious case of sunset vertigo.

The sun was starting to go down. Fresh-faced people were emerging from the hotels. And there I was rinsing someone else's puke off my shirt in the middle of the street. I backed away from the turnstile and headed for the Wild Orchid. I'd had enough adventure for one day.

When I got to the hotel, I stopped in the huge bar that separates the dining room from the pool for another bottle of cold water. When I ordered, the girl behind the bar chirped, "What? No beer?"

I waved her off and said, "No thanks barkeep, I've had my fill of San Miguel for the day".

When she brought me the water and a food menu, I couldn't help but notice how petite she was. In Thailand, the women come in two sizes, small and smaller. In the Philippines, I notice there is a considerable population that could be categorized as "extra-small". Her nametag said "Ivey". She was an attractive and shapely young lady, but I'm sure she didn't weight more than 35 kilos.

After scrolling through the menu three times, I decided I wasn't that hungry and ordered a mango shake with two shots of Tanduay rum in it.

"You must have eaten already, and this is dessert, am I right?" Ivey said.

"No, I've had kind of a rough day and I'm thinking ice cream and mangoes will make it better".

"The rum will help for sure" Ivey said with a big friendly smile.

She sat down on a stool behind the bar across from me and said, "So, what made today so rough?

"For starters, I got drunker than I expected to. Then I got puked on. And to top it all off, I met the most beautiful woman in the world and I'm sure I made a fool of myself in front of her".

Ivey rubbed her chin and said, "Well, probably most of this town will get drunker than they expect today. If you don't want to get puked on, I recommend you stay away from drunk people. And to be honest, a lot of beautiful women like to see men acting foolishly; something about vulnerability."

"Wow Ivey! Did you learn that in bartender school? I feel like I've been to a therapist."

"No sir. No school. I'm a natural. It's a gift from God".

Ivey skipped away and tended to the handful of customers at the bar but kept circling back to me and hanging out for long stretches of conversation. Her cool confidence and sense of humor were as soothing as the mango ice cream.

"So, who is this beautiful woman you met? Which bar did you meet her in?" she asked.

"Not a bar girl Ivey. She works for the real estate company I came here to write about. JS Realty".

Ivey rolled her eyes. "Oh, you must mean M. Orasco".

"M, yes that's her name. It's short for Minerva".

"Yes, here we say "M" is short for "Maneater"".

"Do you know her?"

"Sir, everybody knows M. She is a celebrity. M is from here in Pampanga province and is a supermodel. Or, I should say she was a supermodel for many years. Look, you can see!"

Ivey directed my attention to a framed travel poster hanging on the wall next to the men's room. On it was the image of a slinky dark-skinned Filipina in an electric yellow bikini lying on the beach in Boracay. A big hat and sunglasses partially covered her face, but there is no doubt it was M. The poster was signed, *"Love to all my homies, M"*.

"Don't worry sir, she won't "man-eat" you unless you are rich" Ivey said.

"What makes you think I'm not rich?"

"Why would a rich man stay at the Wild Orchid sir?"

"Maybe that's how I got so rich, not wasting my money on extravagant things".

"Sure" Ivey said. "And maybe you are the one out of all the rich men who have come here and tried to marry her who will succeed. Maybe you are richer than that Italian guy with the private jet. Maybe you are more charming than that Swiss guy who keeps flying her to Zurich. You, with your jean shorts and vomit on your shirt. Sure, I can see it. Why not?"

She said it all with such a pleasant smile on her face. Backhanding me to reality with a velvet glove.

"Goodnight Ivey", I said, and slunk back to my room.

I had only been in-country half a day and already I'd been emasculated twice.

I woke up at 6 AM rolling around in discarded junk food wrappers. Apparently, I had a bag of Cheetohs and a Slim Jim for dinner when I got back to the room, along with a giant Three Musketeers bar for dessert.

I rummaged through the well-stocked medicine cabinet in the bathroom and found Alka-Seltzer tablets. Magic! Listening to the crushed-up tablets fizz in a half-full bottle of water I patted myself on the back for not going through the turnstile the night before. Suffering through a day of meetings with these property monkeys would be trying enough without having a double hangover.

I opened the sliding door to my balcony and could hear the clinking of plates and silverware. The staff was setting up for breakfast.

The Philippines is not known for its cuisine. It's poor people food. Shitty cuts of meat. Everything soaked in vinegar to kill bacteria then over sweetened to kill the sour taste. They are good at roasting a whole pig and they have one good breakfast dish.

After being out on the lash in AC, I always order Daing na Bangus and garlic rice. It's sun-dried milkfish, fried and served over rice that's been stir-fried with garlic. At the Wild Orchid, they put a sunny side up fried egg on top of the whole mess. Protein, fat, carbs ... the perfect hangover cure. I splashed some Tabasco sauce on it and inhaled.

Three cups of crappy drip coffee later, I was showered, shaved, and wearing long pants. It felt terribly unnatural. Jack sent a car to pick me up at 8 AM and I soon entered the gates of the old Clark Air Base. Me and the crew of four realtors were meeting with the head honcho of a big development company called Peregrine Engineering. I hated the asshole the moment he walked in the room.

To start with, he had some ridiculous American nickname like "Flip" or "Chip" or "Tug". I renamed him immediately. *"Henceforth"* I thought to myself ... *"His name is "Smug" ... "Smug Fuckerson""*. He was a caricature of an American expat in the Philippines.

Highly polished penny-loafers? Check. Over-starched and creased khaki trousers? Check. Over-starched and creased Ralph Lauren dress shirt? Check. Gaudy gold Rolex watch? Check.

I'd say Smug is pushing 70 but trying hard to hide it with an awful dye-job on his tight little helmet of hair. Why can't they make hair dye in colors that hair comes in? Smug's lid was kind of burnt orange with flecks of brown and green. Hair is supposed to be blonde or brown or auburn, not tweed. To his credit, he didn't forget the eyebrows like many old guys. His looked like they'd been colored in by a three-year-old, slightly outside the lines.

He introduced himself and gave us a brief resume. He's originally from Cincinnati. He came up working in refineries and oilfields. He spent a lot of time with big engineering companies like Brown & Root and Schlumberger in Africa and Southeast Asia. He wound up in the Philippines three years ago and got this gig with Peregrine, an American firm backed with Arab money.

Smug didn't have to tell me where he was from, I already knew. Early in the briefing he informed us that the "commode" was down the hall and to the left. Nobody but a Southern Ohio shit-heel calls a toilet a "commode".

He proceeded to bore me with a slideshow of Peregrine's pet project, a "Medical City" complex not far from where we were sitting. There was a massive medical and research facility planned as well as several housing projects aimed to serve the wave of new residents that were sure to arrive. The whole thing hinged on the Philippine government continuing to develop the old air base into an international transportation hub.

I set myself to "note-taking" mode and tried not to nod off. The four property monkeys were buying every bit of what Smug was selling. They enthusiastically asked questions and collected brochures. I had to remind myself that my job was to record what was happening, not educate Simon,

Gavin, Ian, and Nigel on the pitfalls of development projects in Southeast Asia. They'd have to learn the same way I did.

I took a deep breath to send my sleepy brain some more oxygen and when I did, I got a nose full of Coco Chanel perfume. I didn't need to turn around to know that M had walked in the back of the meeting room. I was immediately energized. The day wouldn't be a total waste after all.

When the show was over, we moved to an outer office where M was waiting. She flashed me that million-megawatt smile and said, "Good morning Mr. Orlando. So nice to see you again. Please introduce me to your friends".

The four Englishmen were standing with their faces hanging out; probably the same look I had when I first laid eyes on M. She looked spectacular in a perfectly tailored navy-blue skirt and jacket. Hair up in a French twist. A dainty set of pearls around her slender bronze neck.

On that day I could see her eyes. Chocolate bullet holes framed by high arching brows that could go from sexy to furious in a millisecond. Something about her look was classic, timeless, almost ancient. You'd expect to see her image painted on the walls of an Aztec pyramid or in a relief carving on a Cambodian temple.

"Mr. Orlando? Your friends?"

"Oh, shit, sorry. M, this is ... uh ... um ... John, Paul, George, and Ringo. Boys this is M, my future ex-wife".

The ice was broken, everyone had a good chuckle and M piled us into her SUV to transport us to the next meeting. I was so proud M chose me to ride in the front passenger seat next to her. It separated me from these goofy Brits in their cargo shorts and golf shirts. They looked like people dressed as tourists for Halloween.

M stopped in front of a non-descript building on a street running parallel to Fields Avenue. She said Jack was waiting for us inside where he had lunch all set up. It was well past 2 PM and we were starving. There was a simple sign that said "pizza" with a red arrow, so we followed it like swarming piranhas.

We entered through a door that looked like the backdoor of a bar or club. When my eyes adjusted to the dark, I saw we were in a cavernous room with some unusual furniture. My first thought was, *"I wonder what this was before it became whatever it is now?"* It looked like a college lecture room with terraced levels of long tabletops in front of fixed swivel chairs. There were about eight rows and they got lower and narrower until they reached the floor where a live band was set up and playing. Whatever this place had been, the acoustics were good, and the band sounded great.

Jack appeared from a side door all smiles and handshakes. He's a jolly old sixty-something Englishman with a craggy face and some kind of strong regional accent I can't quite place. "Sit down mates, pizzas are on the way". We all sat, ordered some beers, and slipped into a nice, chilled groove with the band that was playing an old Van Morrison tune. It felt good to be out of the heat and not hearing any real estate jargon.

I wasn't expecting much from the pizza, but when it came, I was surprised to see my favorite style. Super-thin crust cut into little bite-sized squares ... back home we call this party-pizza. The Englishmen were all waiting to be given utensils. I guess where they come from it's okay to eat something called "spotted dick", but a mortal sin to eat pizza with your hands. I relaxed with my beer and enjoyed the atmosphere. I was glad to be with them, but not one of them.

As I reached for my fourth pizza square, I heard someone sound checking a microphone, "One, two ... one, two". I looked down to the stage area and it was Jack, chatting with the band and apparently getting ready to say something. My heart sank. "Fuck me" I thought, "not more real estate bullshit".

To my surprise and delight, Jack started tapping his foot and counting down, "One, two ... one, two, three, four" and he and the band launched into the old Tom Jones classic, "What's New Pussycat?" I looked at the English crew and they were as shocked as me. Watching this pot-bellied old goat in his too-tight designer jeans and short-sleeved cowboy shirt blast out the classic tune was like watching "Planet of the Apes". You just couldn't believe that sound was coming out of his mouth.

At first, we thought he was lip-synching, but he had arranged a whole medley of tunes for us. He did "She's a Lady", "It's Not Unusual" and of course "Sex Bomb". At the end he had all the English lads up and singing "Why oh why, Delilah?" It was outrageous.

When he was finished, he came to sit with us as if nothing had happened. I had to ask, "Jack, where the fuck did you learn to sing like that?"

He looked at me and matter-of-factly replied, "I'm Welsh".

"Finish up boys, on to the next stop".

We didn't go too far. Jack led us like ducklings about a hundred meters down the same street to a place best described as a "honky-tonk". The sun was just starting to go down, but the neon sign over the door was already lit that read, "Midnight Rodeo". A smile crept over my face as I heard the sounds of "real" American country music wafting through the door.

As we shuffled in, the familiar aroma of draft beer being spilled on a sawdust-covered floor filled my nostrils. More neon signs hung behind the bar touting long-extinct brands of beer. I was gripped with nostalgia to see old school brand names like Pabst, Stroh's and my all-time favorite, Miller High-Life.

It was only about 5 PM but the place was packed with people. We appeared to be the only single folks in the place. The remainder of the crowd were all couples made up of old expats with their Filipina wives. I'd say the average age of the crowd exceeded 65 years old, and that includes the band. In fact, I'd say the band members were all over 70.

We occupied a couple of tables near the band and ordered beers. I splurged and got a longneck Budweiser. I sat right in front of the lead singer, a tiny old Filipina in skin-tight jeans and a rhinestone bedazzled western shirt. She sported thick cat-eye glasses crusted with matching rhinestones. With her hair twisted up in a tight mini-beehive and a fresh smear of red lipstick, I couldn't help but think, *"I bet she was hot about 50 years ago"*.

She was belting out the old Patsy Cline tune, *"Walking after Midnight"* like she owned it. Her band, a handful of leathery old Filipinos, defied their age and had plenty of bounce. The dancefloor filled up with old couples getting their two-step on; boots were scootin' all over the floor. If you closed your eyes, you could swear you were in Houston, or Nashville or Atlanta or, anywhere but the Philippines.

The band played a tight set of old country tunes from artists like Loretta Lynn, George Jones, and Willie Nelson. I looked over at Jack immersed in the atmosphere and digging every bit of it. I could see this was one of his favorite haunts. John, Paul, George, and Ringo were lost. I guess back in jolly old England they've never experienced the American phenomenon of line-dancing or seen a banjo before. They wanted to make fun of it, but they were outnumbered about 100 to 4. Seeing them out of their element made me feel more in mine. I could have sat there all night.

The young Englishmen may have thought this cartoonish American enclave was funny, but I was a little jealous. "I'm not that far behind this bunch in age" I pondered. "It would be nice to have somewhere to go and someone to dance with". I hadn't made any moves to secure such a comfortable future. For the hour or so we stayed at Midnight Rodeo, I secretly wished I were one of them.

Before the second set began, we tabbed out and huddled in the street in front of the bar. The younger guys were planning to head back to their hotel for a shower, power nap and then a night on Fields Ave. Jack was heading home to his 23-year-old Filipina wife. And I was characteristically on my own. I bid them all adieu and strolled on back to The Wild Orchid with that song in my head, "Walkin' after midnight, searchin' for you-oo-ooh."

My plan was to get a power nap of my own, have a decent meal and visit some of my old haunts, hoping to serendipitously run into any old friends that might be out and about. On the way through the hotel to my room, I spied Ivey working at the bar. She saw me and pointed to the chair where she wanted me to sit. I complied and ordered a beer.

It was dinner time, so the bar and restaurant were quite busy. Ivey popped by every few minutes before scurrying around to service her customers at the bar. My head was down rewriting the notes from the meeting at Peregrine when I felt her approach again and stop. When I looked up, she put a cold San Miguel in front of me with an uncomfortable look on her face.

"Someone bought you a drink" she said in a quivering voice. "It's a man. He says he wants you to meet him in his room. He said to give you this".

Ivey handed me a Wild Orchid Hotel key with a jittery hand. I took the key and put it in my shirt pocket.

"Is he handsome?" I asked.

The look on her face became even more uncomfortable.

"Um, actually yes. He is quite handsome".

"Well tell that good-looking motherfucker to come over here and kiss me on the lips then".

Ivey's head was spinning.

"Uh, uh, ok" she said as she turned to go.

But by then the joke was revealed. Standing right in front of me was my old friend, the Latino lady-killer, the scourge of Dade County, none other than Ruben Ramirez.

"Ruben the fucking Cuban! Fuck me man ... I can't believe it"!

We had one of those "I never thought I'd see you again" hugs and he did kiss me, right on the lips. That's just how he rolls.

I first met Rueben in Angeles City five years earlier. I was fairly new to the Philippines and desperately trying to figure out the language. Tagalog and Visayan sound like Spanish, so I was trying to speak Spanish to the cute barmaid at the swim-up bar.

Rueben heard my pitiful language skills and knew from my accent that I had learned it from Cubans. He's from Miami, I'm from Daytona ... we were friends in an instant. He is without a doubt one of the most entertaining people I've ever met, and I was beyond thrilled to see him again.

We stood at the bar and caught up on each other's lives in a frenzy. After about twenty minutes Rueben said, "Ok, wash your ass. Let's get our balls in play". I knew the power nap and good meal thing was scrubbed from my schedule at that point.

When I went to pay my bill, Ivey said, "Be careful tonight. That guy seems dangerous".

"Don't worry Sweet Pea. I'll be home early".

She blushed bright red and said "Ok. I'll be here waiting".

Walking past the pool to the room my inner voice said, "Knock, knock asshole. That little chic digs you. Hello? Earth to heartless cad. Real girl alert. Hello, you aren't so old and jaded you don't see it, right?"

I showered up and put on my new white linen shirt. It's that shirt you take on a trip just in case you're going to go out and want to take your look to another level. A crisp white shirt, a good tan from my daily walks on the beach and a pocketful of pesos; I was ready for action. A few squirts of cologne and I was on the prowl with the infamous Reuben-the-Cuban.

We started at Roadhouse for their notorious 3-for-1 happy hour. Rueben doesn't really drink much, so it was mostly for my benefit. We sat in the corner furthest from the speakers blasting out AC/DC and schemed the night ahead.

"What are you in the mood for Rueben?" I asked.

"I haven't been here since I last saw you" Ruben replied. "I don't know which bars are good now. Some that I liked before are closed or changed names".

"Well, what kind of girls are we looking for Ruben? Old girls, young girls, sweet girls, nasty girls ... pick your poison".

"You know me brother, I'm all about that ass. Let's find a club that has girls with asses big enough to show a movie on. Asses you can see from outer space. Asses that cannot be ignored. Asses that show no mercy. Asses that challenge you as a man".

"Well then, the choice is simple" I said. "We go see Black Jimmy".

Black Jimmy and I had become friends a few years earlier. I was barhopping with my old friend Gordy Gale and expressed a desire to hear some old Motown tunes. He took me to The Bunny Ranch and introduced me to the owner, Black Jimmy. We hit it off in an instant and sat drinking Courvoisier and listening to Curtis Mayfield all night. I came to see him every time I went to AC.

Jimmy's father was a black guy from the US who was stationed at Clark AB. His mom was a Filipina from somewhere near Manila. Jimmy is a dead ringer for NBA superstar Charles Barkley. Legend has it that Jimmy was a bodyguard for some big Filipino politician in Manila. One night some guys came to murder his boss and Jimmy left both of them shot to death in the stairwell of a hotel. Jimmy's employer set him up in AC with The Bunny Ranch in gratitude for saving his life. Sometimes it's hard to reconcile that story with the soft-spoken gentle giant I know. But every now and then, you can catch him looking at someone he doesn't like, and you can see the killer in there. I'd never want to get on the wrong side of Black Jimmy.

I walked Rueben to the Bunny Ranch, and he was smiling before we even got in the door. Outside there were two "Hello Girls" holding signs touting drink specials and shouting, "Welcome to Bunny Ranch sir!" Rueben had them turn around to display their backsides and confirmed my call on the place.

"Fucking Lando!" Ruben exclaimed. "I knew I could count on you".

Walking into the club was like entering a midnight carnival. Bunny Ranch is deceptively large and voluminous. The ceilings are three stories high, there's a big stage on the left with a sea of high-top tables and barstools. The bar is towards the back and there is an elevated VIP area with a live DJ. The music shifts from old school Motown to R&B to Hip Hop. There are no lazy shufflers in Jimmy's place. Every girl in the club can dance, twerk, and otherwise pop that coochie! The place was filling up with people and much of the crowd was already well-lubricated.

I had sent a text to Jimmy earlier to tell him we were coming. He greeted us a few meters inside the door with his arms spread out in a Christ-the-redeemer pose.

"Welcome friends ... to Jimmy's House of Ass".

Rueben looked like the Cheshire Cat, with a blacklight illuminated grin so big I couldn't see the rest of him. Jimmy took us up to the VIP loft where we could talk and have some drinks from his private stock. He summoned a couple of cello-shaped Filipinas to keep Rueben company and handed me the fixings to roll a joint.

"Roll up a big spliff Lando. I got some boys waiting on the roof".

Rueben can't smoke, so we left him with the girls while Jimmy and I climbed the fire escape four floors to the rooftop. When we got there, I saw four big, yellow-eyed black dudes, all with long braided locks, standing around on the roof drinking beers. As we approached, I recognized one of the guys as my old friend "Gritty" from Detroit.

"Well, well, well. Look who's slumming in the 'pines! Lando, where you been brother? How are things in Thailand?"

Even though I was with Jimmy and Gritty knew me, the other three were giving me the gangster stare.

I took a look at all four of these black guys with their fancy braided hair, gold teeth and premium Nike sneakers and smirked.

"What happened? Did somebody's wife get a job in a weave factory?"

Gritty blew beer out through his nose laughing. The others couldn't help but smile. The ice was broken. Smart-ass white boy accepted. We fired up the joint I rolled that was as big as my middle finger and tuned up our attitudes right there on the roof of the Bunny Ranch. I found out Gritty's Filipina wife had just had another baby. So had Jimmy's. Two of the other guys were twin brothers from Philadelphia. All of them were retired military. All of them had Filipina wives.

We smoked, talked about American football, and cackled like idiots about absolutely nothing. Good weed. There aren't many things I miss about the US, but I couldn't help thinking how I actually missed hanging out with black Americans. I grew up with a lot of different races of people. I was bussed to a black high school to lighten up their mix of students. I played a lot of ball with black guys and I was in the military with a lot of people a different color than me.

In Thailand, you see Africans but there aren't many African Americans. That part of my upbringing didn't travel with me, and it isn't until I get to the Philippines and around a group like this one that I realize I miss it.

"These guys have rather good lives", I thought to myself. Like me, they had all escaped whatever places they grew up in by going in the military and seeing the world. Now they had monthly checks coming in that probably wouldn't support a family in the US, but here in the Philippines, they were respected middle class. They had beautiful young wives, adoring families, and steady income. I must say, it looked like a plan well-executed.

Just as I was about to grow some jealous feelings, my self-awareness kicked in. While I might envy the apparent comfort and stability of their lives, I'm not sure I could stand it. I'm not so good at being married, and in the Philippines, that can get you killed in your sleep. I don't think I could stand to have any more children. I've already proved I'm not a good father, so there is no need to make that point again. And doing the same shit every day with the same idiots until I die doesn't appeal to me either.

Being "content" is not really my thing. The anticipation of what's next and the thrill of each new experience is what makes me feel alive. As Jimmy and I descended the stairs back to the club, I concluded, "It was good to hang out with these guys tonight, but I'm not one of them".

When we walked into the VIP lounge through the backdoor of the club, we could see that the main floor had become packed with people. Jimmy looked at his watch and said, "ten o'clock ... time for the pole show". Jimmy told me that he had installed two mechanical chrome poles on the stage among the 4 dancer poles. There was a team of Filipina performers that came at 10:00 to perform a 30-minute show using the poles. I could see the girls taking the stage in some colorful native Filipino dance costumes.

"They do the show with these costumes to help us with our licensing" Jimmy said. "The minister of tourism is kind of uptight, but if the girls start out in traditional costumes, it doesn't matter how much of it they take off or how nasty they dance".

The two dancers on the special poles were extremely professional and put on a hell of a show. They climbed the poles, hung upside down, spun around slow and sexy, then so fast you got dizzy just watching them. The amazing part was you couldn't see the poles moving. The girls just seemed to be floating around under their own power. If Jimmy hadn't told me the poles were powered by a motor under the stage, I would have been fooled by the illusion.

We were standing about ten meters from the stage behind the first row of high-boy tables. A crowd of people had pushed between us and the stage to get a closer look. The performers had tight bodies from working on the poles every night and a group of drunks was near the stage whooping and hollering for them to "take it off baby... take it all off!" I craned my neck to see who it was and was not shocked to see the three Navy kids I'd seen before in Gecko's. Bama Boy, Baby Giraffe, and the Black Nerd were all there at the stage barking like seals in the circus.

The music was building up and I could tell it was the big finale. As the music got more frenetic, the dancers became more acrobatic, spinning rapidly and at one point, jumping from one pole to the next. When they finally finished with some dramatic spins and dropping to the floor in full splits, the crowd went wild, hollering and whistling and throwing 100-peso notes on the stage. The dancers bowed repeatedly, scooped up the money in one of the costume headdresses, and scrambled off the stage.

Bama Boy continued to whoop and holler long after everyone else and ultimately barked out, "I can do that shit ... I can do that shit!" Then, he jumped up on the stage and ran towards one of the two middle poles and leapt onto it.

When he first hit the pole, he was grinning like an idiot. But when he felt the sensation of the room moving his expression turned to terror as the pole whipped around and flung him off the edge of the stage and crashing onto the high-boy table loaded with drinks, cell phones, ashtrays, and handbags right in front of me.

I was surrounded by people and it all happened so fast, I couldn't move to avoid the flying debris. I just closed my eyes and braced for whatever disaster might come my way. I could hear the table give way with a thundering "CRRRRACK!" I could hear the orchestra of glass shattering and scattering everywhere. And all at once I heard a double splash-splash and felt my belly get soaked with yet-to-be-identified liquids.

When I opened my eyes, it looked like the scene of a plane crash. The table was splintered and broken into three big pieces with a mangled barstool on top. Glass and debris were everywhere. Bama Boy was face down in the middle of it not moving with one arm splayed out at an unnatural angle. At least a dozen people were standing around his body with their phones out taking pictures.

I looked over at Rueben and he hadn't moved a muscle from his perch 20 meters back. Still chaperoned by "the legion of ass", he seemed content to watch the spectacle from afar, and he still had that Cheshire cat grin on his face. When he saw me, he stuck out his hand and made a mock pistol and shot at me twice. I looked down at my front to see that the previously unknown liquids that splashed me during the melee appeared to be a Bloody Mary and a Singapore Sling. Judging from the amount of liquid, both were in big tourist-sized glasses. I looked like I'd been blasted with both barrels of a shotgun. My first thought was, "Who the fuck drinks a Bloody Mary at night?"

I looked over at Bama Boy all twisted up on the floor. I wanted to kick him in the head, but I figured he'd been punished for his assholishness enough. I looked over at Jimmy and he was frantically directing cleanup efforts and bouncer maneuvers. I looked back at the unscathed Rueben-the-Cuban, dramatically shrugged, and gave him my "whaddya gonna do?" face. Then I weaved my way through the crowd and out the door. My night was over.

As I walked down Perimeter Road towards Santos Street, people kept stopping and staring and pointing at me. I must have looked like I'd just walked off the set of a Tarrantino movie. My crisp white "special occasion" shirt was trashed. My buzz was thoroughly killed. I just wanted to get back to my hotel, crank up the aircon and lay there in the dark.

I walked through the lobby of the Wild Orchid and stopped all conversation with my appearance. When I got to the restaurant area I could hear "Oh my God ... Oh my God!". Little Ivey came running from behind the bar. "What happened? Are you okay? Oh my God!"

"No, I'm not okay Ivey. My best shirt has been murdered. It was awful. There was nothing I could do". She walked me over to the bar and began frantically trying to clean the front of my shirt with towelettes from behind the bar.

"Stop, stop, stop honey. My best shirt is gone. I just have to let it go. Mango Shake, two shots of Tanduay please".

Ivey brought my mango shake and I told her the story. Then I told her another story. And another. Then she told me her story.

She was the youngest of three sisters. When she was four years old, her mother murdered her father for cheating. Ivey's mom went to prison and all the kids were split up. Her sisters went to different family members. Ivey went to an orphanage.

When she was sixteen, one of Ivey's sisters found her and she ran away to live with some cousins in Samar, the poorest province in the Philippines. Two years later, Ivey and her sister came to Angeles City to do what province girls do when they come to Angeles City. Lucky for Ivey, she could speak English better than the others and she landed a job at the Wild

Orchid as a server in the restaurant. She had worked her way up to bartender. Ivey was only 24 years old.

We talked about our families and our lives until after midnight. I forgot all about my ruined shirt and my ruined night out. Somehow it had all led me back to this bar talking to this charming young woman and everything seemed just as it should be. I slept a motionless, dreamless sleep that night. I woke up feeling a lot better than expected.

The plan for the day was to accompany the real estate crew down to look at some properties near Subic Bay, about an hour and a half away. I packed a small overnight bag because I wasn't sure if we would stay the night or not. When I got to Jack's office, M met me outside and said there had been a slight change in plans.

"I'm hot to sell this resort near Zambales" Jack said. "I want you to see it, take pictures and write a few thousand words to put on the website". I looked over at the four hungover Englishmen in their mismatched shorts and t-shirts, clutching cups of 7-11 coffee and moaning about the heat. They were standing next to a travel van that looked like a big toaster.

"I don't have to ride with them?" I asked.

"No mate, you go with M and this buyer from New Zealand in M's car. We'll meet you at Baloy Beach later."

I couldn't hide my relief. I was overjoyed to hang out with M all day. Unfortunately, I wouldn't have her all to myself. A skinny, balding, forty-something guy appeared from Jack's office wearing an outfit right out of a yuppie travel magazine. A tech-vest with about 50 pockets, hiking sandals with Velcro straps and those awful water-repellent pants with zip-off legs that turns them into shorts. He said his name was Derek and he was from New Zealand. He gave me a firm handshake and I spied a ten-thousand-dollar Brietling wristwatch on one arm and an apple fit-bit on the other.

I smiled. It's not that I didn't like him. I just felt for him. I remember being that guy. I remember thinking I needed to own everything you see in a Sharper Image catalog. I remember having all the stuff I thought would make me happy. I also remembered the day I emptied out my storage unit and got rid of all that shit. I remember the day I sold my $90,000 car. I remember the day I sold all my property. I remembered the day I quit the club that this guy Derek was a card-carrying member of. The "relentless consumer" club. Poor guy, he didn't know he was miserable yet. We piled into M's Pajero and headed for Subic Bay.

Derek sat in front with M, and I sat in the back hoping to witness M's sales prowess. For the first 30 minutes Derek gave a speech about how he had built his software business from nothing and now had a big building with his name on it. He told us about his houses, his cars, and his expensive Irish Wolfhounds. He told us about the extravagant holidays he'd taken

in France and Tahiti. He'd been on safaris in Africa.
He'd swam with whale sharks. Blah-blah-blah.

When he ran out of things to impress us with, M
launched into her subtle sales pitch about this eco-
resort in Zambales that was for sale. The word "eco"
triggered another soliloquy by Derek on how he had
converted his house to solar power, and his Range
Rover was a hybrid, blah-blah-blah.

When he was done, M calmly guided the conversation
back to the resort. It went on like this the entire trip.
She let him blab and then patiently guided him back
to the subject she wanted to talk about. By the end, he
was asking her questions about how many rooms the
resort had, what the beach access was like and where
most of the guests were from. She was masterful.

Derek also threw in a few personal inquiries along the
way. He wasn't blind and he wasn't gay. I don't
imagine they have many women as striking as M in
Christchurch. His advances were clumsy, but M
showed him that heart-stopping smile and flattered
him with polite compliments. She baited the hook by
telling Derek that if he decided to buy the resort, they
could celebrate at a great little restaurant she knew in
Zambales. His nose was wide open.

When we arrived at the resort, I was grateful to get
out of the car and escape Derek's pompous voice. I
wandered around the property taking pictures while
M showed Derek the particulars. It was a rambling
unkempt property with overgrown gardens and
ramshackle nipa huts. It had potential, but that's
about all it had. It was clear that the current owner
was either absent or out of money to keep the place

up. I walked down to the beach and was unimpressed. It was a long wide stretch of coastline to be sure, but there wasn't a tree or any other form of shade in sight. The sand was that volcanic gray-brown color that made it look like a big ashtray. A couple of teenage boys were surfing. They looked Aussie or Kiwi. The constant 2-to-3-meter waves appeared to be the only real charm this property had.

I tromped back to the resort where I found Derek and M in the small bar drinking iced tea. When I walked up there was a silence like I'd just interrupted an intimate or otherwise private conversation. Derek was clutching a folder with copies of land titles sticking out of it. M was reeling him in.

We got back in the car and were backtracking up the coast towards Subic Bay. Derek had finally run out of mindless jabber and the ride was mercifully quiet. Out of nowhere I heard a distinct "arf ... arf" sound like a dog barking. When I looked up, M was rummaging through her purse for her phone. The barking sound was her ring tone for SMS messages. She took a quick look at her phone and put it in her lap. Every ten minutes or so, more messages came in "arf ... arf". It would have been comical except for the fact M had suddenly become quiet and cheerless. We arrived at The Blue Rock dive resort around 4 o'clock under a stormy cloud of mood change. Derek seemed worn out and M suddenly preoccupied with her mobile phone.

The Blue Rock is a crusty old hotel on the end of Baloy Beach in Olongapo. It has a handful of nasty little rooms attached to the real reason it exists, a big-ass bar and restaurant. I was happy Jack chose this place to regroup because Blue Rock has great food, and I was in the mood for a grilled grouper sandwich. The English lads were already into their second beers and chattering merrily when we arrived. Jack attached himself to Derek as soon as we walked in, and M headed for a deserted corner of the bar to focus on her phone.

I sat by myself on the opposite corner and ordered a sandwich. Trying hard not to stare, I could see M frantically texting, then setting her phone down, then snatching it back up when she heard "arf ... arf". There was some kind of drama unfolding with her. I hated to see her in such an agitated state.

Jack, Derek and "the lads" were planning to stay the night in Subic so they could look at some more properties in the morning. Jack asked if I would be joining them. I wasn't sure I had a choice. I was hoping to ride back to Angeles City the same way I had come.

I got up to go ask M what her plan was, but she was up and heading for the mini mart near the front door of the hotel. When she returned, she was carrying a small plastic bag that appeared to contain a box of tampons. I felt for her. After entertaining this knob Derek all day, she has some kind of texting drama with a man, or family, or whatever. Now she's got to contend with hormones and stomach cramps. She didn't sit down but headed straight towards me.

"Will you ride back to Angeles City with me?" she asked.

"It would be my pleasure and much to my relief princess. Are you ok?"

"A-Okay Mr. Orlando". Fishing the keys out of her purse, she handed them to me. "Do you mind driving?" Before I could answer, she shoved the keys into my hand and headed for the lady's room.

"I'll bring the car around", I said to her back.

While waiting in front of The Blue Rock in M's car, I figured out how to synch my mobile phone to the sound system and put on this smooth kind of jazz reggae playlist I found on Spotify. I figured it would sooth M's nerves and be a good background to any conversation we might have.

When I saw M appear from the hotel, I jumped out to open her door and held her purse while she climbed in. When I got in the driver's side, she was switching off her phone and taking off her shoes. She reclined the back of her seat, let out an exasperated sigh and said, "Home James".

She closed her eyes and took some deep breaths. "Nice music" she said.

"You look like you could use some "Don't worry, be happy" tunes. This playlist always works for me".

"Do you know the way back?"

"Yes, of course".

She fetched a Pokémon shaped pillow out of the backseat, pulled herself up into a fetal position and said, "Good. I knew I could count on you".

All the things I wanted say and all the things I wanted to ask seemed unimportant. I was completely content to be cruising down the highway with her next to me, shielding her from any pain and ugliness that might come her way. It was as peaceful as I've ever felt in my life.

When we arrived in Angeles City and I turned down the street where my hotel is, the jostling of the car on the pothole-pocked road woke M up.

"Wow, we're here already?" she said.

M checked her face in the vanity mirror and slipped her shoes back on. I pulled up in front of the Wild Orchid and went around to open M's door. I helped her out of the car, and we stood there under the bright lights of the portico. She wrapped her arms around me and gave me a good squeeze. She grabbed my face with both hands, kissed me on my cheek, turned my face and kissed me on the other cheek and whispered in my ear, "You're a sweet man Mr. Orlando. Thank you for taking care of me".

With that, she walked around to the driver's side and gave me one last little finger wave and that whiplash smile. In that moment, I knew my place. I knew that was a close as I would ever get. White knight. Guard dog. Champion. Tireless defender. But never a companion or sweetheart. And certainly, never a lover. I knew my place and somehow, I was completely comfortable with it. I smelled her perfume on the collar of my shirt. *"If that's as close as I ever get to her"* I thought to myself. *"I'll take it"*.

I walked through the lobby of The Wild Orchid and headed towards the bar, but Ivey's shift hadn't begun. I needed a drink and her soothing voice. I'd have to wait until later.

Back in my room I shed my clothes like a reptile skin and took a long hot shower. Feeling vulnerable, I put on my "comfort clothes". My baggiest drawstring shorts. My favorite surf shop T-shirt from back home. My $150 Olukai leather flip flops just to keep me from looking like a total vagrant. When I walked out the front door of the hotel, I had no idea where I wanted to go, so I shuffled across the street to The Black Pearl.

The Black Pearl looks like a movie set for a skanky dive bar in the Philippines. It is a tiny hole in the wall with three different colors of linoleum on the floor and a raggedy ass pool table sitting inconveniently in the middle of it. The room is so small you need the "short stick" to shoot every shot. The only saving grace of this place is the old-school juke box packed with classic rock, soul, and Motown. I've been known to pull up a creaky stool, slurp cold beers in front of the fan, and contemplate life for hours at The Black Pearl. It seemed like as good a place as any for the mood I was in.

I plopped down on what looked like the sturdiest stool and ordered a beer. After giving several of the girls working there my *"no I don't want a blow job"* look, I settled into the music and my thoughts.

I used to be a playboy. I used to be a lady killer. I used to land women like M for sport. "What the hell happened to me?" I'd pushed all the right buttons.

I'd said all the right things. I'd been charming as fuck! Why had she not thrown herself at me? Why had she not at least dropped some flirty little hints? How did I get cast in this avuncular role of guardian angel? I'm not a fucking "sweet man".

It's not like I hadn't seen that move before. Many times, when the dynamic is "older man" and "younger woman", sliding the man into the advice-giver and protector slot is the first move. It's like a modern American relationship where you get put into the "friend zone". But normally, it's just a precursor to the real show. Normally, you get called up from that position during a crisis and "wham!", you're in!

But this time was different. I took my eye off the ball. I shifted my focus to what she needed rather than what I wanted. Or to be more accurate, I didn't require her to give me what I wanted to get what she needed. My priority was her happiness ... her comfort ... her peace of mind. And I'd taken that relegation like it was a gift. I'd actually felt warm and fuzzy about being the guy who got her home safely.

Playboy? Lady killer? Pussy-hound? Guess I'm not one of them anymore.

Suddenly I heard a thump and rustle coming from the stairwell in the rear of the bar. I may have forgotten to mention that The Black Pearl is a blow job bar. For the nominal fee of 500 pesos, one of the ladies will take you upstairs and relieve you of your poisons. It's 750 for a "double-header". I could hear someone stomping down the flimsy stairs and some girls chattering in Tagalog.

I recognized the drawl before I saw him. "Hey, one a you bitches get me a beer". It was Bama Boy, and he sounded like he'd started day-drinking pretty early. He staggered through the doorway with his left elbow wrapped heavily in an Ace bandage and gave me a look that said, "I recognize you, but I don't know from where". He flopped down in an ugly orange chair with duct tape on the armrest. I turned my attention to the NBA game playing on the ancient TV above the bar.

The two girls that had come down with Bama Boy were huddled in the corner with the mamasan and three other girls. One of the girls was holding out a 500 peso note, and they were all discussing something in hushed urgent tones. Finally, the mamasan came around the bar and started pulling out shot glasses. Another girl pulled several bottles down from the shelf and commenced making some kind of drink in a big metal shaker.

In a moment they all magically changed their moods from whispering conspirators to happy party girls. The mamasan lined up seven chocolaty brown B-52 shots on the bar and bellowed, "Happy Birthday Nina!" The girls all echoed her call and gulped down the shots in unison. The mamasan refilled the glasses and one of the girls went over to Bama Boy and pulled him from his chair.

"Come on man, have a shot. It's Nina's birthday! Have a shot with us man!"

Bama Boy perked up. "A free shot? Fuck yeah I'll take a free shot!"

The girls lined up near the bar, grabbed their glasses and the mamasan handed one to Bama Boy as he neared my corner of the bar. They sang out "Happy Birthday Nina!" and raised their shot glasses in a toast. Bama Boy looked at me. I raised my stubby brown bottle of San Miguel and nodded.

As the girls slammed their shots Bama Boy did the same. When they sat their glasses down, all the girls stared at Bama Boy. He stared back, wretched, bent over and spat the entire contents of his mouth onto the green linoleum floor right next to where I was sitting.

He stood up straight, took a deep breath and screamed, "You cunts! That shit ain't funny!"

He hocked up fluid from the back on his throat and spit on the floor again.

"That shit ain't funny you stupid fucking whores!"

For a moment, I thought he might get violent, but the look on his face was more hurt than angry. He spit one more time, wiped his mouth on his arm and stormed down the steps and up Santos Street.

As soon as he was gone, the girls erupted with laughter. Giggling and chattering in Tagalog and giving each other high-fives. They lined up one more round of shots and ask me if I wanted a free shot.

"No thanks ladies. I saw the last guy who took a free shot, and he looked none too happy".

They all started cackling again.

"That's because we drink B-52, but we gave him the "cement mixer" the chubby little mamasan said.

One of the girls started mopping up the floor where Bama Boy had spat.

"What's a cement mixer? Do I want to know or not?"

The mamasan explained, "It's Bailey's Irish Cream, lime juice and Cointreau on top. It looks like a B-52"

"I can see it looks like a B-52" I said. "But what does it taste like?"

The girls all look at each other and grinned. Then one girl with a nose ring and a sleeve of bad tattoos blurted out, "Sperm! It tastes like a big mouthful of salty, gritty speeeeerm!" With that they all burst into giggle fits again.

The mamasan brought me a fresh beer and explained what had happened. Apparently, Bama Boy came to The Black Pearl a couple of days ago. She said he was already drunk at 11 AM and took two girls upstairs for the "double-header" special. He was having a hard time finishing and was quite rough with the girls. They finally got him off and he refused to pay the full bill saying, "One blow job, 500 pesos, I know the fucking price". He stormed out, cheating the girls out of 250 pesos.

The next night he came back, hammered again, and a different crew was working. They didn't know about his stunt the day before and he did it again. Took two girls upstairs, rammed his cock down their throats for the better part of an hour, then refused to pay the full bill.

Today he came back and tried it again. This time he got the cement mixer.

I bought the mamasan a drink and asked her, "Mama, am I wrong, or did he look like he'd had that taste in his mouth before?"

She chugged a bit of her beer, smiled broadly and said, "Well, he is in the Navy".

I finished my beer and was in a mind to bar hop for a little while. But when I got up, I realized that one of my swanky leather flip-flops was stuck to the floor. It appears Bama Boy got me again when he sprayed out his shot on the floor next to my foot. The sticky gritty concoction was all over my shoe and a little on my foot. Once again, I wanted to tear out his larynx, but took consolation that he'd probably spend the rest of the evening trying to get the taste of jizz out of his mouth.

Me and my sticky flip flop shuffled back across the street to The Wild Orchid. I spied Ivey at the bar, so I went over and blew her a big kiss when I sat down. She ignored me. In a few minutes she came over with her order pad in hand, stood in front of me and said nothing. She just stood there waiting for me to order.

"Uh, SMB please" I said sheepishly. Ivey wrote it on her pad and walked away. I didn't have to guess. I already knew what this is called. In the Philippines, when a woman is angry with you, they give you "tampo". It's Tagalog for "the silent treatment". Only, Filipinas have refined it to an art form. I once knew a guy whose Filipina wife didn't talk to him for four months. Not one word. For whatever reason, Ivey was demonstrating her prowess at tampo on me.

Just like she wanted me to, I sat with my beer alone trying to figure out what I had done to deserve it. Let's see ... I just came from across the street at a blow job bar. That probably doesn't make her think too highly of me, but I doubt it caused this reaction. Perhaps it was the small public display of affection earlier with M in front of the hotel. I tried to disregard this notion. Surely everyone could see this wasn't a lover's embrace.

Unfortunately, I know and understand how gossip works in the Philippines. From the time I said goodbye to M in front of the hotel and she kissed my cheek to the time Ivey arrived at work, the staff on duty at the hotel had built the innocent goodbye into a lurid and shameful act of adultery. We might as well have been banging in the swimming pool. There was no doubt she thought I had hooked up with M. There was no doubt that was the reason for the tampo.

I sipped my beer and considered what a twisted trip it had been. Coming to Angeles City on business had changed my normal whoremongering behavior. I was acting and reacting like I was in a normal place and I was just a regular guy. I should have put on my sex tourist hat and kept it on. At least that approach was predictable. This regular girl thing was confusing and exhausting. I paid for my beer and went back to my room. I stood in the shower rinsing the "cement mixer" off my favorite flip flops and then put them on the balcony to dry. I pulled my suitcase out of the closet and started to pack.

In the morning I woke up once again when I could hear the staff setting up for breakfast. As I walked to the door, I noticed a lavender colored envelope had been shoved under my door with my name, "Mr. Orlando" on it. I picked it up and noticed it smelled like a girlish perfume; something sweet and inexpensive. Even without opening it, I knew it was from Ivey.

I carried the envelope with me to the restaurant and took a seat facing the pool. I ordered a pot of coffee, some toast and fruit. Upon pouring my first cup of joe, I opened the envelope and took out a one-page letter that was handwritten in red ink on pink paper. Here is what it said:

> *Dear Mr. Orlando,*
>
> *Of course, you know I am in love with you. I want to tell you, so you don't think I am a crazy girl. I know that you were with M, but I don't care. I can love you more than her. I can love you better than her. I will not man-eat you. I will be yours forever.*
>
> *When we talk, I know you listen to me. I know you care about me too. I can make you happy. I can be your wife forever. We can have sex any way you like it. We can live at any place you want. I will follow you. I will take care of you when you are old.*
>
> *Please Mr. Orlando, I know you are the man for me. I want to be yours forever.*

I love you,

Ivey

I put the letter back in the envelope. I knew what this was all about too. Along with tampo, Filipinas have a rich tradition of going all-in on a relationship right away. Back in the west, women generally play it coy, hold back on their true feelings until they feel safe, then throw in some sex to secure the deal. In the Philippines, they are prone to going all-in right from the beginning, banging your brains out on the first date, and then hanging on like a remora, even if they end up disenchanted with you later on. I'd experienced it firsthand with a Filipina schoolteacher I dated in Bangkok. So, I was neither shocked nor inappropriately flattered. In my mind, all this meant was that an offer was on the table.

I finished my breakfast and took my pot of coffee back to my room. I sat on the balcony and read the letter again. I couldn't dismiss it. Ivey was a fascinating young woman. She was beautiful, clever and she had a calming effect on me that I could not deny.

Hadn't she made the events of this trip seem more funny than bizarre? Hadn't she endured my pining for an unattainable woman without judgement? Hadn't she listened to my boring-ass stories? Hadn't she revealed secrets about herself? Hadn't I searched her out every day I'd been in town?

I considered it for the rest of that pot of coffee. I could take her back to Thailand. I could move to the Philippines. Waking up next to that toasted cinnamon skin and warm smile is something most men can only dream about. Come on, *"Sex any way you like it"* ... what's wrong with that? An offer was on the table and I had to admit, it was awfully attractive.

Jack Seymour had a 23-year-old Filipina wife. Black Jimmy had a 24-year-old Filipina wife. Even Smug Fuckerson, who was at least 70, had a young Filipina waiting at home for him. They all seemed happy as hell. They all seemed secure and confident in their homelife. They all seemed completely at peace with their decision to go all-in.

As I zipped up my suitcase and rolled it towards the door, I crumpled up the letter and threw it in the trash.

Apparently, I'm not one of them either.

Crimes of Opportunity

"Go to Bangkok". It had been on my list of things to do for a year. I hadn't been back to Bangkok since Mina died. My friends said I was "grieving", but it wasn't true. I was avoiding grieving. That's the half-step between "denial" and "grieving". But I had to go. It had been three years. I had friends there. I had history there. It is my favorite city in the world. I couldn't just erase it from my life. So, I got up early on a Tuesday morning, took a Xanax, and got in the car.

I'd booked a room at The Ambassador Hotel on Sukhumvit Soi 11. It's centrally located in the farang zone and close to all my old haunts. The moment I got on the motorway from Pattaya my brain started plotting all the places I would go and people I would surprise. It felt good to be excited about Bangkok again. To be honest, it felt good to be excited about anything.

Just as I'd gotten up to motorway speed, my phone chirped that I had a new incoming email. I took a peek, and I could see the email was from Credit Karma, an agency in the US that keeps track of changes in your credit score. Normally I got an email every few months confirming that my credit was still shit. But this email had one of those red exclamation marks next to it and a smiley face emoticon. I was intrigued.

When the traffic thinned out, I opened the email on my phone and in big bold letters was an announcement that my credit score had rocketed from *"you must be joking"* to *"hey there handsome"*. I didn't have to read any further or go to the site to find out what triggered the dramatic change. I already knew. I started counting back how many years it had been since the credit-wrecking judgement against me had come down. It was so long ago I'd stopped thinking about it. It took me back more than a decade.

Right around 2000, I was in transition between my old life and a new life in Thailand. My partner and I had agreed to wind down our business. Nobody knew what my future plans were. But everyone knew I was tired of enabling a bunch of dirtbags to steal old folks' retirement savings. It had made me soul sick.

Officially we were known as an "investor relations" company. Investment bankers and individuals who had taken big enough positions in public companies to control the board of directors came to us. These were usually OTC bulletin board companies, NASDAQ listed firms, or somewhere in between. Occasionally we did AMEX firms. Most of these companies had been approved to issue additional shares of stock to raise money. Our job was to create an increased volume of buying to soak up the additional supply of shares. My partner did all the schmoozing, back-slapping and deal making. I ran the publishing and marketing operation to make the promotions work.

It was an oddball business marriage to be sure. My partner was a silver spoon fed Annapolis, Maryland rich boy. I'm an ex-military Florida redneck from the dark side of town. It was an unlikely pairing that worked like a well-oiled machine for nearly ten years. Once at a party, someone said to my partner, "Wow! You and Lando have been partners for a long time. You must be really good friends." My partner replied, "Not really. I just can't do it without him." That was the secret to our success. Neither one of us knew or cared to know what the other guy did.

Parts of this business were very prone to illegal activity. When companies paid us, it was usually a combination of cash and stock. Because I had to pay vendors, I took the cash. My partner took the stock, and that's where the illegal stuff happened. Promoters like us weren't supposed to own, buy, or sell stock in the companies we were promoting. It was a flagrant conflict of interest and someone could sell all their shares according to the price fluctuations resulting from the promotion. And that's exactly what my partner did every time. It affected me in no way. We operated separate companies. He did the dirty stuff on his own.

That's really not the part of the business that bothered me. I couldn't stand the sleezy people we dealt with and the idea that I was setting up innocent investors to buy some really shitty companies. We did have a handful of clients whose shares actually gained in value and things worked out well for the buyers we brought in. But for every good deal there were at least three slapped together shell-company-charades or Canadian moose pastures touting themselves as prospective natural resource bonanzas. Gold mines, oil fields, sometimes both located on the same property. People desperate for a big win will believe anything.

As my partner's illegal shenanigans got bolder and the clients got sleazier, I opted out. When we closed down our office, we both still had individual companies running. My partner was determined to do deals without me, and I had a company that owned lists of prospective investors. I generated a nice income renting the names to publishers and marketing companies.

I'd been back in Bangkok laying low for a few weeks when I was contacted by some of our old clients in Vancouver. They read our operation closing down as a breakup and said they wanted me to work on a promotion for them. I had a long think about it. These guys in Vancouver were my least favorite clients, but the deal was fat, and I could most likely pull it off with minimal contact. So, I flew to Vancouver to talk about details.

The main player on this deal was a shifty-eyed twitching weasel named John Gorwin. His nickname was "Johnny Go". He was the quintessential Vancouver conman. A silk suit and cufflink wearing chain-smoker who never stopped talking. He wanted to pick me up at the airport, but I didn't want him to know I was coming from Thailand. We met at The Four Seasons. We had a three-martini lunch and walked to his office up the hill. Johnny had set me up an office space in the group of office suites he occupied at the Marine Building. He and his young Indian partner were pushing me to move to Vancouver and work for them full-time. I acted flattered. I acted like I was considering it. They thought I was buying their bullshit. I knew they were buying mine.

The company they were touting was a pharmaceutical manufacturer that had cloned a handful of drugs whose patents were expiring. They had a good story, an impressive board of directors, and they were traded on the AMEX. The real players behind the deal were some shady-as-fuck Pakistanis funneling money through banks in Barbados. Combine that with these Vancouver crooks and the deal was extra-greasy. I agreed to conduct the promotion at the end of a ten-foot pole. This was the kind of shit that can get all over you.

So, we made a deal that was all handshakes and phony smiles. I estimated the cost and drew up a payment schedule. Johnny Go didn't bat an eye.

"A third to get started, a third when we are ready to drop the mail and activate the phone room, the final third upon receipt of the first lead. Just like before", I said. The first payment was in my offshore account by that afternoon.

That night I had an early dinner alone on the veranda at the Pan Pacific hotel. Perfectly seared wild salmon with a Margaret River Sauvignon Blanc, watching the float planes land and take off in the harbor. I considered what a good life I'd been leading. I considered how much money I could make staying in the business. I considered how nice it would be to live in Vancouver. I spat the notion out like a mouthful of spoiled milk. *"That's not the plan asshole"*, my inner voice scolded. *"One more deal and out. That's the fucking plan"*.

I had a number in mind. I knew exactly how much I needed to make my escape to the next chapter of life.

It wasn't a massive fortune. It was enough to survive on until I got some traction in Asia. This deal would top me off perfectly. Two hundred and fifty thousand dollars would be the final installment in my getaway fund. That's exactly how much I stood to walk away with on the deal.

The next day I worked out of the office Johnny Go had set up for me. It was comfortable. I had a good view of downtown Vancouver. I had a hot Korean girl bringing me coffee. What's not to like? I started the ball moving on the promotion we'd need to create new buyers for the avalanche of new shares hitting the market. Writers were lined up. Graphic artists alerted and standing by for details. I started the list selection and prepared to produce a nice tight promotion.

Late in the afternoon I got a text message from an old friend in Vancouver, Jeffrey Dixon. He heard I was in town and wanted to get together for drinks and dinner. He's one of the only Vancouver dudes I genuinely like, so I set my mind for an evening with my old pal Jeffie D.

We met at Cardero's on the water, a restaurant with a singles bar that had been the scene of the crime for me on more than a few occasions. I saw Jeff at the bar and I almost didn't recognize him. He'd lost about 20 pounds by my estimation. His retreating hairline had been styled into a modern Caesar-cut and his weak chin was covered by a bristly short beard. With his perfectly tailored sport coat and Persol sunglasses, he looked like a movie star.

"Goddamn Hollywood! You look like you just stepped off the movie set!" I said.

"Gimme a hug ya handsome hillbilly" Jeff replied, with a big goofy grin.

It was great to see him in such good form and good spirits. When I first met Jeff, he was a wreck. He was a working-class dude who came out of the mining business in Western Canada. He'd decided his path out of the field was to become a stockbroker. Jeff studied hard and passed the Canadian and American Series 3 exams and was poking around for a firm to hire him. He ended up in a boiler room cold-calling clients, pushing sketchy bulletin board stocks. He made just enough money to buy a sport coat and get a hot girlfriend. Then he lost it all in a deal that fell apart.

Jeff was an old friend of Johnny Go and he hit him up for a job. Johnny sent him down to us as a liaison for a handful of deals we worked for natural resource companies. His job was to train teams of brokers we set up and oversee lead contact. Johnny paid him just enough to get by.

When he walked into our office, he was a mess. He had lost all his money. He had lost his hot girlfriend. He had lost his mojo. His first remark was how much our receptionist reminded him of his former girlfriend. Pitiful.

I could see that Jeff is one of those guys who takes everything personal. And it was clear that he had way too many scruples to be swimming in the shark tank he found himself in. He was simply too good of a person.

I was living in a big-ass condo on the beach. I figured Jeff could use a friend and some ocean air. He moved in with me for three months and came out a changed man. He learned about walking meditation. He read some Jack Kerouac. He learned how to let things go. We smoked a lot of weed. We talked about women. We would have been friends in any century.

Jeff went back to Vancouver with some money we put in his pocket and started his own operation. He gathered some like-minded brokers and only worked deals they believed in. They built their client base and got rich slowly. Jeff got a tattoo of a turtle on his arm with the caption, "slow and steady", a mantra he lived by.

We ordered a bottle of champagne and a dozen raw oysters. Jeff caught me up on everything Vancouver and I caught him up on everything Florida. Somewhere in the middle of our second dozen oysters Jeff got serious.

"I need to talk to you about Johnny Go", he said.

"Oh fuck. I don't like the sound of that Jeffie, what's up?"

"Are you doing the Biomed AMEX deal?"

"Yes, but don't bother warning me how greasy it is. I know about the Pakis. I know there's a boatload of unaccounted for shares. I don't give a fuck brother. Just between you and I, this is my farewell voyage. I'm out after this deal."

"Well,", Jeff said. "Just between you and I, you're going to get fucked".

"Really? How's that?"

Jeff told me that Johnny Go had invited him and some other brokerage firms to a dinner meeting the night before. He wanted to pitch them on working this Biomed deal.

"He always tries to pull me into these deals" Jeff said. "I know it isn't out of courtesy. He just wants to pollute my book. I always go. It's good for a free meal and a laugh. He's keeps redefining the meaning of the word 'douchebag'".

According to Jeff, Johnny Go had reserved a private dining room at Imperial Dim Sum downtown. Once everyone had arrived, he closed the doors, dumped a big bag of cocaine in the middle of the table and said, "Dig in boys, it's snow-time!"

"Whisky and blow were flowing. Everyone was loud and proud", Jeff said.

"Especially Johnny Go. He was more loose-lipped than usual and pounding his chest about how he had bought the golden goose with the secret formula, meaning you. He was telling all these hard-ons that the Biomed deal was a slam dunk because he had the infamous Orlando Braxton, Market Media's secret weapon".

"I was surprised that you were on this deal" Jeff said. "I got next to Johnny to get a better read. I asked him what was up with you and your partner. I hadn't heard you had parted ways."

"Oh yeah" Johnny Go said. "It was a big ugly divorce. The redneck came running to me with his tail between his legs begging for some work. He's broke as fuck. He can't make it without his partner. Now he's gonna be **my** new bitch".

Jeff said when he pressed Johnny for more information, he spilled it all out in one long cocaine and whisky infused stream of hyper-consciousness.

Johnny said, "We usually pay them a third, a third and a third. Up until now, we always came through with that final third once the promotion started to kick in. I know the cash part of that last third is the redneck's profit. This time I'm gonna string him out. Gonna make him stay here and work our next project to get paid. Greed and need will make him my bitch. He needs a new daddy, and it's me".

Jeff went on to say that Johnny Go rambled on and on about my partner being the brains of the operation and how I was a one-trick-pony. He called me an ignorant rube that was like a country dog in the city.

I'd stopped paying close attention. My mind was already churning. My internal fire department had detected an adrenaline rush. That telltale electro-chemical crackle across the back of my tongue. Heat in my cheeks. Nostrils flaring. I took a couple of imperceptible deep yoga breaths and a sip of champagne and said, "Thanks for the heads-up brother. Let's talk about pussy".

Jeff read the signal perfectly. We settled our bill and walked towards Gas Town. We hopped from one wine bar to the next. We smoked a joint. We talked about pussy.

The next morning, I woke up early and headed to my favorite coffee shop in Vancouver for breakfast. A big doughy bagel topped with a pile of wild sockeye smoked salmon and cream cheese. I savored it slowly and with purpose. I knew it would be the last time I ever set foot in Vancouver.

I called Johnny Go and told him I had a family emergency back in Florida. I told him my son was in jail and I had to go help him. My oldest son Jay was in jail, but that is a normal occurrence. I had no intention of bailing him out, but I made use of the situation to add believability to my story. I'm an ignorant redneck, of course my son is in jail.

Later that morning I flew to Panama to meet with my banker. I closed my accounts and exchanged the cash for a more "travel friendly" asset. For the next week I stayed in touch with Johnny Go by email. I went through all the motions of getting his approval on documents and copy for the big promotion. To him, it must have looked like I was going full steam ahead with his project. I was in fact spending most of my time at the horse track with my lawyer and rolling around in Columbian hookers at various brothels around Panama City.

When all my loose ends were tied up, I boarded a plane for Bangkok. Upon landing in Thailand, I invoked total radio silence. I closed my US mobile phone account and destroyed the SIM card. I closed my email account. I left no forwarding address. Not even my family knew where I was.

It took Johnny Go five days to smell a rat. He started burning up the phones to everyone he knew I knew. He bombarded all my associates with threatening emails trying to find me. He contacted my banker in Panama and was informed that there was no one by my name or company name that currently had an account there. He even called my mother and went ballistic. First, he threatened her and said he would have her arrested as an accomplice to fraud. Then, he tried to bribe her and said he would give her $10,000 if she told him where I was.

My mother gave him some motherly advice.

"Mr. Gorwin, if I knew where my son was, I wouldn't tell you, so you can stop making a fool of yourself. And I can tell you from personal experience, if that boy doesn't want to be found, the FBI, the CIA and Sherlock Holmes couldn't find him. Whatever game it was ya'll were playing is over and you lost. Get over it".

But he didn't get over it. He filed a lawsuit against my company in Florida. The paperwork was delivered to my lawyer, a cranky old Florida Cracker named Dave Buster. Dave looks like a shit-kicker, but he went to law school at George Washington University and had been the President of the Florida Bar for several years. When the lawsuit came, he got in touch with me through my secret email address and we had a teleconference.

"How bad is it Dave?" I asked.

"Well, that depends. Do you have any assets in the US?"

"Nope"

"Then this is pretty much an exercise in futility unless someone wants to press criminal charges, and I don't see them pursuing a criminal case. This is strictly civil".

"Dave, I read the complaint. It says ugly words like "fraud" and "breach of contract".

"Yes, but there is no filing of a criminal complaint. There's no report to any police department or policing agency. There's just this case claiming you clipped them for about $275,000. They are claiming that and all kinds of damages. But, for now, no criminal complaint."

"Ok Dave if you say so. But how is this not fraud?"

"Well, first off, there is no contract. No one can say for sure what the arrangement was. Second, according to the document, you began work on the project in question and just stopped. So, it isn't like you set them up knowing you weren't going to deliver, that would be fraud. For whatever reason, you didn't finish the job, and kept the money. There was nothing premeditated about it. Maybe you thought you'd fulfilled the "contract". This could all be one big misunderstanding. If there was a crime, it was a "crime of opportunity", not fraud.

"I should add", Dave continued. "This guy Gorwin is a total bag of shit. He was the main player in a stock manipulation case last year and plead guilty to a lesser charge and paid a bigass fine. Two years before that he got busted for another securities fraud violation and turned prosecution witness against his partner. The partner went to jail and Gorwin walked. He won't go the criminal route because he knows lawyers on your end would start digging and reveal this group of players as a den of thieves with no regard for law or doing business in good faith. Nobody cares about crooks screwing crooks, especially if they're not American citizens. Even if a criminal case was filed and you were convicted, you going to jail doesn't bring his money back".

I thanked Dave for his expert advice. I told him not to reply. Just let the case run its course. They'd get a judgement for an outrageous amount of money. There was no way for them to collect any of it. I hung up the phone and put it out of my mind. I had beaten Johnny Go to the punch. I fucked him before he could fuck me. Most importantly, the money I took was the last piece of my getaway puzzle. It set me free.

I had not thought seriously about it until my phone chirped telling me I had an email from Credit Karma. There was one giant blemish on my credit history, and now it had been erased by time.

"Hello handsome. Would you like a credit card? How about ten?"

I should have just let it flow in and out of my mind, but I didn't. Back then, I'd felt righteous. Johnny Go had insulted me deeply. He thought he was somehow superior to me. He sought to enslave me. So, I did him dirty. I kicked him right where it hurts the worst. Not only did he lose face, but he'd have to come up with the money to continue the deal. Those yellow-eyed Pakistanis funding the deal weren't going to understand he'd been ripped off. Not only did I pull his pants down, but I kicked him square in the balls. Ouch!

But, I had some regrets. I didn't feel bad about doing him dirty. I just wished I had been smoother. I wished I had found a better, cleaner way to turn the tables, without any negative impact on myself. At the time, I was prone to making decisions charged with emotion. The satisfaction of revenge meant more to me than the money.

Back then, I couldn't have walked into that office every day without throwing Johnny Go out the window. If I were in the same situation today, I would play it cool and maximize the final take away. I'd draw him in deeper and fuel his overconfidence. I'd convince him to expose himself even further. Looking back ten years, I still didn't feel guilty. I committed a crime of opportunity, but I probably should have made more of it.

Starting to see signs for Suvarnabhumi Airport, I could see the hazy Bangkok skyline coming into view in the distance. I let out a long sigh. Back to Bangkok. It felt like time travel.

I checked into the Ambassador in a breeze. They upgraded me to the new tower, and I got a spectacular city view. Pulling back the curtains, I could see the whole picture. Bangkok, my favorite place on this planet. I couldn't believe it had been three years. I lived less than two hours down the road, and I hadn't been there in three years. At that moment, if someone would have asked me why it had been so long, I would have had no answer. There was no logical reason.

I dropped my bag and headed out into the sweltering afternoon heat to get my Bangkok on. First stop was at my skanky old salon near Soi 5. It's sandwiched between two ladyboy salons, so I had to endure the whole "Hello handsome man, where you go?" charade every time, but it's worth it. The girls at Tik Salon were all shocked to see me. I flopped down in a big reclining chair for a simultaneous manicure, pedicure, foot massage and facial. It felt like I was being worked on by a Formula One pit crew. An hour later, I looked and felt like a new man.

Next stop, Let's Relax, a proper Thai massage place. For those who have never had a real Thai massage from a masseuse trained at Wat Po, it is life changing and addictive. My brother visited me a few years ago in Bangkok and called it "assisted yoga". You get bent up, stretched out, walked on, and kneaded like a big blob of dough. Two hours at Let's Relax and I felt like I was two inches taller and could hear better.

With my body now the consistency of a boneless chicken, I floated on over to the last stop on my "me day" afternoon, Ranahan Suda, the quintessential indoor/outdoor Thai shophouse restaurant. It's just inside this little side soi between Sukhumvit 14 and Asoke, near the Sheraton Grande Hotel.

Suda is a legendary old place located in a low, flat one-story building about four shophouses wide. There are long tables covered with those hideous plastic tablecloths you see all over Thailand. Half of the available tables are outside and that's where I always sit.

One of the stoic old Thai ladies that runs the place sees me, walks over with her order pad, and almost cracks a smile.

"Where you go?" she says.

"I go Pattaya", I said.

Okay, conversation over. Let's eat!

I get a draught beer Chang, order my favorite three dishes, and just soak in the Bangkok vibe. There's a table full of Chinese tourists with a pile of dirty plates. It looks like they put on an eating clinic. There are some Korean girls taking selfies with their mango and sticky rice desserts. There are some smartly dressed young Thai office boys with their ties tucked into their shirts and slurping down big bowls of Tom Yum Gung. They're dressed in full business attire in the withering heat and not a hair is out of place nor a drop of sweat to be seen. I've been waiting to get used to this heat for 15 years. I've still got to put ice in my beer and sit in front of the fan.

When my food comes, I shamelessly plow through it in a panic. If I hadn't eaten it all, I might have rolled around in what was left. Belly full and all of my afternoon activities checked off, I waddle back to The Ambassador Hotel for a nap.

I woke up as the sun was going down. I slept so hard I didn't even wrinkle the bedspread. A shower, a shave and on with the night. I had a plan in my head. I'll work my way up Sukhumvit, hop over Asoke to Soi Cowboy and surprise a few old friends in the go-go bars. Then I'll crossover on the Sky Train bridge near Exchange Tower and end up on Soi 22. I couldn't manage going there right away.

I couldn't return to that soi without having a few cocktails in my system. Any other part of town would be a piece of cake. Soi 22 is the boogey man. It's the reason I haven't been back in three years. It's where I met Mina. It's where her spirit lives for me.

Strolling up Sukhumvit brought back a rush of memories. The footpaths were already crowded with vendors and shoppers on both sides. The aroma of grilled meat, the cacophony of languages, the toothless old man offering me Viagra for "good price". When it comes to blissful chaos, Bangkok never fails to satisfy. I break a sweat. I stop for my first beer. I am home again.

When I got to Soi Cowboy, the street was already alive. Soi Cowboy reminds me of the old strip in Las Vegas back in the 80's. There's so much neon you can feel the electricity in the air. You can literally hear the buzzing of all the lights. It's kind of early, so I have to weave down the soi in an out of food carts parked haphazardly to feed the minions of bar girls fueling up for the night. It doesn't matter what vocation Thais are involved in; the first order of business when you get to work is to eat.

I strolled into The Doll House and the staff acted like they'd seen a ghost. They weren't sure if it was me or someone who looked a lot like me. I sat at the back bar and ordered a double Jack on the rocks, in a tall glass, with a bottle of water on the side. "Now they know it's me" I chuckled to myself.

Within minutes a guy who really does look like me appeared. It was Dirty Daryl, the owner and manager of this place. DD is an old paratrooper from Texas. He and I have seen the sun come up together through the window of many an afterhours joint in BKK. I always start my night in the ruts getting an update from him.

Daryl gave me the run down on what managers are where, which clubs are doing well and who's screwing who. While he was talking, I kept scanning the room. When a new team of girls took the stage, I perused them all.

"I know who you're looking for dude. She ain't here anymore", Daryl said. "She had a fight with my mamasan. Now she's down at Tilac Bar".

He knew I was looking for Wan. For some reason, I always find one particular girl I like at a bar. Even though there are literally hundreds to choose from, I find that one who trips my trigger, and then I don't see any of the others. I guess in some twisted way, I'm a "one-woman-man".

Wan was a special creature. She looked more like a Latina than a Thai girl. Powerfully built body with curves everywhere, long wavy black hair, and bottomless brown eyes. The best part about Wan was her laugh. She was so funny she made herself laugh ... and laugh ... and laugh ... and giggle ... and snort. I had never seen her not smiling. I was disappointed. I was hoping to soak in a little of her charm. I finished my drink and headed down the road.

I settled outside at Toy Bar. I hate going in Toy Bar because it is one of those bar-in-a-hallway arrangements. All the patrons smoke like Chinamen, and the girls never stop plying you for a lady drink. So, I sat at one of the stools outside and ordered a drink. The only reason I stopped there was to stare at the blinding pink lights of Tilac Bar, on the opposite side of the street. Daryl had told me Wan was working there. The only problem is, I hate that bar. I hate how brightly lit it is. I hate the array of chrome and pink stools and tables. I hate the music they play. Most of all, I hate the memory of the last time I was there.

A few years earlier I had been on a similar solo sojourn on Soi Cowboy when an old friend texted me to meet him at Tilac Bar. I really wanted to see him, so I endured the bright lights and pounding dance music. I already had a good buzz on, so it didn't seem so bad. The place was packed with customers and I saw one particular guy staring at me like he knew who I was. I didn't give it a second thought. A lot of guys have a shaved head and a goatee; it's a popular look among expats. And, when you have a lot of tattoos, you get used to people staring at you. In the middle of my first drink, I went to the men's room to pee. While standing at the urinal I heard a voice from my past piercing the din.

"Well, well, well. Look who it is. Big bad Lando. Stealing money from any innocent girls lately Lando?"

I looked towards the voice and I could see who it was. It was one of those moments like having a dream and you suddenly know it's a dream because the person you see doesn't belong in the setting. Standing by the sink, drying his hands was Ben Mackay, aka Benny the Weasel. He was my former business partner in Phuket. What the fuck was he doing in Bangkok?

I first met Ben early in my Thailand adventure when I moved to Phuket. I was poking around on the southern tip of the island near Nai Harn beach when I stumbled upon this cool little low-rise condo complex called "The Sands". I went to the manager's office and asked if any were for sale. She showed me one that was nice, but on the ground floor with not much of a view. I left my name and number in case any other units became available. Twenty minutes later my phone rang, and it was Ben Mackay. He lived in the building and just happened to have a unit for sale.

We met in the parking lot. Ben's a skinny little red-haired prick from western Canada. He was sporting stylish tropical clothes and some knock-off designer shades, but I know a Canadian four-flusher when I see one. I played the rube. He played the seasoned real estate mogul. He had no idea about the ordeal I'd just been through in Vancouver. He thought I was a dumb redneck too.

The condo for sale was a third-floor unit right underneath the one Ben lived in with his wife, daughter, and sister-in-law. The unit was perfect, so I bought it cash with very little negotiation. It seemed to be worth what he was asking, so I paid it. I think this reinforced his notion that I was a dumbass American with too much money.

We were neighbors. We became friends. We became business partners. Ben was a real estate agent and managed a few properties. I helped get his brand formulated and his website up and running. In truth, it was just a way for me to get a work permit and a long-stay visa. I showed up at the office a few days a week for a few hours. Ben's sister Nat was our assistant and Thai interpreter.

Nat was an interesting girl. She was from Trang, a coastal province deep in the south of Thailand. In Thailand, the further south you go, the darker skinned the people get. And the natives of Trang have a completely different look than other Thais. At the risk of sounding racist, you can definitely see they are from a different tribe than the population further north.

Nat was very petite with chocolate skin and short cropped hair. She had sexy almond shaped eyes, big juicy lips, and a big juicy butt too. I lusted after her secretly because she seemed like such an innocent girl. She was nearly thirty years old, but Ben told me she was still a virgin. I'm not sure I believed it, but it was good enough to keep me at arm's length. I mean, who wants the emotional headache of a thirty-year-old virgin, right?

Although she looked full-grown, much of her demeanor was little girlish. She was however a great assistant and helped sort out any and all paperwork I needed for immigration, the land office, even my driver's license. And to be honest, Nat was just a pleasure to have around. She was cute, efficient and she had this high chirping little voice that sounded like windchimes on a blustery day.

One morning, Ben called to ask a favor. He was on the other side of the island and had received a call from someone on our end that wanted to sell their house and land. He wanted me to take a look at it and assess the value. I drove to the site and knew within ten minutes that I would buy it.

It was a big rectangular piece of land surrounded by jungle on two sides and a quiet little Muslim fishing village on the others. The owner had started construction on a big house and got about 90% finished when his romance and his money ran dry. He was desperate to sell this big lot and the house. I made him an offer. He accepted it. Ben tried to collect a commission.

For the next 18 months I was fully engaged in building my own little housing development. I finished the big house, put in a swimming pool, and moved in. I divided the remainder of the land into three smaller lots and built three three-bedroom/three-bathroom pool villas. It was the most fun I've ever had working. To this day it is the accomplishment I am most proud of.

Ben was stunned that I'd had the wherewithal to start up such a business. He was clearly jealous. He had neither the balls nor the money to pull off such a project. I had appeared in Phuket out of thin air and become a developer. I could feel his envy, but I just let it slide. I figured he would get over it.

In Thailand, foreigners aren't supposed to own land. Just like every other unreasonable law, there was a cottage industry built on getting around it. I formed a Thai company to buy the land and Nat was my co-director. It was very convenient as she could sign any necessary documents while I was away. Nat began working more for me than Ben.

It caused an uneasy friction between Ben and me. I just kept plowing forward figuring he'd get over it. Ben stewed and seethed in a passive-aggressive soup of jealousy and self-loathing. When I announced that an offer had been accepted on the last house in the project, Ben was elated. He knew I'd be leaving the island and heading back to Bangkok.

A week before the final closing, I got a panicked call from Nat. A new director for the Phuket Land Office was taking charge and his first move was to try and crack down on all the illegal companies set up with nominee shareholders just so foreigners could get around the land ownership laws. This is a cyclical event that happens every time a new head honcho comes in at the land office. They like to flex their muscle and talk tough about "cleaning up the corruption". It usually lasts a just long enough for their first graft payment to come in, and then it's all over.

But Nat is afraid of everything, and she said we need to take "action" to avoid having my assets seized. In a flurry of paperwork, I was removed from the company as co-director and in fact I didn't appear anywhere in the ownership of the firm. The last payment for the final sale was due to arrive in my account at the end of the week. I saw no reason to worry. I trusted Nat. She had always done me right.

Friday came, the money arrived, and I celebrated my last night in Phuket. I paid my taxes. I paid Nat a nice bonus. I pocketed my profits and moved back to Bangkok. I never thought I'd hear from perky little Nat or Benny the Weasel again.

A year later I got a panicked email from Nat. "You owe many taxes" is how the email started. She sent me some paperwork in Thai that she said showed that I owed twelve million baht in taxes from the sale of my houses. I sent her a copy of the taxes I had paid the year before. She claimed the accountant we hired had made a mistake and now the revenue department was hounding my company for taxes.

I waited a few days to think about it and I got another email from Ben. He was ranting and raving about how I had left Nat in a tough spot. He said the revenue department was threatening to seize her bank account. He said she was trying to sell her car to give them some money. According to Ben, they were after Nat because she had been left as the director and my company had a big tax bill. He also said that if they started legal action, it would be discovered that I was a co-director and they'd come after me as well.

"You better pay your bills buddy. The tax people don't fuck around", Ben warned.

I felt like something was fishy about the whole deal. First off, I told Nat to close the company as it had no more assets and no reason to exist. Apparently, she didn't do that. I contacted our old accountant for details and got the cold shoulder. "We no longer work with that company" was their response. The taxes I had paid seemed like a proper amount. Twelve million baht was three times what I had already paid. This deal was more than a little smelly.

I looked up an old friend in Phuket named Karen White. She had been one of my other neighbors while living at The Sands in Nai Harn Beach. She knew Ben and Nat as well. I ran down the situation to her and asked for a little research help. Karen despises Ben. She in fact gave him the nickname, "Benny the Weasel". A week later, I got a call from Karen. She'd put her Thai lawyer on the trail and learned that indeed the department of revenue was after the company I used to own. She also learned that Ben and Nat had kept the company open and run several real estate transactions through it in the past year. That's what the taxes were owed on.

Karen's lawyer also pointed out that I might be on the hook if the tax people filed a lawsuit against the company within 18 months of me being a co-director. If that happened, I'd have to lawyer-up and fight it out in court.

I was not surprised that Ben was trying to fuck me. I was shocked that Nat was part of it. I had the feeling that she had been pulled into it by Ben. She's just not that devious and she is highly manipulatable. It saddened me to know that little Nat was being used in this way. She might be a virgin, but she was definitely trying to screw me and it kind of hurt my feelings. I thought we were friends.

I wanted to get on a plane, fly to Phuket and snap Ben's neck. I wanted to fuck his wife and burn his house down. A dozen revenge scenarios played out in my head. But, with my recent experience in Vancouver in mind, I made a play that was much more satisfying.

I sent an email to Ben and Nat begging for their understanding. I told them I would like nothing better than to sort this all out and "do the right thing". But I was in the US. My son was in jail and I had to help him. That's right. I used the old "I'm not there I'm here and my family needs me" story. They had no idea where I was. That's the beauty of conducting a ruse by email.

I told them I couldn't access my money in Thailand. I couldn't do anything until I came back. All I had to do was stretch things out for three more months. If the revenue department filed a suit after that, I would be in the clear.

So, for three months it went on like this. Every week I'd get an email from Ben scolding me like he was my daddy and shaming me for causing such a poor innocent girl like Nat such anxiety and stress. He'd get drunk and send nasty messages in the middle of the night calling me a douchebag and threatening me with all sorts of civil lawsuits. All the while, I stalled and ask for his understanding and patience.

The day the 18th month was over, I stopped
responding and blocked his email. Two months later I
got a message from Karen White saying she heard that
the revenue department had sued my former company
and that Nat and Ben had negotiated a settlement and
paid the past due taxes.

Benny the Weasel. He'd tried to commit a crime of
opportunity, but he wasn't very good at it. He didn't
pay attention to the details. He could have pulled it
off, but he was lazy and haphazard about it. It was my
fault the opportunity was there. I hadn't followed up
to close that company. But I read the situation and
escaped unharmed. I was proud of myself. I hadn't
been emotional when the weasel came trying to hump
me. I side-stepped his attempt like a nimble
quarterback avoiding a blitzing safety. He was
outclassed at the "fuck you" game.

And there I was. Standing at a urinal in the men's
room of a go-go bar in Bangkok five years later,
staring at Benny the Weasel. He was drunk, leering,
oozing with malignant jealousy. "Fucking douchebag!
You ruined that girl's life!" he slurred.

I looked him straight in the eye for what I'm sure was
an uncomfortable length of time for him. Then I just
turned my head and looked straight into the wall as I
finished my pee. "Benny the Weasel" I sang. "Can't
believe someone hasn't killed you yet".

I zipped up and leisurely washed my hands as Ben
stood there staring and fuming. I wanted to headbutt
him in the face. I gave him one last look and said,
"Your fly is open". When he looked down, I walked
back into the bar.

The friend I had come with was standing out in front of the bar talking to one of the "hello girls" that lure customers inside. I paid our bill and waited for my change. Looking behind me, I realized who the guy that was staring me down before was. He is an Aussie named Brett who is a friend of Benny the Weasel. They must have come up to Bangkok together. Benny joined him and now they were both staring and pointing. The moment of truth. I wanted to stay. I wanted to see where this little macho showdown might lead.

He was still pitching that bullshit game. He was still trying to make me believe his lie. I felt that electric adrenaline crackle on the back of my tongue again. Jack Daniels was telling me to stand up for myself and call him on it. But I knew where it would lead.

He's drunk and he thinks his Aussie friend will back him up. He'll push it too far and I'll have to splatter both of them. Getting into a fist fight in a go-go bar on Soi Cowboy was a stupid idea and would serve no purpose for me. I got my change and walked right by them on the way out.

Even though I'd done the prudent thing, my pride was hurt. A man should be able to stand up for himself, right? I should have stepped off in that weasel's ass. I know I did the right thing, but it felt like defeat. It felt like I was retreating, not winning.

That's the taste Tilac Bar left in my mouth years ago, the taste of defeat. As I sat across the street nursing my beer at Toy Bar, I weighed the decision. Should I go over there and slay that dragon? I hated that place. Did I want to see Wan that badly? I paid up and moved on. I had other dragons waiting for me on Soi 22.

I crossed over Sukhumvit Road using the Sky Train bridge at Asoke. I stood on the bridge looking down on the sea of cars and red lights. I took in Bangkok with all my senses. The trip down Soi Cowboy had made me feel old. It had made me remember that not all my time in Thailand had been pleasant.

Guys like Benny were clumsy amateurs, but there were other players out there that didn't wait for opportunity, they created it. Evil people who ambushed unsuspecting foreigners as a means of commerce. There were real thieves out there, and I had met some of them.

When Mina and I moved away from Bangkok, I was in the middle of renovating a bare shell condo unit twenty minutes south of Pattaya at Ban Ampur Beach. The building was a spooky survivor from the currency crash and Asian financial crisis of 1998. The original developers weren't an experienced real estate company. It was a Thai man and wife team that owned a big waterfront lot and were keen to maximize its potential. They put up this 15 floor, 270-unit condo building set 100 meters back from one of the most picturesque beaches on the Eastern Seaboard. It should have been a goldmine.

Unfortunately, the crisis hit just as the building was being finished. Buyers who were finishing out there units suddenly stopped. Deals that were in the works collapsed. Everything in the building came to an abrupt stop. The building was virtually empty and unpainted. It looked like a hairless dog shivering on the beach.

I saw nothing but potential. The unit I bought was on the 13th floor corner with a 70 square meter balcony and a 270-degree sea view. It was breathtaking. The best part was that it was a bare shell. It didn't even have windows or doors yet. I could create my dream condo; and I did. I designed it specifically for Mina and me to live in. With the sand-colored tile floor and sea-green walls, we called it "green heaven".

Before we moved in, we stayed at a hotel in Jomtien Beach. Every day I would come to check on the buildout progress. It was then that I met a Thai woman named Sunisa. She and her husband were the original developers of the building. Sunisa was a fat little fifty-something woman with that birdhouse of puffed-up hair all the rich Thai ladies like to wear. She was the quintessential wannabe "hi-so" (high society) Thai. Her husband was a General in the Army (like about 14,000 other Thai men).

She told me the story of the building and how the financial crisis had sucked all the air out of their plans for the place. She also showed me dozens of available units. Some were finished, many were bare shells like the one I was finishing. She was friendly and flattering. She took me to lunch a few times at the Navy Base in Sattahip. I knew she was massaging my ego and trying to make a sale on some of the other units.

I was blinded by the potential of the property. That building could be spectacular, and I knew it. When I finished my big condo, it was stunning and the finished product cost less than half of what it would have cost in any building that wasn't as distressed. In my mind, I had found a hidden gem. I thought I was way ahead of the crowd that was sure to find this place and gobble up whatever was available.

And my imagination was running wild with what I could do with some of the other units. Building those houses in Phuket fed my desire to do something creative. I can't paint, play music, or write poetry, but I build one hell of a nice house. Blowing out these bare shell condos was irresistible.

Every day or so I would see Sunisa trotting some more prospective buyers through the building. I figured my window of opportunity was closing fast. There was a group of units available on the top floor facing right up the coastline towards Pattaya. The sunset views were incredible. The price Sunisa offered me was too good to pass up. I explained to her that I had three condos for sale in Bangkok and I needed the money from them to pay for her units. She told me to put down one million baht and she would hold them for six months until I got the money. I didn't hesitate one bit. I was over the moon. I sat up at night designing and redesigning what I would do with those four units on the top floor.

Then I met Ray. One day I was walking through the parking lot of the condo, and I saw this skinny little forty-something foreigner riding around and doing tricks on a BMX bicycle. It was kind of odd. I said "hi", he said "ssup" and I stopped. "Do you live here?" I asked. It turns out he did live there and had lived there for over one year. His name was Ray, and he was from California.

We stood outside the building talking for the next 45 minutes. Ray told me a horror story about Sunisa and our building. He'd been drawn in by the promise of a turnaround in the building too. He had a small unit on the sixth floor but alerted some friends who came in and bought 4 unfinished units with plans to finish them off and rent them out. But, when they tried to get the title deeds from the land office in Sattahip, they were told that all those properties had liens against them. Sunisa had gotten loans with all four properties as collateral.

When they confronted her and demanded their money back, she took off to see her daughter in the US. According to Ray, there were at least a dozen unsuspecting foreigners who had the same experience. They put money down on units they couldn't get title to and then were ignored. "See you in court" was Sunisa's response.

Ray told me that I was lucky to have bought my place from an original investor not related to Sunisa's family. At least I held title to my condo. The rest of them were hung up in court trying to get their money back or their title deeds.

"She's made a business of selling property she has loaded up with debt. That's her business model" Ray said. "Another big problem is, it isn't under the jurisdiction of Chonburi, the big province where Pattaya is located. It's in Sattahip, a province dominated by the military bases and full of Generals like Sunisa's husband. The chances of a farang winning any type of lawsuit in Thailand are slim already. But in a place like Sattahip ... forget about it."

My heart sank. I had no doubt he was telling the truth. I should have seen it in Sunisa's eyes. She saw what I did with the first unit, smelled money, and all she had to do was show me the others. I sold myself.

Just to make sure, I called Sunisa and told her I had the money to finish purchasing the other group of condos. I asked her to show me the title deeds. She gave me copies. I asked to see the originals. She told me they were at her lawyer's office. When I told her that I wouldn't transfer the money until I saw the originals. She hung up on me and wouldn't return my calls or emails. Jay was right. She'd tried to sell me properties she had leveraged to the max. She had no intention of transferring the property to me. It was all a scam.

For the next five years Mina and I lived in this abandoned building with about five other tenants. The building limped along, slowly deteriorating, but functioning. It was like a haunted old mansion. To be honest, it was kind of cool. It was deadly quiet at night and we were right on Ban Ampur Beach. But the fact that I'd been ripped off still burned. A million baht at the time was about $25,000 USD. Not a king's ransom, but enough to piss me off. I'd been set up and robbed by a professional. Not a crime of opportunity, but outright fraud and larceny.

Sunisa could be spotted every now and then around the building. She and her family were in control of most of the units. The handful of foreign owners who did hold title made futile attempts to improve the building. Sunisa controlled the board of the condo association and was the de facto Juristic Person. We were helpless. Besides the fact that I lived in a really nice place that I had designed, it was miserable.

Then Mina's illness started. When she had to be put in the hospital in Bangkok, I was left all alone in my beautiful condo. That's when the whole situation really started to break me down. Every day I woke up alone in a haunted building. Every night I witnessed spectacular sunsets over the Gulf of Thailand by myself. I did a lot of day drinking during that time. And I lived for the weekends when I'd drive up to Bangkok to visit Mina.

When Mina died, I went to Chiang Mai and stayed with my friend Lester for three months. I couldn't bear the idea of going back to our place on the beach. Ultimately, I knew I had to sell it because I was nearly broke. I'd sold my properties in Bangkok and invested the money in land and a couple of houses in Buriram where Mina's family lived. Her sister and brother-in-law worked farmland we bought growing limes and casava. We built her mom a small house. There was a modern three-bedroom place we had just finished.

I lost it all. Mina's family blamed me for her death. The property was in her name. They took it all. I was left with this white elephant of a condo at the beach and a couple of rental units in Jomtien.

There was no way anyone would even consider buying a condo in the building the way it looked. And none of the wannabe real estate agents from Pattaya had a snowball chance in hell of selling it. I knew I had to be there to get it sold. So, I went back.

I suffered for nearly a year living there. I was like a ghost living in a ghost building. Every morning I'd wake up, make coffee, and burn incense in front of my big buddha. It was the ultimate irony, my big atheist ass standing in front of a statue I bought to complete my Asian modern décor and praying for mercy. Praying to any power in the universe to get me out of the repeating nightmare I was living.

One day, I got my coffee brewing, took out my incense and walked towards my buddha. I stopped short and said out loud, "Fuck you buddha! Your shit is way overrated. I've been burning these sticks for you almost a year and nothing. Compassion my ass!" With that, I moved my incense burner in front of my statue of Ganesh, another decoration.

"Alright Papi Ganesh" I said. "You're supposed to be the 'remover of obstacles', let's see you do your thing". I lit the incense, fired up a joint and went for a walk on the beach.

The next day I got a call from a real estate guy I did not know, working for a company I had never heard of. Somehow, he had seen a listing for my condo somewhere and had a prospective buyer. I spent the rest of the afternoon getting my place in showhouse condition. I put out some chocolates and a glass of wine in front of Ganesh. He had impressed me with his prompt response.

The agent and his buyer came at sunset, the perfect time to show my condo. I greeted them with the lights perfectly dimmed, incense burning and cool jazz emanating from my bad-ass audio system.

The agent's name was Larry and to my secret delight he was a Canadian from Vancouver. His buyer was named Chad and he was a Canadian too. My inner voice said, "What's up with all the Canadians?"

I gave them my sales pitch standing in the living room with the mango-colored sun melting into Gulf of Thailand behind me. I invited Chad to just roam around while I chatted with Larry. I watched Chad on the balcony. He actually stepped it off to measure how big it was as if he didn't believe me when I told him it was 70 square meters. He checked the second bedroom. He surveyed the TV and audio system. But, when he stepped into the master bedroom, I knew I had him.

Chad stood staring at the jacuzzi I had built in the corner of the room. There had been a small round balcony and I'd enclosed it with glass and installed a jacuzzi tub big enough for four people. Many nights were spent with Mina, sipping wine in a burbling tub of bubbles, with a 13th floor view straight up the coast on Ban Ampur Beach. Whenever there was an occasion that involved fireworks, we always watched them from there. Chad stood there looking at the tub for a good ten minutes. I could read his mind. He was imagining his own adventures there. I knew it was over. I knew he would buy the place right then.

Chad only had one question. "Is the furniture included?"

"Of course," I said. "The only thing I'm taking with me is my Ganesh".

Two days later I was sitting in Larry's office drafting up an agreement between me and Chad. It wasn't exactly a straightforward deal. Chad agreed to my price, but he had to pay in installments. He worked on offshore oil rigs all over the East Asia region and made good money, but he didn't have any money in the country.

He'd been living in the Northeast of Thailand in the city of Khon Kaen with his Thai wife. Unfortunately, they'd ended up in an ugly divorce and Chad had to be careful about showing any assets in the country or having a significant amount of cash in any bank accounts. The case wasn't settled yet, and his wife's lawyer was out for blood. He wanted to pay lump sums of cash he'd bring in periodically until the condo was paid for. We could transfer the title after his divorce settlement.

Chad handed me an envelope with enough Singapore Dollars to make a 20% down payment. He wanted no trace of electronic transfer of funds, so we agreed that he could make payments every six weeks or so when he came in from a rig. There was no contract in writing, only a sales contract form with information filled in by hand.

I moved out of the condo and Chad moved in. I was free. I took my Ganesh and moved into a one-bedroom condo unit I owned in Jomtien Beach. I felt reborn.

I never saw Chad in person again, but his agent Larry would call and say there was an envelope for me at his office. There was always a thick stack of Singapore dollars which I converted into Thai baht.

About six months into the arrangement, I got a call from my brother in the US. My oldest son Jay was in serious trouble. He had become a heroin addict. He started with prescription opioids and ended up shooting street heroin into his veins. My brother said he wouldn't live to see his next birthday if someone didn't intervene. I dropped everything I was doing in Thailand and went back to Florida to save my son.

I ended up spending nine months back in the US. I was resigned to living there as long as it took to get him straight. There was detox, and rehab and relapses. It was emotionally exhausting and expensive. In all I spent about $300,000 on hospitals and housing for my addicted boy. In the end, none of it worked. The last time I saw him, he was in the hospital in Miami recovering from surgery on his hip and leg. His crazy junkie girlfriend had tried to run him over with her car.

It was then I realized I'd just wasted nine months of my life and a big bag of money on a hopeless cause. Knowing that I had tried to do the right thing was no consolation. I had failed. So, I came home to Thailand defeated and broke.

Chad made the final payment on the condo I sold him soon after I came back. I couldn't transfer the title to him because I'd borrowed money from a finance company in Bangkok with the condo as collateral. I hadn't made the payments in four months. When I explained the situation to Chad in an email he went berserk. The mild-mannered Canadian turned into a complete asshole over the matter.

I told him I'd sell one of my other properties and pay off the loan, but it would take a little more time. I was in touch with the finance company, and they were very understanding. The last thing they wanted was to take possession of my property and try to sell it. The condo market in Thailand was flooded with unsold inventory. We devised several paths to paying off the loan and transferring title to Chad.

Chad was having none of it. He hired a lawyer and started threatening me with a lawsuit. I put up with his daily emails and threatening letters from the lawyer for a few months. Then one day I woke up and decided, "Fuck that guy. If he doesn't want to be reasonable, I'll just walk away from the whole deal and he won't get anything".

I cut off all communication with Chad and his lawyer. I knew how it was going to play out. He'd have to pay a big chunk of money to get the court to hear his case. I could stall for a long time until the court would finally looked at it and say, "Take this to arbitration, we don't need to clog up our courts with your farang bullshit". Then it would go to arbitration, and they would say, "Where is the contract? What agreement was violated?" Chad would have to argue we had a verbal contract and that he had paid in cash.

The real estate company that transacted the deal had gone out of business already. His agent Larry had gone back to Costa Rica where he lived before. Chad had no chance of getting his money back or obtaining the title to the property he was living in. Yet, he persisted with the legal threats until one day it went to court. They threw it out and said, "go to arbitration" just like I predicted. The issue died when the arbitrator said, "Show me the contract".

I felt bad. I'd screwed him. I didn't set out to screw him. But my situation changed drastically during the year. I needed money to pay for what I thought was lifesaving treatment for my son. I leveraged the property I sold him to get that money. When Chad got shitty with me, I got shitty back.

His whole game of clandestine payments and handshake deals to evade his gold-digging ex-wife had backfired. He made it possible to fuck him over, so I did. It was a classic crime of opportunity.

Standing on that bridge and breathing in Bangkok, it occurred to me that everyone back in the US thought I was living a charmed life here in Thailand. All they knew were the happy stories I'd tell about the good times. What they didn't know was, I was just living life the same as them. A life with ups and downs ... ecstasy and agony ... glorious victories and humiliating defeats. A life where you have to face your demons, or they will consume you.

As I approached the corner of Sukhumvit Road and Soi 22, my face became flush, and I felt hot. I could feel my breath quickening. I stopped on the corner, took a deep breath, and said to myself, "Here we go".

I was a little stunned to see some of the changes on the street. A brand-new Holiday Inn dominated the corner and nasty old Washington Square had been demolished. Still, some of the old hole-in-the-wall bars were there like Honey House and Lek's Place. Titanium appeared to be getting ready for a night of revelry with a half dozen pretty Thai girls standing outside to greet passersby. My buddy Lester's old place "Larry's Dive" had been blown out and converted to a posh eatery called "No Idea". Some things about the street were different, but it still had the same feel. It still smelled the same.

With the Queen's Park Hotel in sight, I crossed to the other side of the street and stood at the entrance of Queen's Park Plaza, a cluster of bars and restaurants that had survived the gentrification of Soi 22. They are drinking bars with pool tables, pub grub and sexy barmaids. It's not a place for in-your-face prostitution, but you can certainly find as much companionship as you want. This is where it all began. This is where I met Mina.

Mina and two friends from her hometown in Buriram had spent a year working in Singapore and saved enough money to buy a bar. It had one of those bullshit Thai names like "Up to You" or "My friend You" or "Mai Pen Rai". An old friend of mine was a regular at this tiny little bar and he invited me for a few games of pool. When I got there, he introduced me to Mina. She looked right through me, flashed her crooked little smile and I was hooked. Mina and I drank and played darts until closing time. By the end of the week, we were inseparable.

We had our ups and downs over the years, but when we finally gave in to each other, it was as solid a relationship as I have ever had. Even through the years we lived in the ghost building on the beach, we were happy. Standing at the entrance to Queen's Park Plaza, I realized those were probably the happiest years of my life. To be sure it was the last time I remember being inside out and head-to-toe happy. And there I was, returning to where it had all begun.

Most of the bars had changed owners and names. The only place I recognized was Moonshine Pub. I was happy to see the plaza was alive with music wafting out of each bar, customers shooting pool and watching sports on giant flat screens. I started to feel more at ease. It almost felt like a homecoming. I worked my way to the back of the plaza and sat down at the outdoor beer garden.

A cute little cat-faced waitress brought me a cold beer and I soaked up the atmosphere. It sounded like a block party and smelled like a carnival. I remembered coming there every night to see Mina. I remember how lucky she was at pool, shooting with reckless abandon on every shot. I remember one of her bartenders getting so drunk she stripped down and ran through the plaza completely naked. I remember Mina and I discovering our mutual love for raw oysters at this very beer garden, her picking out the big ones for me and the smaller ones for herself.

I closed my eyes, and I could almost hear her voice. Taking a deep breath, I wanted to seize the moment, freeze it, and keep that as my static memory of her and this place for all time. Yes, I could almost hear her voice. In fact, I could swear that I did hear her voice.

My eyes snapped open. I tilted my head to hear better. Yes, I could have sworn I actually heard her voice. *"Fuck! I'm not drunk, what's this all about?"* I've never been one to say, "my mind is playing tricks on me", but this was a peculiar feeling. It's one thing for someone to sound like someone else, but that's not what I heard. I heard her laugh. I heard her speaking Thai. It wasn't someone who sounded like Mina, it was her!

Reflexively, I stood up and started to move towards the sound. My inner voice stopped me in my tracks. *"Hold on now big boy ... where are you going? Let's sit down and collect ourselves, okay? You're out here wandering around in the Bangkok heat drinking alcohol and grieving over your long-lost love. You should expect to be emotional. Maybe you will even imagine you hear her voice. Sit down. You're okay."*

But I didn't sit down. I walked towards the sound. I stood at the corner of the walkway in the back of the plaza. I could see the reflection of people drinking in the window of a bar down the walkway. I could see a woman in a flowing white dress with long black hair and brown skin. I heard her laugh again saw her flip her hair back. It was Mina, alive! My feet turned to stone. My breathing stopped. I couldn't trust what I saw. It was just a reflection in a window from across the way.

I stepped out onto the walkway far enough to see the little bar full of people with my own eyes and there she was. Those brown legs. Those six-inch-high heels.

And wearing the Longines watch I had given her. I felt sick to my stomach.

Suddenly I was back at my table in the beer garden. I didn't remember walking back there. I felt like I had passed out and just woke up. I had no idea how long I had been sitting there staring at my beer. I snapped out of it when the waitress asked me if I was okay. I took a hundred baht out of my pocket and put it in the drink bin. "No" I said. "I'm not okay".

I walked out to Soi 22, turned left, and just kept walking. I don't remember my feet touching the ground. I was just floating aimlessly through the sweaty crowds. I crossed over Sukhumvit Road at Nana Skytrain station and found myself making a beeline to the Eden Club. I returned like an opium sparrow to my safehouse.

The manager Miki greeted me with his sleazy smile and immediately read my face. "My friend, you look live you've seen a ghost", he said. A double Jack Daniels appeared in front of me. I was left alone in my special corner, under the broken television.

I was numb. My emotional circuit breaker had been tripped to control the damage. Thank God I had gone into survival mode and removed myself from a situation I had no idea how to handle. I didn't know how to feel. I should have wanted to confront her. I should have wanted to shame and humiliate her. I should have wanted to know why she would do such a thing to me. I should have wanted to kill her.

But I didn't want any of that. My first reaction was an overwhelming feeling of relief. Yes, she had betrayed me. Yes, she had stolen more than half my wealth. Yes, she had crippled me emotionally for the past three years. But there I was, shedding tears of joy because she was still alive. I felt like a colossal fool.

For the next two drinks, I bashed myself. How could I have been so stupid? I put a big bag of money down to pay for property in her hometown to show I was committed to *us*. I put it in her name because it gave her big face with her family. She never gave me any reason not to trust her.

When she got sick, I was frantic to help her get better. I took her to the best facility in Bangkok for patients with her type of psychosis. She was there for nearly a year. It was impossible to tell if she was getting any better. Sometimes I would visit, and she was sweet Mina. Other times, I didn't recognize the person in the room with me. It was gut-wrenching.

It appears however, that somewhere in the middle of this ordeal, she emerged from her psychotic malaise long enough to fake her own death and steal half my shit! Her family played their parts perfectly. Her sister hysterically berated me on the phone, saying I had killed her baby sister. Her brother-in-law told me if I came to Buriram again he would bury me in one of my own casava fields. They blamed me. I blamed me. And it was all a lie.

As I started my third double Jack, I tried to coerce myself into being angry. I played it over and over in my head, trying to whip myself into a frenzy. But the outrage was canceled by the relief. Three years of soul-crushing guilt had evaporated. The emotional vacuum left behind sucked up all my indignant rage.

I couldn't help myself. I was happy she was alive.

And why should I be angry? She didn't intend to do me wrong.

It was just a crime of opportunity.

Professor Thailand

Americans represent less than 10% of the expats in Thailand and that's if you include Canadians. If I find myself within earshot of a conversation, it is most likely not in English, so my brain just tunes it out. I don't speak or understand Russian or German or French or any of those Scandinavian languages. If I overhear a conversation in Thai, I can choose to decipher it or not. They are usually just talking about food anyway.

Even if I hear people speaking English, I can ignore it if it's that mishmash of colloquialisms and idioms people from the UK call a language. I can also tune out that profanity-laden gibberish Aussies and Kiwis speak. But, if there is a conversation being held in squawking-honking blah-blah-blah American English, I can't not hear it. It will cut through even the thickest barroom din and go right into my auditory canal.

One night I met this naïve young American in a bar. My favorite bar. My neighborhood pub. I go there when I finish work in the evenings to unwind, have a few glasses of wine and flirt with the barmaids. If I'm there after work it means I just spent at least five hours teaching English to Chinese people online, so not hearing my own voice is welcomed relief. Usually, this bar is pretty quiet so it's like my own little decompression chamber.

I was sitting in my favorite spot at my favorite bar, and these three belligerent Americans were bleating on and on about what they knew about Thailand.

Apparently the youngest and fourth member of the crew was new to the kingdom and the others were trying to impress him with their wisdom and knowledge. The three pontificators were all semi-veteran expats. I say "semi" because you could add all of their years in-country up and it still didn't exceed mine. None of them had seen more than one of Thailand's bloodless coups, so "semi" veteran at best.

The horseshit these guys were shoveling into the newcomer's ears was astounding. One guy was preaching about Thai women.

"They're all whores at heart" he insisted. "You've got to keep 'em down and not give 'em too much money or they'll just piss it away on their Thai boyfriends. They're stupid money-grubbing whores ... all of them".

Another guy was prattling on about Buddhism and the Thai mindset. "Remember, they aren't Christians like us" he advised. "Thai people are devout Buddhists, and you really should learn something about their religion to understand them".

Another guy offered to download his extensive list of blowjob bars and happy ending massage joints to the young guy's phone. I secretly wished I had a big Japanese sword so I could lop off all their heads in one fell swoop.

I didn't want to listen, but I couldn't not hear them. This little "Thailand 101" clinic went on for at least an hour. Mercifully, the lecture began to break up as one guy peeled off to pick up his daughter from school and another was off to a neighborhood whorehouse. In the end, only the newcomer was left nursing a beer and pretending he was watching a rugby match on the TV. With the others were gone, it was just me and him at the end of the bar furthest from the door.

Still staring at the TV screen, he said in a voice loud enough for me to know he was talking to me, "Man, those guys like to talk, don't they?"

I just stared straight ahead pretending to watch a tennis match on another TV and replied, "Some people come here to talk. I come here to drink". Inexplicably, he took my reply as an invitation and moved three stools down the bar across the corner from me.

"I'm Hank. You're American?"

I did my best not to recoil from his outstretched hand. Facing him for the first time and shaking his hand, "Guilty" I confessed.

Then, seemingly out of the blue he asked, "Are you from Florida?"

While I was prepared for the *"where ya' from?, whaddya do?, how-long-ya-been here?"* battery of questions, this on-the-nose query caught me off guard. I must have had a stunned look on my face, so he clarified by pointing at the logo on my t-shirt.

"Red Dog Surf Shop in New Smyrna Beach. I know it well" he said. I'm from Jacksonville".

It was such a blast of freshness to hear a Floridian accent and to have someone other than me say the words, *"New Smyrna Beach"*. I cracked my first smile of the day and countered, "I'm Lando, from Daytona, pleasure to meet you Hank".

For the next hour we existed in our own little Floridian bubble, coming out just long enough to order fresh drinks. There is just something cool about running into a person from your sliver of the globe halfway around the world in a strange land. It is a comforting confirmation of the notion *"it's a small world"*.

Hank is a mechanic on heavy equipment like bulldozers and cranes. For the past few years, he had been working all over the middle east and Asia for several big engineering firms. He had just finished up a project in Papua New Guinea and was taking some time off in Thailand.

"I learned about this place on the internet" he said. "Two of those guys I was talking to are members of the board I follow".

As I suspected, young Hank was being wooed by a "he-man whoremongers club". There are dozens of these websites frequented and supported by men who travel the world banging hookers and telling stories about it. They share information like where the best go-go bars are, what the girls charge for a few hours of fun, where the cheapest beers can be found, etc. They crave new members to fund the sites and supply fresh titillation for their daily pleasure. Hank didn't seem like the type, but I'm sure most of those dudes started out young and naive before immersing themselves in the "sexpat" lifestyle.

It was Hank's second trip to Thailand, and he said he might want to make this his home base.

"I really like Thailand" he said with childlike enthusiasm. "The food, the culture, the people ... it's all so exotic. And the women ... man how can you not love Thai women?"

I listened to Hank make list after list of things he liked about Thailand. In my head I journeyed back to my early years. It really was like landing on another planet. I felt like Captain Kirk on Star Trek when be beams down to some uncharted orbiting rock and all he really knows is that the air is breathable. I envied his unjaded and naïve state of mind. Those were simpler happier times for sure.

Normally I would have just let a guy like Hank get on with his journey. No words of wisdom. No sage advice. Just a pat on the back and a heart-felt *"good luck buddy"* would usually be my approach. I had to earn my stripes in this nutty-ass country, why shouldn't he?

But, since Hank is a fellow Floridan, I felt a little responsible for making sure he got set on the right path. The world doesn't need another know-it-all sexpat asshole. I would hate to see this intelligent and sensitive young dude fall into that lifestyle trap. The world also doesn't need another Yankee Pollyanna trying to "fix" things or show Thai people the "proper" way to do anything. That's the other side of the sexpat coin ... the "do-gooder" or the "missionary". I don't know which I despise more.

"Hank, your friends are idiots" I said. "All that stuff they said is absolute horseshit. They don't know anything about Thailand, Thai people or Thai culture, and neither do you".

Hank made a face like he'd just been slapped. He shot back sarcastically, "Do tell Old Asia Hand ... what is the secret Old Master?"

The compulsion to say what was on my mind overwhelmed me so I said, "I don't pretend to know it all dude, but I have lived all over Thailand for 20 years. I can speak Thai. I've taught in a Thai university. I've had real Thai girlfriends and a real Thai wife. Those motherfuckers landed in Pattaya less than five years ago and haven't left a five-mile radius since. "Walking Street Warriors" ... they know fuck-all".

Hank leaned back in his chair and rolled what I'd just said around in his head. After a few minutes he leaned forward and said, "Alright then Professor. If you are a teacher, then teach me".

I rejected the idea immediately. "I'm not your daddy" I spat out. "And I am not inclined to mentor some newbie. You're not an idiot ... figure it out for yourself".

Hank shrugged and said, "fair enough". After some thought he took a nostril-flaring deep breath and said, "Man, don't sit up there and tell me my friends are idiots and bullshitters when you aren't prepared to provide me with better information. How is a guy like me supposed to know what's what in this bizarre-ass country? If those guys are all I have to go on, then I'll probably end up like them. I feel like we crossed paths for a reason. If you don't set me straight, it's kind of your fault. How are you not as bad as them?"

It appeared that alcohol had emboldened my new young friend, but he did have a point. I tried to counter by saying, "Alright then young buck, what do you want to know?"

"Ahhh na, na, na" he said as he waived me off. "I want a syllabus and a course outline Professor. Please, enlighten me with what you consider to be the coursework for Thailand 101".

I wished I'd never told him I was a teacher. I wanted to blow this whole conversation off and get home to my bed, but the prospect was too intriguing to let go. I went to the bathroom and mulled it over leaned up against the urinal with my head on the cool tile wall. This guy was about the same age as I was when I got to Thailand. He's from my neck of the woods. We see many things the same way. I'd certainly had the benefit of several mentors along the way. I hadn't gone out of my way to help anyone in a long time. I had some relevant information to impart. I had the free time. Why not?

I knew what he was really after. He didn't like those assholes he was with any more than I did. He's realized that it's hard to make real friends in places like this. He was interested in me for the same reason I was interested in this silly proposition. I wanted him to be my friend. We needed a premise to start our friendship, and this was it.

When I came back to the bar I said, "Ok young Hank, here's the deal ... you meet me here next Sunday night at 9 o'clock. We'll meet for three consecutive Sundays. It will be like a lecture series you get three credit hours for. During these Sunday meetings I will teach you about three separate aspects of life in Thailand. You can choose the three subjects. There will be no quizzes or term papers. Let's call it a one-way conversation. You can take notes if you like. Drinks are on you. Agreed?"

Hank broke out in a big southern grin, stuck out his right hand and said, "Professor, consider me enrolled!"

For the next week I prepared for our first meeting just like I would a lecture at the university. For the first few days, I was putting a lot of pressure on myself to give him valid and usable information. I'd promised to give guidance that was more practical and realistic than that offered by his sexpat companions from the pub.

But, about mid-week, I had a revelation about the whole process that refocused me and made me relax. I realized that no matter how sage my advice, odds were that young Hank would probably make all the same mistakes most of us old-timers made when we landed in the Kingdom. He'd trust the wrong people, choose the wrong girl, and more than likely end up owning a beauty salon, a pig farm, or in the worst-case scenario ... a bar. I chuckled to myself as it dawned on me that it's a lot easier to give advice than to take it. I wanted to make a difference in Hank's Thailand experience, but it was more likely that I was just reserving the right to say, "I told you so".

Hank had phrased his topics as questions. The first was: *"What are Thai people really like?"* A broad and objective topic indeed.

My idea was to paint the picture in broad strokes for Hank but give him real stories and examples as illustration. I wanted to debunk any myths and preconceived notions he may have picked up from his ignorant cohorts. Most importantly, I wanted him to have a realistic view of what it is like to deal with real Thai people on a daily basis and not just the staff at his hotel.

Hank showed up right on time, bright-eyed and eager. After some polite chit-chat, I opened a nice Margaret River Cabernet and began to talk.

Lecture One - Thaiworld

Please understand something Hank; I don't want to sound like a person that comes to live in a foreign country and bad-mouths its people. I like most Thai people. I admire Thai people for a myriad of reasons. People from our country could learn a lot from Thai people. If you stay here long enough, you will learn a lot from Thai people too. And ... here is a warning ... if you stay here long enough, you'll become a little bit Thai yourself.

First of all, Thai people are just people. People with families and jobs and problems just like you and me. They are motivated by many of the same dreams and desires as we are. But, after a while you will notice that their priorities are arranged a little differently than ours. The subtle differences between the workings of Thai society and that of our own country will become not-so-subtle.

Here are three things you must remember when trying to understand Thai people. Number one don't be fooled by the show. Number two, Thais aren't "big picture" people. Number three, Thai people live in Thai-World.

Live here a while and you'll soon learn; the smile is a mask, the genuflecting "wai" their shield and no deals are ever really "done". Whether it is a business deal or a love relationship or any other interaction with a Thai person, one should always remember that Thais are mostly motivated by things they think have a direct impact on them personally and in the present tense. Here are some examples.

At the end of 2004, as a monster tsunami devoured chunks of Southeast Asia, the world witnessed the alleged caring and selfless nature of Thai people on CNN every night. During a news interview with a nearly drowned Aussie, the tourist gushed about the fearless Thai hotel manager that risked his own life to pull him out of the churning abyss. As a longtime resident of Phuket, I remember thinking *"That Aussie probably hadn't paid his bill yet."*

While driving to the market one morning I witnessed an unfortunate dog that had lost his life attempting to cross three lanes of morning traffic. All week I passed this site, wincing a little more every day as the dog's body bloated grotesquely and slowly succumbed to the elements.

"Why doesn't someone take that dog away?" I asked my Thai wife.

Incredulous, she answered, "Why I'm gonna get that dog? Not my dog".

I had just assumed that in a Buddhist country with all that compassion and temples and monks and such, someone would take it upon themselves to take care of the poor creature. Ask ten Thai people the same question that I asked my wife and eight of them will answer the same way: *"not my dog"*. The other two would say, *"How much you pay me?"*

In Bangkok, the Skytrain makes a slow curve right over the shrine of the four-faced Buddha in front of the Erawan Hotel. Any day of the week you can witness throngs of faithful burning joss sticks and kneeling before the giant icon. At first glance one could easily be moved by their devotion. They suffered the Bangkok traffic, the crowds, and the stifling heat to pay homage to a higher power. Well, here's the real story. That four-faced statue is the "money buddha". Most of them are praying for good luck in the lottery.

The myth that all Thai people are rabidly compassionate and devout Buddhists should be debunked right away. Like most American Christians who go to church twice a year, Thais pay lip service to being Buddhists. In fact, I probably know more about the teachings of the buddha than the next five Thais you'll meet.

302

The idea that Thais are somehow more compassionate or caring than we are because of their spiritual beliefs is laughable. And all those spirit houses and statues you see all over the place are mostly throwbacks to old animist beliefs and one form of Hinduism or another. They are at best good luck totems. They've got nothing to do with Buddhism. So, get it out of your head that Thais are somehow more spiritually connected than you or I. Like most religions in most countries, it's total bullshit.

There is also a vast difference in perspective between Thais and us. While we can be quite selfish and self-serving, we do have the capacity to step back and gain perspective. We do have the ability to see the forest and not just the trees. Thais are not "big-picture" people. For Thais, there are only trees. They don't know what the fuck a forest is. Here are some examples.

While visiting a friend who runs a property development firm in Pattaya, I saw him close a huge deal for 63 units in his off-plan condo project. With that deal he had the funding to break ground with confidence immediately. He danced around the office in his bare feet and sent one of the staff out for champagne.

The remaining staff members observed his antics like cows watching a train pass. None of them cared but the salespeople; and they were unhappy. That would make 63 units they couldn't sell and collect commission on. They could care less about the success of the company or financial health of the project. The idea that "a rising tide lifts all boats" is lost on them. For the Thai sales staff, it was money out of their pocket. They were however happy about drinking free champagne.

I've seen waitresses quit their job at a restaurant that was "too busy". I've seen office workers quit one company to work at a company where they have friends they can have lunch with.

There is no reason to arrive at a Thai place of business the minute they open. You will probably have to wait for whatever goods and services they offer until after they finish eating. That's the first thing Thai people do when they come to work ... eat. You could walk into a jewelry store that opens at 9 AM at 9:01 intending to make a large purchase. The staff will most likely ignore you until they have finished their somtam. If you leave in a huff and go to another shop, they could care less.

You can't expect them to see "the big picture" because they live in their own little bubble. Walk around in Bangkok long enough and you will be rammed, full-stride and headlong, buy a Thai person that apparently could not see you. Invariably they will dust themselves off and look at you as if to say, *"What the hell are you doing on my planet?"*

You are not invisible; you have entered Thai World. We may live in Thailand, but Thais live in "Thai World". And, apparently, Thai World ends about three inches from the surface of a Thai person's skin. The phrase "self-absorbed" doesn't even begin to describe it.

Westerners would like to pigeonhole and label this pathology as "insular" and "self-centered". Those are western ideas. For Thais, it's more like "self-preservation" and "survival techniques". It's not that they don't care about you. They care about themselves more. Unless they perceive some benefit from being drawn into your personal drama, they see no reason to consider you anything other than another creature breathing up their air.

Perhaps the best example of this compassion vacuum was an experience I had a few years ago. I was standing on my eighth-floor balcony in downtown Bangkok, drinking wine with my best friend and his Thai wife.

It was rush hour on busy Soi 16 and we could see the traffic building up to a jam. As the sun went down and the brake lights came on, we noticed a commotion several blocks away. A fire had started beyond some low-rise condos and the flames were soon licking into the air more than seven stories high.

Within minutes we could hear the howl of fire trucks and police sirens. As the blaze built to three-alarm status, we could see all the rescue vehicles stuck in traffic. No one pulled over to make way for the emergency team. Vehicles crept forward, nose-to-tail, as if the blaring siren and flashing lights did not exist. It took 20 minutes for them to move 100 meters.

When the fire truck and support team finally arrived at the fire, I used my binoculars to see what was happening. Under the billowing black smoke, I could see fire suits being donned, and hoses being reeled out ... but none of it in a hurry. One fireman, whose job it was to connect a big hose to the hydrant was standing there smoking a cigarette and talking to another fireman ... right over the top of the hydrant ... someone had to remind him to hook up the hose to the water source.

I handed my binoculars to my friend's wife and exclaimed, "Those guys don't seem to be in a big hurry to put out that fire". She looked for a moment, shrugged and said, "Not their house". It was just that simple. I felt stupid for saying anything.

The next day I went to the site of the fire. I could see that it had been the site of what we in Thailand call a construction camp. I walked by it almost every day. When high rises and other buildings are being erected, huge teams of nomadic construction workers set up what looks like a shanty town to house themselves and their family. This particular construction camp had stood for over two years and serviced three building sites nearby.

A fire in such a ram shackled cluster of half-assed sheds and tents, complete with propane tanks, gasoline, and other flammables, must have been devastating. I couldn't help wondering if anyone died.

Stopping at a somtam vendor on my way home I asked the owner what happened. She explained that all three construction projects were finished. The lease the developer held on the land where the construction camp had stood expired. To evacuate the site of the camp more expediently the owner had torched it. They gave no warning. I still don't know if anyone died.

Please don't get it twisted. I still choose to live here above any other spot on the planet. But those considering a long stay in The Kingdom should not expect to be bathed in the light of neighbor-loving Buddhism.

Now, it may seem like I hold a negative opinion of Thai people, but that is not the case. I'm simply being realistic and relating my personal experience. There are unique and positive features of the Thai mindset that are so superior to our own it makes me jealous. Here is an example.

During my early years in Bangkok, I was a fan of the party zone known as "Patpong". It is a wild and decadent section of town known for go-go bars and a bustling night market. I arrived one Saturday night and Patpong was going full throttle. Music from the go-go bars was pulsing out into the street, offering a soundtrack to the frenetic market where shoppers could buy anything from bootleg DVDs to exotic pets. Barking dogs, screaming vendors and Thai hip-hop music was producing such a din, I literally held my hands over my ears as I negotiated the gauntlet on my way to meet my friends at a French restaurant.

I stopped on the corner to get my bearings and I noticed a girl. She was a young teenager, probably about 13 years old. The girl sat motionless on a tall stool between two knock-off vendors with her legs pulled up under her yoga style. Her back was erect, hands resting lightly on her knees and her face slightly tilted upwards. She looked like a slinky Siamese Cat. Her eyes were closed, and she was breathing ever so slowly with a cat-like smile on her face. In the middle of the full-blown bedlam of Patpong Road on a Saturday night, she just wasn't there. She had turned off the outside world as easily as switching off a light.

I thought to myself, "The genius of that ... what would I give to have that move?" If I had the ability to just disconnect, I'd probably stay in that mode most of the time.

Thai people have a saying, *"You think too much"*. And they are right. We westerners think too much and obsess over things we have no control over. We are missing the switch that turns off all that noise. Regret and anxiety rule us like tyrannical overlords. We lay in our beds replaying all the mistakes we've made and gnashing our teeth about the future. But I've never met a Thai insomniac. It must be nice to come equipped with an "off button".

You've asked the question, *"What are Thai people really like?"* They are gracious and accommodating hosts to us barbaric foreigners. Some like us. Some loathe us. Mostly, they tolerate us, and I am grateful for that.

What you should concern yourself with is how Thai people and their actions relate to you. Make no mistake, you should expect Thais to be Thai. They are not ashamed of being Thai. They don't feel guilty about being Thai. If you have it in your head to change the way a Thai person is behaving, you should get on a plane and go somewhere else, Thaiworld is not for you.

And that concludes our lesson for the day young Hank. Do you have any questions? Hank smiled and shook his head.

"No questions professor. I think I understand".

"And tell me Hank", I said. "In one sentence, summarize what you have learned from our lesson today?"

"We live in Thailand, but Thais live in Thaiworld" he replied.

"Good boy! See you next Sunday".

Lecture Two – Free Sex

Hank showed up right on time the next Sunday. He had given me his question for the week a few days before. *"What's with all the sex in Thailand?"*. I found it to be an odd question. Surely the boy had experienced sex in Thailand. Surely those cackling hyenas I saw him with had shown him the ropes in Pattaya.

When I sent an email asking for further explanation, Hank said he had been exposed to the soapy massages and go-go bars, but he wanted to know what the sexual atmosphere outside the two-week-tourist's world was like. Thailand's global reputation as "Freaky-deaky Sexland" seems well deserved to the casual tourist. He wanted to know what it's like for people who live here.

Not knowing Hank's personal preferences or depravations, I thought it would be good to give him a wide-spectrum overview. Here is what I presented in the second session.

Straight, gay, male, and female; this is the basic set of variables we grew up with in America-world. In Thailand however, sexuality is measured on a sliding scale with more dimensions; a prism would be a more accurate way to describe it. Expats, sex-pats, and locals come in all the colors of the rainbow. When I first arrived in Thailand, I thought I was ready for anything. My re-education started right away. Here is a story to illustrate.

Sitting in a ramshackle seafood restaurant by the river in Bangkok, my friends and I are approached by our server, "Bee". Bee appears to have started out as a squatty little Thai man and now is in mid-transformation to something else. Since "Bee" is a nickname usually given to a beautiful young woman, we'll refer to Bee as a "she".

From the waist down Bee is dressed in smartly pressed black trousers and highly shined shoes. Above the beltline she sports a bright pink blouse, full-blown make up, false eyelashes and hot pink nail polish. Bee speaks in a falsetto voice and is dramatically effeminate. After she takes our order and swishes away, I asked my friend's wife, "What do you think that is?"

With typical Thai nonchalance she replied, "I think that is Bee".

Trans-genders of all description abound in Thailand, in fact "katoeys" or "ladyboys" are literally recognized as a third sex and given different consideration under Thai laws. Where I come from, the only trans-anything I saw were employed in places like record shops or night clubs. In Thailand, katoeys are respected and revered at many levels of society.

Take a stroll through the cosmetic department of any major department store in Thailand and you'll see some convincing examples. The more adventurous should take in a Cabaret Show in Pattaya just to see how complete the illusion can be. Once you've got the hang of identifying them, you'll see the "third sex" is woven seamlessly into Thai society. After twenty years here I hardly take notice.

In the early days, I also had to adjust to the total lack of "gay-dar" in Thailand. Where I come from, gay men just seem to know I'm not gay. Even in an environment where I may be the hetero minority, nobody approaches me, and no one thinks I'm open to suggestion.

The first time I went to a big commercial gym in Bangkok I realized that gay Thai men either did not sense my straightness, or they did not care. At first, I was unnerved, but ended up taking their advances as a compliment. (At my age I embrace flattery no matter what the source).

Besides having a wider selection of players on the social scene, there is the pervasive pay-for-play arena that exists in labyrinth layers all over Thailand.

Bangkok's legendary nightlife could more realistically be called the "night market". You want to see naked girls? Aisle four, Soi Cowboy, Nana Plaza or Patpong are for you. What's that? You want to sip a nice scotch, fire up a Cuban cigar and have a persuasive "hostess" talk you into drinks, dinner and whatever? Aisle seven, swanky private gentlemen's clubs are all over Bangkok, some with legendary status. Soapy massages, blowjob bars and just plain old whorehouses are woven seamlessly into nearly every neighborhood in a city of 12 million people. From all-boy go-go bars to champagne sipping sirens in evening gowns, there is something for every taste.

What makes it so bizarre is all ages, genders, nationalities, and fetishes are well represented and thoroughly mixed. It's like a big human aquarium that comes alive when the sun goes down and the lights come on. Grab a strategic perch in Nana Plaza or Patpong on a Saturday night and witness some of the world's finest people watching. I assume you've already witnessed Pattaya's Walking Street in person. As you have seen, it's like an open-air sex convention.

Eighteen to eighty; blind, crippled, and crazy they come ... from every corner of the globe. Not just middle-aged men ... young guys ... couples of the same sex ... couples of the opposite sex ... Russian girls on holiday ... whatever! They all come to quench everything from innocent curiosity to decadent cravings.

If point-and-click sex isn't your bag, just head to local hotspots, nightclubs in big hotels, or the old reliable Hard Rock. You'll find a kinder-gentler version of the skin game with plenty of girls, boys and whatever looking for a friend for a night or two, maybe even a modicum of romance.

When I lived in Bangkok, my wife called these the home of *"secretary hookers"*; girls (and boys) who work a day job and supplement their income a few nights per week. Some are looking for love. Some are looking for money. To be honest, love and money are pretty closely related in Thailand.

If you find such a relaxed approach to sex morally repugnant, you'll have a problem in Thailand. You must get used to seeing it or you can't live here. I know of no expat living in Thailand against their will. And I don't know any who are vehemently opposed to what goes on here. Whether you get involved or not, most folks live and let live. The Thais certainly do.

Ask ten expats living in Thailand why they live here, and chances are nine will respond "freedom". You can pretty much live however you want as long as you aren't hurting someone who doesn't want to be hurt or insulting the royal family. For most expats, the freedom to explore one's sexual identity is part of Thailand's charm. As a group, Thais can be a little stodgy about some moral issues but being hung up about sex is not part of the Thai psyche.

With that said, this much freedom is not for everybody. Some folks get lost along the way. Tell your average westerner they can have any kind of sex they desire, pretty much on demand, and observe their behavior. For most, the novelty eventually wears off. For some, when the thrill of the chase is removed, so is the desire. Others develop what

Bangkok author Christopher G. Moore called *"the sickness"*.

Walk down to the open-air bars on Beach Road in Pattaya and you'll see them; old guys bellying up to the bar at 11 AM, waiting for the girls to wake up. Viagra-Bags; hollowed-out men who have wasted decades chasing the pink dragon. The sickness is a slow, self-inflicted death by obsession and excess.

You'll see good men, old and young, living "the life" in Bangkok; making good money during the day and handing it all over every night to whichever venue scratches their particular itch. Some choose to burn the cash they saved for their old age. Some sell everything they have and arrive ready to commit "Siamese Suicide". None of them are able to carry on normal relationships ... the substitute is too accessible and satisfying. If you meet someone with "the sickness" you'll know. All conversations will lead to the subject of sex of some description in very short order.

For others, a little bit of freedom is just what the doctor ordered. A few years ago, I met a forty-something English couple in Phuket. Kathy was a barrister from London and Jack a Brigadier General in the British Marine Corps. They owned a condo in my building and visited there frequently.

Kathy came for months at a time and I'd see her out on her big Harley motorcycle cruising up and down Rawai Beach, stopping to frolic with the local bar girls here and there. Jack came to town less frequently and favored the glitzy go-go bars in Patong. Sometimes they'd be out together, other times alone.

One evening we were all drinking wine and watching the sunset at Nai Harn Beach; me, Jack, Kathy, and Kathy's new Thai girlfriend Poo. Kathy sensed my confusion. Over the second bottle and some grilled squid, Kathy revealed to me the secret to her and Jack's unusual marital arrangement.

It seems that Jack and Kathy were grade school sweethearts, had been married for over 25 years, and raised several children. Kathy had built up a big respectable business in London while Jack had been out conquering for Queen and country. They had planned all along to retire at 50. When it came time to find a winter getaway and retirement home, they chose Phuket.

Kathy began to spend most of her time in Phuket, exploring property investments. One evening while Jack was in town, Kathy called him down to the beach and uttered those dreaded words ... *"Jack, we need to talk"*.

According to Jack, here is the how the conversation went:

Kathy: *"Jack, I believe I like girls"*

Jack: *"Too right darling ... me too!"*

And so, they bought a two bedroom/two bathroom near the beach and lived happily ever after. Kathy has a steady girlfriend riding around on the back of her chopper. Jack retired from the military and now performs some kind of "private consulting" for an undisclosed middle eastern state. When he comes to town, he usually looks up an old friend or finds a new companion. On occasion I would see Jack and Kathy out "on the lash" together, partying with the bar girls, cackling like magpies.

Such a display back in England would surely have lost Kathy clients and cost Jack a promotion. Here in the Land of Smiles, no one bats an eye. They are a sweet and loving couple. Theirs is a relationship only someone looking through the bent light of Thailand's sexual prism would call romantic. But, at a time in their lives when many couples experience turbulence, they've found a way to be happy together. Nobody can deny that a little shot of freedom changed their life.

When most people are considering other countries to live in, they ask about the weather, the health care, the public transportation systems, etc. Rarely does anyone think about sexual morays and practices that may be drastically different than their home country.

If you find such a wide-open approach to sexual behavior offensive, I'd recommend scratching Thailand off your list. If you fear that access to unlimited sexual escapades is your own personal kryptonite, beware of how quickly "the sickness" can get a grip on you.

Before considering a long-stay Thailand, you really must know your own tolerance for freedom. Everything all the time ain't for everybody.

As I concluded Lecture 2, I realized Hank had not moved a muscle. No notetaking. No head-nodding. He hadn't even finished his pint of beer.

"Hello, earth to Hank. Are you there Hank?"

"Sorry professor. I heard every word you said" he offered. "Man, I've got a lot to learn".

Lecture 3 - Fear the Genie

For the third and final installment of this lecture series, young Hank had posed the question, *"What should I know about Thai women?"* I knew this question was coming. Everyone who starts out as a tourist and dreams of becoming an expat of some description wonders what it's like having a real Thai girlfriend or wife. Or, at the very least, what they should expect from dating Thai women.

First of all, Hank, they're just women. If you've had problems understanding women in your home country, you are going to have even more trouble here because of the language barrier.

Secondly, refer to our fist lecture and my axiom, "don't be fooled by the show". Shy ... demure ... coy ... uber-feminine. When you compare Thai women to the trolls we have back in the US, it may seem like they are superior in every way. I certainly prefer them.

But buyer beware. You probably have never encountered a person that can keep a placid demeanor in the face of adversity like a Thai woman. You probably have never met a person that hides their emotions as effectively as a Thai woman. The only thing you know for sure with a Thai woman is ... you'll never really know what the fuck is going on. You are best advised to just give in to it and hope the lady has your best interest in mind.

With that said, a person could come and go here in Thailand for years without ever seeing the dark side of a Thai lady. They are gentle loving creatures with soft voices, soft skin, and heart-melting smiles. But, if you plan to stay for an extended period and become involved in a long-term live-in relationship, you will eventually find out who your dream girl really is. Here are some stories to illustrate:

I woke up one morning at 6 AM. As is my custom, I made coffee and opened my balcony doors. Normally I hear the pleasant cacophony of birds squawking, roosters crowing and the occasional kick-start of a motorbike. When I hear water splashing, I know the foursome of baby elephant statues surrounding our swimming pool has been turned on, spewing tinkling streams of water onto the surface of the pool. Peaceful.

But this morning's placid din is brutally interrupted by squawking of another kind. My neighbor on the ground floor across the corner of our L-shaped building has some guests, chain-smoking and slamming whisky-cokes on the balcony. It appears Michel from Switzerland has had a long night. And it looks like he's in for an even longer morning. The girl that I can see is extremely animated, extremely drunk, and extremely loud. Her flat staccato delivery echoes up to my third-floor balcony as if we are in a canyon.

I can't get a full understanding of what she is on about, but I did hear those three words you never want to hear come out of a Thai woman's mouth; the dreaded *"listen to me"*. I can hear her desperate demand over and over again, *"listen to me, listen to me Michel"*.

"Listen to me" signals the end of civility. It means she has lost all inhibition and restraint. It means that all that pent-up emotion from maintaining her polite Thai public face is about to come tumbling forth. *"Listen to me"* is the sound of the genie escaping the bottle.

I have found that the best strategy for coping with a *"listen to me"* conversation is to nod agreeably and let her roll. Don't interject. Don't offer your two cents. And by all means don't disagree with her. Keep sharp or heavy objects out of her reach. If you are at home, keep her drink topped up and shoot for the knockout. (Be forewarned, this strategy can backfire)

When a Thai woman gets drunk and set off, there is simply no getting that genie back in the bottle. If you are in a public place, God help you. Play it cool until you can plot an escape, then run. Run like you are being chased by flying monkeys.

My poor neighbor hasn't learned this lesson yet. Every few minutes I hear him try to chime in, drawing an immediate *"LISTEN TO ME"* from his belligerent companion. I'd love to be all indignant and bitch about the interruption of my peaceful Sunday morning. But I've been that guy sitting on the balcony at 6 AM with an alcohol-infused time bomb. I've been the guy waltzing into a restaurant thirty minutes from closing with three drunk Thai girls. I've been the guy excusing myself to the bathroom and escaping out the back door.

There is nothing I can do to help my poor neighbor, so I close my doors and turn on some nice jazz. I am thankful to have learned those lessons a decade ago. Good luck with that genie Michel.

My friend Tom is a seventy-something American ex-ship's captain. He's a handsome old devil that keeps in good shape. He likes to be the envy of other men, so he sports and supports a 25-year-old Thai girlfriend. If you had to guess what nationality she is, you would have a tough time. She has dark skin, long straight black hair like a Thai girl, but she has a body straight out of Columbia. Big melon-like breasts and a rear end like ... well ... it's like heaven isn't it? Her name is Dow, she is from Korat.

I would describe Dow as shy and reserved. Her English comprehension seems limited and her speaking ability almost non-existent. She is glued to Tom's side whenever I see them, pawing at him constantly. She is what many guys who have never been here think of when someone says, "Asian woman". Beautiful and subservient.

One evening I joined Tom and Dow for dinner on Pratumnak Hill. When we ordered I got my traditional glass of red wine, Tom and Dow followed suit. Tom and I chewed the fat about work. We are both teachers. Dow listened attentively, cutting Tom's food, and lining up the next bite of whatever he was eating. Mid-dinner we got another round of wine.

Once we'd finished our meals and the dishes cleared, I ordered one more glass of wine and asked Tom and Dow if they wanted another. Tom took in a deep breath, gave me a pensive look, and said *"uh, I don't know ... Dow ... uh".* I missed his signal and insisted we all had one more. Dow just smiled and nodded.

During our continued conversation, I noticed that Dow had become a little more involved. She interjected and spoke to me in Thai. She knows I can speak Thai and seemed happy to have me there to interpret her comments. About halfway through our third glass of wine, something changed dramatically. As if a switch had been flipped, the shy and demure village girl suddenly spoke pretty damn good English.

Suddenly she had something to say about everything. And it didn't matter what the subject was ... she disagreed. At one point she reached out and grabbed my arm and said those dreaded words, *"Listen to me".* Her grip was incredible. I took notice of how toned her arms were. Only when I was this close to her did I realize how big Dow is. Usually in Thailand, women only come in two sizes ... small and extra-small. Dow is a large Thai girl without an ounce of fat on her. And now this big-ass country girl was drunk, and the genie was coming out.

When I looked at Tom, he just gave me a tight smile. He looked genuinely frightened. It took every ounce of his diplomacy and persuasion to get her up and out of the restaurant. As they walked up the hill ahead of me, I could still here Dow ranting, *"Listen to me ... listen to me Tom".* He turned around to give me a look that said, *"Thanks a lot buddy!"*

Both incidents involve alcohol, but Thai women can be set off by any number of things. One day she's a purring horny kitten who *"love you too much".* The next day she's goes totally silent and starts sharpening all the knives in the kitchen.

Get over the whole *"subservient Asian woman"* myth. Get over the idea that a relationship with a Thai woman will be easier than with a westerner. Get over the idea that Thailand is a man's world.

Get over it and fear the genie.

Bonus Lecture – The Reinvention Game

So, Hank and I concluded our deal; his three questions got answered. But I had one more nugget of wisdom to impart. To be quite honest, I was a little disappointed at the predictability and shallowness of his questions. I wanted to answer the question he should have asked, so I did.

"Hank, I'm going to give you one more session, are you up for it?" I asked. He looked stunned. "Sure Professor. I'll take whatever you got". I ordered a double Jack in a tall glass and began.

After twenty years in Thailand, I finally figured out what the best part is. After two decades I have discovered what keeps me here and what attracts so many wandering souls. After sacrificing my 40's and 50's to this kooky country, I finally understand what I'm doing here.

When I first got here, I had a pocketful of cash, a hard dick and no restraint. I was so happy to get out of that nanny-state I called home and I couldn't wait to be run amok. And run amok I did. A candle burning that bright and at both ends is doomed to flameout in short order. After six months of Bangkok life, I moved to Phuket to slow down and chillout. That's where I discovered what I was really looking for.

Because I was getting bored and needed something to do, I paired up with a dirtbag Canadian real estate agent which led me to buy a really sweet piece of land on the southern tip of Phuket near Nai Harn Beach. I went to look at this parcel because my "partner" was too lazy to drive across the island. I was supposed to evaluate it but instead bought it immediately. The moment I set eyes on the property I knew what I wanted to do.

To the rear of the plot was a nearly finished three-bedroom house sitting in the middle of the Phuket jungle. I moved into the house, dug a big-ass swimming pool, and began construction of my own little property development. After about 16 months I had erected three more houses clustered around mine and sold every one of them. I drew the floorplans up on notebook paper, found a local architect and builder and was responsible for every tile, every fixture, every last centimeter of those four houses. When I cashed out, I had doubled my money in less than two years.

The point is, I had never been a builder in the US. I had never been a property developer. I had never dreamed of designing and or building one house, let alone three. Creating something that was not there before was a feeling beyond description. The thrill of accomplishment was exhilarating. I felt like an artist. I felt like a visionary. I'd made money doing something I was actually proud of.

Standing in front of my little village and looking at it one last time before I handed over the keys to the last buyer, I realized something very important. I would never have been able to do this in the US. Too much red tape. Too many barriers to success. Too many motherfuckers with their hands out along the way. And who was I? I didn't know anybody. I didn't have any "connections". All I had was a sack of money and an idea. I stepped off the plane in Phuket and acted like a property developer ... so I was one.

About ten years ago, I met a guy who owned and published a magazine. He said he liked the way I told a story. He said he thought I might make a good journalist. He asked me to write some articles about real estate. Since then, I've been published in dozens of magazines and on even more websites. I've written 15,000-word exposes on travel locations. I've written entire magazines about interior design. I've written series upon series about music and entertainment. Last year I wrote a 60-page brochure for the Tourism Authority of Thailand. I don't have a journalism degree. I'd never been published before. Now I am a freelance writer with long string of accomplishments. Somebody said they thought I was a writer, so I became one.

Five years ago, I met a guy who said he thought I would be a good teacher. He offered me a job teaching some test taking courses for his company. I took a 120-hour course on teaching English as a foreign language and went to work. Eventually I ended up teaching English, Public Speaking and Academic Writing at a major university in Bangkok. I taught business English classes to employees at Honda Motors and the Civil Aviation Authority of Thailand. Now I've taught over 25,000 individual

English lessons to Chinese students on-line. Someone said they thought I'd be a good teacher, so I tried it. I liked it. Now I teach almost every day.

Property developer? Journalist? Professor? Before I landed in Thailand in 1999, I would never have imagined any of these job titles appearing on my resume.

And that young Hank is the best part about living in Thailand. Cheesy as it may sound, you can be whatever you want to be. You are who you say you are until someone proves that you are not. I grew up believing I lived in the "land of the free" overflowing with opportunity. Well, now I actually do.

This reinvention game does however come with a warning. When you can change who you are like putting on a new hat, it can be a crutch. Sometimes when I change direction, I feel like a quitter. Sometimes I feel like I'd be a lot better off if I had just picked a lane and stayed in it.

But if I'd played it safe, I wouldn't have all of these stories to tell. And now that I'm a writer, well ... you never know ... these stories just might come in handy one day.

Class dismissed.

Made in the USA
Middletown, DE
26 February 2022